The Trouble With Fairies

Emma Bradley

For Emily

Happy Reading!

DEDICATION

For all the relentless dreamers out there, and those that still look behind and beyond hoping for magic. You can often find it in the simplest of things, the nicest of people and the most teetering of TBR piles…

CHAPTER ONE
ARCANIUM

A dilapidated amusement arcade in a seaside town didn't seem like the right place to find a portal hub to Faerie. The high street was full of people on their way back from the beach, with seagulls lurking beside bins and the overwhelming smell of candyfloss and fried food hanging in the air.

I stared up at the neon sign hanging over the arcade's double doors – *ARCANIUM*.

The bulbs for the second A and the N weren't working, and the grime on the windows didn't exactly scream 'here's the entrance to a mystical realm'.

I checked the address on the back of my acceptance letter again, but I was definitely where it told me to be. With a deep breath, I squared my shoulders and faced the doors. This was my chance to make something of myself, and I wouldn't achieve anything dithering outside. After one final look at the dingy exterior, I covered my hand with the cuff of my sleeve and pushed open the door.

The arcade machines flashed and pinged as I dragged my suitcase inside, but I couldn't see a single soul amid the gloom. As I looked around, the scent of something awful wafted up my nose, like the dregs of stale cider usually found growing mould in my sister Jenny's room on cleaning day.

Okay, not exactly what I was expecting.

A cold draught sent shivers over me as doubt tiptoed into my mind.

Still, all secret organisations had a well-disguised entrance in stories. I just needed to figure out where to go next and not do anything dim.

I rubbed my face with my free hand and peered between the machines. I'd heard the many stories and rumours about Arcanium, the headquarters of the Fairy Deity People, or FDPs for short. Now here I was, barely sixteen and ready to start my training as one of them. The fact I was a fairy had come as a shock when I turned thirteen, especially as my mum and two sisters weren't anything ethereal at all. I glanced around the deserted arcade again.

Not what I expected from what they told us at fairy class.

Over the past three years, I'd been going to fairy classes on weekends to prepare myself for this very moment. I made every effort to study hard and learn all I could about fairies and the histories, until my only goal was to train as an FDP. I could only hope that Arcanium would give me somewhere to belong among my own kind. Or at least a space to exist where I wasn't being relentlessly chased with hockey sticks.

My skin prickled a warning and I turned my head to see a boy to my left. He stood leaning against a claw-grab machine, arms folded and his gaze fixed on me. He certainly hadn't been there a minute ago. Curly, honey-brown hair spilled out from underneath a dark blue baseball cap, framing turquoise eyes and a pale face peppered with freckles. The sleeves of his unzipped dark blue hoodie were rolled up to the elbow, and he wore jeans that hung baggy over a pair of black boots. In my anxiety, I even checked his ears, despite knowing that fairies didn't have pointy ones like the Faerie tales sometimes suggested. His ears were as normal as mine. Finally, I eyed the *Demon Babies* logo scrawled across his t-shirt, just visible beneath the front of the hoodie. Relief flooded through me. Even I knew that *Demon Babies* were a famous band throughout Faerie.

At least I've come to the right place.

The boy stood staring back at me as much as I was taking him in. I ignored the flush that crept across my cheeks and faced him, waiting.

"Here for training?" he asked.

I nodded. "How did you know?"

He pushed himself away from the machine. "Your book is showing."

His top lip twitched into a one-sided smirk as he nodded at my satchel. I looked down to see my well-worn fairy manual peeking out from beneath the flap.

Oh, hell. I pushed the book back in, my cheeks burning with embarrassment. *Two minutes in and I'm already making a mess of things. What if someone had seen, or it dropped out and someone found it?*

I guessed the boy was roughly the same age as me, but I wouldn't be caught dead asking him. Given his amused smirk, he'd probably make fun of me or assume I fancied him. I gripped the handle of my suitcase tighter so he wouldn't notice my hands shaking.

"I'm Demi Darcy. You didn't answer me either."

My stomach crunched into a knot at how rude I sounded, but the boy just raised his eyebrows. I noticed one of them was pierced through with a small black hoop.

"I was just passing through, but I'll show you down to induction," he offered. "They'll explain all about what the FDPs get up to. FDPs are-"

"I know it stands for Fairy Deity Person. I've read the manual from cover to cover. Twice. Did you know they changed it officially from Fairy Godmother to be more inclusive in the nineties, but nobody upheld the new term until at least 2003?"

My cheeks burned as I babbled, but my mouth wouldn't quit.

3

Instead of answering, the boy laughed and walked away. I followed him toward a metal door near the back of the arcade, almost catching my suitcase on one of the machines.

"Okay, Brainiac." He glanced back at me. "Did you know the Ogle has just found-"

"Realm 313, more informally known as Tentacleville? I heard. It's amazing how much we still don't know about Faerie. Did some people really lose their eyeballs?"

He snorted and jabbed a button to summon a lift. The door opened immediately, and he strode inside before answering.

"Of course they didn't." He sounded almost insulted. "What do you think we are here, amateurs?"

I panicked. "Oh, no, not at all. I've always wanted to see the Ogle if I made it here. Are there really screens that show you every single realm in Faerie?"

"Every single realm so far," he said. "Maybe I'll show you one day, if you're good."

What does that mean, if I'm good? Who is this boy anyway? The flickering thought of not knowing where I was being taken crashed through my head. *What if he's some kind of weirdo? But then he recognised the manual, and I can't exactly alienate the only person here who knows the way in.*

The lift was barely big enough for four people, and I wasn't exactly keen on being stuck in small spaces either, but I'd come this far. I breathed deep, hurried in after him and pressed my suitcase close against my legs as he tapped the lowest button on the lift's panel.

The lift door thudded shut with a clang, leaving us in what could only be described as a rickety metal death trap. Someone had scratched 'Trev woz ere' on one wall and a disconcerting dark patch in one corner looked like it might be sticky, right beneath a missing panel with cables clearly visible.

4

A quick look in the shiny surface and I saw my black hair was escaping its hairband like a tangle of electrical wires. The odd oil-slick tints that shimmered in all different colours when the light caught various hairs were just visible under the white light in the lift.

Pale skin, dull eyes, yep, I look a mess. Great.

I couldn't do anything much about my appearance now, other than a quick smooth down of my hair with my hand, so I racked my brain for something I could say to make a good impression instead. The boy stood with his arms folded, his gaze fixed on the door as the lift started downwards. I remembered what my mum had said many times before about staring, but I couldn't help the odd sneaked glance.

He was only a little taller than me. Closer up, his freckles looked like an explosion across his nose, and I vowed never to use the word 'glitter' when describing him. At least, not to his face.

The lift jolted sideways, and I crashed against the wall with a yelp. I stared accusingly at the boy as he grinned back at me, his legs relaxed to absorb the movement.

"You get used to it."

I rubbed my sore elbow as the lift trundled on. I could only hope someone would explain what was expected of me. My mentor at weekend fairy classes, Xavio, had been surprisingly 'airy-fairy' about the specifics.

"So, did your parents drop you off?" the boy asked.

I shook my head. "No, I came on the train. I have two sisters and both of them are playing in the county Hockey semi-finals, so my mum needs to be there to cheer them on."

"That sucks." He frowned.

"It's okay. I've always been the odd one out at home and my sisters make sure I know it. I'm just glad to finally be here with people more like me. I'm the only fairy in the family, which is weird I guess, but my mentor at fairy class said it happens. He also said a lot of other things about my sisters, but they're not that complimentary."

Aware that my nerves were rambling on my behalf, I faced the lift door again and wondered if I should ask him any questions. Not everyone liked to discuss personal things, or so my mum insisted. The boy gave me a quick, assessing look.

"Okay. So, every new starter here has a meeting with Queenie," he said. "It's more like an audience in her mind. Then I'll take you to the residents' floor. Someone there will show you your room and where stuff is."

"Is it like a test, meeting Queenie?"

My insides started to bubble with trepidation at the thought. Someone called Queenie had signed my acceptance letter, but nobody had mentioned having to meet her.

What do I say? Other than as little as possible without being rude?

I never usually made good impressions, although to be fair to myself it was mostly my sisters making sure of that, but this meeting with Queenie would be vital to my entire future here. In two years' time after training, I wanted to qualify as an FDP. Then I could finally escape home and my sisters for good. Meeting people might shorten those odds considerably if I screwed up.

"Nah, she'll just want to welcome you." The boy shrugged. "All you need to do is smile, don't interrupt and basically be one step short of a wet blank- Actually, I think you'll be fine."

He eyed the doors as the lift came to a stop, but I had to ask while I had a chance.

"What's your name?"

The door opened and he looked me up and down, as if to work

out whether I was worth telling.

"I'm Taz Elverhill."

He strode out of the lift and I hurried after him, my insides sloshing with nerves. A long corridor stretched in front of us, the walls covered in wood panelling with a dark blue carpet underfoot. I eyed the paintings we passed, all of different natural landscapes. A snowy forest, a sun-scorched grey mountain and a rolling green hill down to a lake glimmering silver.

Taz, now several steps ahead, turned back to frown at me.

"These are all places in Faerie," he said, waving a dismissive hand at the paintings. "Some have been here since Arcanium began."

I hovered beside a picture of a cottage by a stream, the very essence of a Faerie tale with its thatched roof and roses around the door.

"I like this one," I admitted. "I wonder if it's a real place."

"Yeah, it's nice." Taz's tone turned softer. "Queenie tried to have them removed or changed, painted over and covered, a bunch of times but they always end up back the same."

I eyed him with a frown. He seemed to know an awful lot for someone who was meant to be roughly my age.

"So, are you an FDP already then?" I asked.

He shook his head. "No, I'm a first year mentee like you, but I came here when I was fourteen on a sort of apprenticeship. I plan to be Head Mentor one day. Anyway, come on, I do have a life to get back to you know."

I grimaced an apology and tore myself away from the painting to follow Taz the rest of the way along the hall. That was one thing I did know more about; FDP's took the assignments in Faerie, while mentors stayed behind to guide and assist them.

Maybe he'll even be in my classes. At least then I'll know one person.

Taz came to an abrupt stop in front of two large doors, and I eyed the FDP emblem carved into the wood, an orb surrounded by ivy strands in the rough outline of an eye.

"So, yeah, this is Queenie's office," he announced. "Good luck. I'll watch your case for you 'til you're done."

Why is he being so thoughtful all of a sudden? I eyed my suitcase with all my possessions in, reluctant to leave it with him. *He was desperate to back to his life a moment ago.*

Taz reached out and banged his fist on the door before I could say anything to stop him. I forced my fingers away from the handle of my suitcase and straightened my back into what my sisters called my 'broomstick-up-the-bum' pose.

Now is not the time to do anything stupid. I smoothed down the front of my t-shirt. *I will be calm, collected and-*

"WHAT?"

The screech from the other side of the doors almost sent me fleeing back to the lift. As much as I'd learned to put on a brave front, to face scary people like my sisters and not back down, a lot of social situations still unnerved me.

Taz stared at me with withering disgust as I hesitated. My throat twinged, but I reassured myself that my lunch had been a long time ago on the train and the chances of plastering the carpet a fetching shade of cheese sandwich yellow were slim. I pushed open the door and stepped into Queenie's office.

Long mirrors with metal frames dominated the walls, separated by swathes of dark purple drapes. Even though the room was large enough to fit a classroom in, there was only one set of furniture right in the middle of the dark carpet. The huge desk had stout legs, all ash grey wood with various spiky carvings sticking out, complete with a wing-backed chair of black leather. The whole effect made the office look more like a torture chamber from a cheesy vampire film. I looked beyond the desk and into the narrowed eyes of the woman sitting there.

She looked regal and elegant, but something about her set my nerves on edge. It wasn't the velvet dress, or the pale face with dark burgundy lipstick. I wasn't even sure it was the sharp eyes, jade in colour and jaded in expression. It was the whole effect together, carefully arranged for maximum intimidation effect.

The backs of my knees began to perspire as we stared at each other. Realising I was being rude, I hurried forward with my hand outstretched, willing my feet not to trip me up. The woman eyed at my hand for several long seconds, so I dropped it to my side again.

"Welcome to Arcanium." She picked up a nail file. "I am Queenie, the Director. You're one of our new mentees?"

Scrape. The nail file started work. *Scrape.*

"Yes," I nodded, my cheeks burning as I forced myself to use my full name. "I'm Demerara Darcy."

Scrape. Scrape. Queenie's nail file went back and forth, the noise making my toes curl. I didn't tend to admit to people that I had misophonia, which meant certain sounds really got on my nerves and made my insides jitter like they were full of electrocuted eels. As for my name, let's just say Mum was doped up in the hospital when I was born and hadn't learned to say no to my oldest sister yet.

Queenie looked me over mid-scrape.

"So, you're the one Xavio chose to mentor?" Queenie confirmed.

I gulped against the dryness in my throat.

"Yes, um, Ma'am."

I wondered if Xavio, my old mentor at fairy classes, had thought to send word ahead about me. It was the kind of thing he might do, if he remembered.

Scrape, scrape. It took all of my willpower not to clench my fists.

Queenie puckered her purple lips, possibly wondering why she had to deal with adolescents like me. I'd been surprised to find out that mentees were sometimes given charges and tasks to carry out in Faerie. Xavio had explained that charges could often be young people, and they tended to trust others who saw things without the "blinkers of adulthood", as he put it. I wasn't too sure about the blinkers, but I couldn't imagine my mum or my sisters making good FDPs. Mum would be too concerned with telling people what to do. My sisters would probably use the charges for target practice like they did with me.

"So, Demerara." Queenie put the nail file down.

"Everyone calls me Demi," I interrupted, relieved the scraping had finally stopped. "I'm very pleased to have this opportunity, and I'm eager to get started and help out all I can."

There, I'd practiced that on the train and it sounded grown-up, even from my lips. Queenie's thin, pencilled eyebrows rose in mild surprise.

"Well, that is a comfort." Her spreading smile held a look of amused mockery. "We set a very high standard here though. Only the best succeed, the strongest, and many students don't even make it past the two years of mentoring."

I heard her loud and clear. It sounded very much like what my sister Mary had said to me before I left.

"Don't get your hopes up. Even if they are 'your kind', they'll still have standards. They'll want the strong, clever ones, and you're, well, you."

Queenie sighed, bored already.

"But I'm sure they find the human world just as rewarding," she continued. "Then there are several supporting roles here for a lucky few that prove themselves useful."

I clung to the strap of my satchel as though it could whisk me away somewhere safe and familiar, like back to Xavio's small garden where me and my fellow junior fairies had gathered on weekends to learn. Even home would have done right now.

I couldn't think of what to say to Queenie without being petulant. Luckily, one of the doors swung open and bounced into the wall, saving me the trouble.

"We've got a situation," the newcomer announced.

I eyed the interruption, a man with a bald head wearing a dark green boiler suit. He flicked the quickest of glances in my direction.

"What is it, Emil?" Queenie snapped.

The man, Emil, rubbed the back of his head.

"There's a new errand come in, but I've got nobody to fill it." He looked my way again. "Are you a new FDP then?"

I shook my head. "Not exactly, I'm a mentee."

I knew I was likely in the way. In fact, Queenie seemed to have forgotten all about me as she tapped her nails on the table with an exasperated frown. I forced myself to ignore the rhythmic clacking and raised my hand hesitantly.

"Um, should I-"

"Volunteer?" Emil locked eyes with me. "What a great suggestion."

CHAPTER TWO
INTO THE UNKNOWN

I froze. "Er, that wasn't what-"

Emil ignored my feeble protests. Perhaps he didn't see the sheer horror scrawled across my face. Even Queenie gave the idea a derisive snort.

"Of course, it wouldn't be an assignment," Emil continued. "It'd be more of a little favour, but willingness is exactly what we want from new recruits, especially the mentees."

His eager tone made me even more determined to stop whatever misunderstanding was currently happening.

"I wasn't-"

"Run along and wait outside now." Emil shooed me away. "I'll just clear up the details and we can whisk you off."

I wilted under the demanding stare. Of course I wanted to prove myself, but after learning from someone much more experienced, with much more training behind me, and possibly even after being given some actual fairy gifts.

One final look at Queenie's narrowed eyes sealed my fate. I wanted to be an FDP more than anything, and to prove that I wasn't the waste of space my sisters thought I was. Besides, if I didn't succeed here, what else did I have? I had to take every opportunity to prove myself, no matter how scared I was.

I scuttled past Emil without a word, and he followed to shut the door behind me. I stared at Taz in bewilderment.

What did I just agree to though?

Taz pushed himself away from the wall and flicked his chin toward Queenie's office doors.

"What's going on?"

I shook my head, scared at the mere thought of finding out the answer to that. He frowned at my hopelessness and pushed past me to get to the doors. A tiny gap was left where Emil hadn't closed them properly, so Taz tilted his head to listen.

"We pay you to manage the FDPs." Queenie's shouting needed no gap to be audible. "It's down to you that there's nobody left."

"If there weren't so many bloomin' restrictions, I'd hire more. As it is, I can't, so there isn't anyone left. Anyway, the girl wants to be an FDP, doesn't she? So send her. It's just a short errand."

Queenie's irritated huff echoed down the hallway, and probably all the way up to the arcade.

"You seriously have nobody else?"

"Mulcet is on long-term sick with a unicorn bite. Baines is on paternity. Stella's on leave. The rest are all still in the field with charges."

"What about Carrigan?"

"Cat's sick. We can't call him in either because it was our manticore that poisoned the blinkin' thing. He could still sue us."

The discussion descended into a furious buzz. I inched backwards away from Taz and the doors. It wasn't that I didn't want to take on the errand, whatever it was, but nobody had mentioned unicorn bites or manticore poisonings before.

"And not a single suitable mentee with actual training?" Queenie pressed.

Emil huffed. "If you want to explain to them that they have to miss the annual object training tournament today, feel free. Or to highlight how short-staffed we are to everyone? It's a quick assignment, in and out, no fussing. I'm sure anyone could do it without causing total mayhem."

"Fine." Queenie sounded like she'd lost the argument. "If

there's really nobody else, then we have no other choice."

"Exactly. What's the worst that could happen?"

Queenie muttered something else in response to that but I couldn't make it out. I wondered if she guessed someone was listening outside the door, or if her words were about something so scandalous that she had to keep her voice down just in case.

"Yeah, true." Emil's voice rose, strident. "But they couldn't prove anything a second time."

"Oh, fine. Go away then and take her with you. I want to watch the latest episode of *Demolition Ducks* and the mentees are your responsibility anyway. On your head be it."

Taz scrambled back from the door and stood against the far wall so fast that I wondered if he had full Fae blood. Fairies were part-Fae, part-human, but those with pure or stronger Fae blood were meant to have various gifts like super-strength or increased speed by birth. I hadn't met anyone like that yet, but I knew that gifts and abilities could only be given to fairies by full-blood Fae.

Either way, unlike some at fairy classes who had a distant Fae relation to bestow small gifts on them as a child, I had nobody Fae at all to gift me any.

Emil emerged from the office and shut the door properly behind him.

"Heard all that?" he asked. Taz shrugged. I gulped. "Right, what do you call yourself?"

I realised Emil was speaking to me.

"I'm Demi, sir."

Emil scratched his chin and looked me up and down, as if he'd only just noticed my entire body quaking.

"I'm no sir. Just call me Emil. Are you up to this?"

I blinked. Weird of him to ask after making so much effort to convince Queenie to let me go, but then perhaps he was having doubts about my abilities too.

14

If I say no now, it'll be branded on me for ages. I'd be the fairy who wouldn't even take a simple assignment.

"Yes," I squeaked.

Emil nodded. "Good. This particular realm isn't too hostile anyway, but Taz will take you to despatch and clue you in as best he can. Welcome to Arcanium, Demi. I'll take your case to your room for whenever you get back."

Emil handed Taz a single A5 page and what looked like a small key-ring before sauntering down the corridor with my suitcase trundling behind him. Every part of me screamed at him to bring it back, and I stared after him as Taz scanned the page. He squinted with one eye shut for several moments, then his mouth fell open. When he looked at me, I saw the worry etched in lines on his face. Without a word, he strode toward the lift. I hurried after him, clinging to my satchel.

"I can't believe they've done this." Taz scowled. "They should have waited, not sent the first newbie they found just because there's nobody else to take the errand. They could have even asked me. Why on earth did you say agree to it when you clearly have no idea?"

Out of breath and out of place, I sagged.

"Oh, that's flattering."

Taz halted in front of the lift, his hands on his hips as he glared back at me.

"A lot of these realms are dangerous," he hissed. "Mentees don't usually go near a realm for a good six months, even then it's easy work. You carry a message into a peaceful realm, or you check up on a previous charge for someone and file a report. You've only been here five minutes! Have you ever even been to Faerie before?"

"Um, no." I shook my head.

Taz looked me over yet again, threw up his hands and

15

stormed into the lift.

I stared after him in horror. *Drama Queen.*

Unable to do anything else, except maybe find the arcade and run screaming to live in a cave somewhere, I followed.

"Can you tell me where I'm going?" I ignored his grumbling. "Or what I'm meant to be doing?"

Taz held out the piece of paper as the lift started downwards. I read it aloud.

"Realm 258 – non-hostile in civilised areas. Deliver new orb to resident FDP. That's it?"

Taz grimaced at me. "Welcome to Arcanium, home of vague instructions. It's a fairly low magic realm and one of the Traditional Lands from human fairy tales."

"Um, isn't all of Faerie a fairy tale land technically?"

I waited for him to huff or grumble at me, but surprisingly he seemed to think that was a perfectly acceptable question.

"A lot fairy tales told in the human world originated from Faerie," he explained. "Cinderella, Snow White, the Twelve Princesses, they all happened in Faerie realms. We call those realms the Traditional Lands. I'm not sure which one Realm 258 is as that's usually strictly a need-to-know basis, but it'll be one of them."

The lift stopped before I could ask anything more, and the door opened to reveal a heaving crowd.

"This is the atrium." Taz raised his voice over the hum. "We need to get a permission form from reception so you can realm-skip."

His words missed me completely. I stared at the vast hall bustling around us, my skin beginning to tingle with excitement.

This is it. I twisted back and forth to get a better look. *It looks exactly the same as the pictures in Xavio's book.*

Thick wooden beams arched high above, with ivy winding its

stems around each one and the wood stained a dark maroon. The colour reminded me of Mum's red velvet chocolate cake and my stomach grumbled in reply. The flattened cheese sandwiches I'd eaten on the train seemed a lifetime ago.

Small flutters of vivid colour caught my eye amid the ivy, until my gaze focused enough to see butterflies weaving in and out. Many were bright flashes of colour, but several others were larger, with wings so pale blue they looked luminescent. Further above the arches, I could see endless space and the glint of what looked like sun on glass uncountable levels away.

People dashed about in a clamour of busy steps and buzzing conversations, making sure to look important with papers clutched to their chests. One woman shot past with a rattling tray of china cups.

Across the pale marble floor, at the other end of the hall, was a large semi-circular desk, flanked by two enormous trees bursting with pale cherry blossom. Two men and a woman sat behind it with varying expressions of boredom, and I could just hear the drone in their voices over the din.

"FDP head office, how can I help?"

"Hold please, I'll connect you."

"His orb is set to DND right now, would you like to leave a vision?"

Taz approached the reception desk at a brisk pace, dodging through the crowd. I hurried after him, trying my best not to bounce into the people I passed.

"Hi." Taz's hands thudded onto the waist-high counter. "We need a slip to go up to despatch. Demi here has been given an assignment."

I tried to untangle my fingers from the strap of my satchel, but by the time I lifted my hand in a tentative wave, the woman behind the desk had swivelled her chair away from us.

"Hmm," she said, rifling through a pile of small, purple papers. "Emil has orbed down approval. I must say, this is rather irregular though. She's meant to be going through induction, not straight on assignment."

She scribbled something on one of the slips and held it out to me. I took it with a shaking hand.

Everything about this has been irregular so far.

As she turned away, I saw the flash of pale gold glinting on her back. I stared at the top of her wings furled into the furrow between her shoulder blades. I knew from research that some could be given wings as one of their gifts, but I'd never met anyone who had them before. The filmy surface of the wing itself was delicate, but given the arch of the sturdy bones in between, they looked powerful enough to carry her weight.

Taz took a step backward, but stopped when he realised I was still standing at the desk with my permission slip clutched tight.

"Come on." He tapped my elbow. "Or people will think you're a normie that's wandered in by mistake."

He swept across the hall and back into one of the lifts. This one only had a delicate brass gate instead of a metal door to separate us from the shaft, little more than a golden cage. I inched in beside Taz and stared at the carvings of birds and grapevines etched into the metal, wondering how long the rails had been there.

The floor shuddered beneath my feet. I grappled to hold onto the bars of the gate as it zoomed upwards along with the floor, the brick lift shaft cocooning us. I had the fleeting thought of sticking out my hand, but with the speed of the lift I would probably smash off my fingers on the wall. The rush of cool air hitting my face was nowhere near as disconcerting as having it whistle up my trouser legs.

Accidental death by kamikaze lift on my first day. I closed my eyes tight. *That sounds like my kind of luck.*

"The offices are squashed in the spaces between actual human world buildings," Taz explained, completely at ease. "I always wondered how they did that, but when I asked your lot, I just got told it was "Faerie magic" and "not my concern"."

I opened my eyes.

"What do you mean, my lot?"

Taz flicked a dismissive look at me. "Quallies, that's what we call FDPs and their mentees. You all think it's too vast and intellectual for mentor minions like me to understand."

"I'm afraid it might be too intellectual for me to understand," I muttered.

Taz gave me a look as if to say I might be right. Desperate to avoid the thought of what I might be about to head into, I fixated instead on the soft whooshing noise around us and toyed with the idea of how likely it was for a lift like this to break.

Taz cleared his throat and gave me a look, as if he'd already figured out just how easily my mind could wander off.

"The trolls will run you into your realm, so just do your best with the assignment and they'll bring you back in one piece."

"Trolls?" I almost fell over as the lift stopped.

"Yes, trolls."

A dazzling light filtered through the golden grill of the gate and I squinted, my mind still hanging onto what Taz had said.

"Wow, nobody said there'd be actual trolls here. How does it work? Do I just hop on and wait for them to start jogging?"

"Don't be crude." Taz opened the gate. "They do an amazing job, and they run faster than the interns do when a new *Carrie's Castle* book comes out."

"I wasn't trying to be crude, but I've heard they use rickshaws to travel? I've just never met one before. How do I greet them?"

"You say hi like a normal person. They're just like you or me, but don't stare or anything."

Taz strode out of the lift without checking to see if I was following. I took a step forward, blinking as my eyes finally adjusted to the bright light seeping around me. I could just see long wooden walkway stretching from the lift to a circular platform ahead.

"Oh, I almost forgot," Taz called back. "Probably best not to look down."

I shaded my eyes with my hand and did the only natural thing that you do when someone says 'don't look down'. I looked down.

The only thing either side of the walkway was air. I gulped as my gaze drifted further down and down. *And down.*

Far below, the atrium looked like a deep pit with the Arcanium employees scurrying about like determined ants. With my insides dribbling to jelly, I fixed my gaze on the platform ahead, but couldn't get my brain to make my legs move just yet.

"Let me guess." Taz sighed. "Scared of heights?"

I shook my head. "Not heights, just freefall drops plummeting several hundred feet."

Taz approached and grasped my elbow with firm fingers, jostling me forward the first few steps. Afraid of stumbling to my doom, I shook him off.

I can do this. I got the train here on my own. I met Queenie and survived, kind of.

I coached myself a couple of steps further forward, aware of Taz now waiting on the circular platform with his arms folded.

My head span with relief the moment I made it. I eyed several wooden rickshaws that created a horseshoe shape facing a vast wall of sparkling white stone, my curiosity growing. I even managed to look up at the glass dome above, but the dazzle from the sun beaming through seemed so close it made my knees go funny.

Taz cleared his throat to get my attention as a troll approached with a rickshaw. I'd seen pictures of trolls of course, in books, but I still had to remind myself not to stare. The troll's head came level with my ribs and he had long, bat-like ears either side of a wrinkled mossy green face. Even the fact he was wearing a beige shirt with the sleeves rolled up and black corduroy trousers over a pair of worn running shoes did nothing to quell my unabashed wonder.

"Oi." Taz clicked his fingers in front of my face. "Focus on me for second. Get in the rickshaw."

I wanted to refuse, but how would that look? Mum had been proud when I said I'd been invited to join Arcanium. I couldn't actually remember ever seeing her proud of me before. Not proud enough to come with me on my first day apparently, but still. My sisters wouldn't even hesitate to dive straight into an adventure. I got into the rickshaw.

Taz stood beside it, his nose crinkling as he pointed to the now grinning troll.

"This is Trevor. He's between FDPs at the moment and owes me a favour, so he'll be taking you to the realm and bringing you back."

I raised my hand in a hesitant greeting to Trevor, but didn't dare say anything as Taz handed me a tiny pearlescent grey ball on a silver keychain.

"Here's your orb," he said. "All you have to do is say the name of the person you want to communicate with. Then you'll see them projected out of it."

I clung to my satchel strap with one hand, the only familiar thing in the swirling vortex of change whirling around me.

"I don't suppose you can access email or the news on it?" I guessed.

Taz rolled his eyes. "No, you can't get email, but it will tune in to Arcanium channels, so you see the latest episodes of *Demolition Ducks* or *Siren Sing-Along*. But focus on the assignment. The one thing you need to know is that you can use it to communicate with anyone at FDP headquarters."

"I only know you!"

"Yeah." Taz didn't sound pleased about that at all. "So, it's me that's stuck with you if you're useless. Try not to be useless please, for me? Now, the FDP you're looking for is called Alannah. She's seventeen, blonde and posing as maid to the realm's future duchess."

Taz held up a second orb between his finger and thumb, this one shining and black. I closed my fist around it to keep it safe.

"That second one is the one for Alannah. Give it to her and only her, no matter what anyone says. Once you've handed it over, you use your one to call me and Trevor will come get you, okay? Good luck."

I panicked and shoved the orbs in my pocket, one on each side so I couldn't risk getting them mixed up.

"How long will it take to get to Realm 258?" I asked.

Taz waved his hand at the sparkling slab of white stone.

"Trevor is the fastest runner at HQ, so about three seconds. The despatch wall is made of pure quartz, but I'm sure you already knew that."

I hadn't known that about the quartz. Nobody had explained any of this in detail to me and I couldn't remember reading anything about it in the manual. Then I realised what Taz had said.

"Wait, three sec-*aaaaah*!"

Trevor took off at speed straight toward the wall with the rickshaw in tow. As I got thrown forward, one hand smashing into the carriage's rail, I waited for inevitable death.

Either the fall from a great height will get us, or I'll end up smashed flat as a pancake against a bit of sparkling rock.

Air rushed cold past my face. I closed my eyes and the sensation of plummeting swirled in my chest.

Something whacked against me and the falling sensation disappeared. Whatever I'd crashed into gave way with a loud squelch.

I flailed but my arms and legs were trapped in some kind of super strong gloop.

Breathless, I stopped struggling and lifted my head. When I opened my eyes, I saw a vast world of muddy brown.

Nope, just mud, and I'm stuck in it.

Trevor was nowhere to be seen, but a few feet away on the edge of a grassy bank, stood a young man. He must have been a good couple of years older than me, and would have been kind of cute if he was smiling. However, he wasn't smiling. He had his eyes fixed on me and looked extremely annoyed.

"You are trespassing," he barked. "State your name."

CHAPTER THREE
OFF TO FIND A FAIRY

I took a long time getting out of the mud. It didn't help that the boy stood watching with a sour frown instead of helping. He wore a deep blue jacket with shiny silver buttons, and britches with leather riding boots that made him look every inch a prince fit for a human fairy tale. Even his curly auburn hair shone in the sunlight. I imagined him charging off on some shining noble steed and yelling something suitably dashing.

The moment I clambered onto the bank, covered in slimy sludge, the boy folded his arms.

"Who are you? What are you doing in the royal garden? There are severe penalties for trespassing."

I eyed my surroundings. The unkempt wilderness of the tall, silver-trunked trees overhead and a lack of anything floral didn't look much like a royal garden, but I guessed mentioning it wouldn't get me off to the best start.

I also had to contend with the fact that fairies couldn't lie. Or rather, we could, but Xavio had warned us that it did something twisty to our brains and each lie would cost us, break us down bit by bit. Every time a fairy lied, the act stayed like a jagged shard of glass inside their mind, gradually scratching deeper every time another lie was added. I could remember dark stories about fairies that had gone mad trying to keep track of their lies and bearing the burden of them. It was doable, but most fairies much preferred the skill required for manipulating a situation to outright lying anyway.

I hadn't told a single lie since then, but we'd practiced word-tangling in class. That at least was something I could do well.

The boy stood waiting for an answer, and I thought quickly for a suitable one. I'd had no time to prepare and no idea if explaining my real identity would make things better or worse.

"I don't know." I made a show of rubbing my forehead. "I think I hit my head. I'm not sure. I might need a minute."

The boy waited and I would have bet on him counting to sixty in his head, assuming this realm kept time like the human world did. I tried to remember the scant information Taz had sprung on me, but all I had left in my head was the sound of my own scream as the rickshaw had taken off.

"I'm looking for someone," I tried. "She's a maid to the future duchess. I've been asked to come and find her. Um, her name's Alannah, if that helps? She's blonde, with blue eyes-"

"I have met her on previous visits." The boy grimaced. "The duchess and her daughter have already arrived at the castle in preparation for the wedding. I will take you personally."

I blinked. "Oh, um, thanks, that's very kind."

The boy frowned and glanced around.

"Do you not know who I am?" he asked.

I shook my head. *Should I just use the orb thing and insist they send Trevor back for me? Then they could get someone experienced to handle this. Or even Taz.*

Only the thought of going home stopped me, the visions of my sisters crowing over how I didn't even last a day dancing in my head.

"You are addressing Prince Lucastrian of Egloriem," the prince announced with a vocal flourish. "You must have travelled far indeed to not know of me or recognise the royal crest."

He tapped a gold emblem stitched on the left side of his chest, a horse's head with two spears crossed behind it.

25

I thought quickly. "Thank you, your Highness?"

The furrow on the royal brow dug even deeper.

"Are you mocking me?" the prince asked. "What has my highness got to do with anything? Are you calling me short?"

He eyed me up and down. Before I could answer him, the prince seemed to take pity on me, the regal shoulders sagging.

"Perhaps it is the bump on the head," he decided. "You are still a lady, despite appearances, and I cannot allow you to roam unchaperoned. You call me Prince Lucastrian."

"Sorry, thank you, Prince Lucastrian."

The prince frowned and unfolded his arms.

"Well, let us away. I do not have much time to spare."

He strode off without a look back and I wondered if I'd manage to get through the rest of the day without another boy doing that to me. I hurried after him toward a tall stone wall, trying to keep my wits and wariness sharp.

The sun emerged from behind steel grey clouds and sent heat beaming down through the trees. Blue cornflowers grew in the undergrowth and clumps of clover stood out like a sea of emeralds against the paler grass. Despite the beautiful setting, my shoes filled the air with a depressing squelching sound, and I was focused more on the disgusting damp sensation from my clothes.

I clutched my satchel with one hand and assessed my options. I still had my spare change of clothes inside, just in case I got separated from my suitcase, my FDP manual and what I considered my emergency survival kit (extra pants and socks, two apples and two big packets of Jelly Babies).

If all goes splat, I just have to consult the manual, and worst case orb Taz to get me out of here. That'll be the last resort though, like if things start exploding or princes start trying to eat my brains.

One thing I'd learned at camp was that all realms were different. Sometimes it would be almost unnoticeable, until an unassuming rose lunged and tried to eat your arm, or a dog told everyone the secrets you'd been muttering to yourself when you thought nobody was around.

Then you get realms full of tentacles, like Realm 313 that they just discovered. I wiped streaks of mud from my nose. *This could be worse I suppose.*

The prince slowed as we reached a wooden door set in the wall, and I increased my pace to catch up.

"So, you are not from any of the villages nearby?" Prince Lucastrian asked.

"No, I'm actually from Salisbury," I blurted out. "Um, you wouldn't have heard of it I don't think. It's far away."

The prince pursed his lips but didn't argue, and thankfully didn't say he knew exactly where Salisbury was.

"And you're not here for the wedding?"

"No, only passing through to see Alannah."

Keep it vague. If you can convince him to get you to the castle, you can find Alannah, pass over the orb and go back a success.

Queenie and Emil would be sure to consider me for a full-time position after the menteeship then. Granted, that would be two years away still, but eventually there would be no more living at home getting chased or sat on.

Prince Lucastrian gave me a final, disapproving once over and opened the door, striding through without looking back. I hurried after him into a rose garden, planted in sections that were split into eight. Without the trees overhead, a dark stone castle loomed above us, like something out of traditional *Disney*. Two guards stood either side of a wide archway on the other side of the garden, their clothing deep blue and covered with chainmail tunics.

The guards bowed their heads as Prince Lucastrian steamed past. I expected them to stop me, but I was part of the prince's entourage now it seemed. Other than casting a few bemused looks in my direction, the guards let me through.

I puffed along behind the prince across a wide bridge that leapt over a moat beneath, stopping only to pull a serviette from my satchel and dab my face. At the foot of the castle, just in front of a long flight of stone steps, Prince Lucastrian came to a stop. He eyed me and sighed.

"You have come to the great city of Eglor," he announced. "Ah, you are in luck. Here is the future duchess now, out for her walk."

A woman glided toward us with effortless grace, her feet hidden beneath the folds of a very impressive purple dress. She looked only a little older than me, but behind the black hair curled around her face and the youthful fresh complexion, were shrewd, orange eyes.

"Prince Lucastrian," she said with uneasiness in her voice. "Your companion appears to need tending to."

Beside her stood another girl, wearing a simpler dress of matching colour. Taz's words about blonde hair filtered to the front of my mind, and my heart rate picked up with hope. The girl looked back at me with even more caution than her mistress did. I caught her eye and tried to subtly lift my hand so she could see the small keychain with the black sphere hanging against my palm. The girl's brow shot up.

"There you are," she exclaimed loudly, startling everyone. "Oh, look at the state of you."

The theatrical tutting must have sounded genuine to the prince and duchess, but I waded through the indignity of how mucky I was with flaming cheeks.

"I landed in a bog."

The girl raised her eyes skywards. "Mistress, forgive me. May I take her somewhere and see to her? We do not want the wedding guests seeing her in such a state."

"Hmm." The duchess narrowed her eyes. "Very well, Alannah, but be quick. I should not be left around the prince unchaperoned."

"Come along then, quickly." Alannah beckoned to me.

I hurried after her, somehow managing to dip a quick curtsey as I passed the prince and duchess. Alannah stalked off out of sight around the side of the castle and pounced the moment I joined her.

"Who are you?" she hissed.

I gulped. "Um, I'm, Demi, um-" I cleared my throat and tried again. "I was sent here to deliver something to you, and to retrieve something also."

I held up the black orb still in my palm. Alannah swiped it from me and studied it before turning her critical gaze back to my face.

"Who sent you?" she asked.

"Queenie. Well, Emil technically. Taz took me up to the big platform and the troll- I mean Trevor, he brought me here."

"Okay, no need to babble." Alannah huffed out a resigned sigh and pinched the bridge of her nose. "I have to get mine from inside to give to you. I'm guessing given the state of you they didn't even bother letting you go through induction before throwing you out here?"

I shook my head, taking Alannah literally about the no babbling thing. Rather than meet her gaze, a task I found daunting when faced with pretty much everyone I met, I focused instead on the cloudy, diamond-shaped crystal pendant around her throat.

Alannah cast one final reproving glance over me.

"Stay here. Don't touch anything. If anyone speaks to you, be polite and say you don't know, you're just visiting. When I get back, I'll show you how to call your ride home."

I nodded and clamped both hands to the strap of my satchel. Alannah swept through a nearby side door and I focused on not taking too much notice of the foul stench wafting over from a nearby hole in the ground.

I wonder if they have actual plumbing and things here. I mused, determinedly avoiding eye contact with a group of people walking past. *It's more like a medieval story book scene. They probably don't have any electricity.*

I looked down at my muddy clothes.

Everyone is still cleaner than me right now though. Once this is done, I can have a serious shower.

I stared across the courtyard to a wooden barn with its doors thrown wide open. A surge of heat emanated out, accompanied by the sizzle and clang of a forge. Intrigued, I shuffled a few paces forward until a lightning fast flash dazzled me. With a hand shading my eyes, I turned back to see what had caused it.

A glass tank nearby had caught the light from the sun. It was sat on the corner of a wooden work bench pushed up against the castle wall but, as I inched closer to have a look, I could see the tank wasn't filled with water.

I bent forward to peer in at six wide-eyed lizards staring back at me.

"Whoa, hello there," I murmured. "You look a lot like chameleons. I'm guessing you might not be, considering where I am. Are you super monster lizards instead?"

Aware I was essentially talking out loud to myself to anyone who might walk past, I pressed the slightest tips of my fingers against the glass. One of the lizards ambled up and flicked out a long, brown tongue at me, it's head tilting to one side.

"What are you up to?" A voice boomed.

I turned my head to see Prince Lucastrian scowling at me. I flinched and scrambled to get away from the tank, my hands flying out.

My palms met cold glass.

I held my breath at the tipping point moment as the tank teetered on the edge of the bench. Before I or Prince Lucastrian could react, the tank sailed sideways and smashed into smithereens on the stone.

"I'm sorry!"

I bent forward and tried to scoop up the nearest lizard, who didn't seem to have noticed anything had happened. Either that or it was still in shock.

Three of them were making a determined bid for freedom up the side of the castle wall, and one was still asleep on a large rock from the tank. The sixth headed for the gap between my feet. I doubled over, my fingers grazing its long tail as it slipped out of my grasp. I stumbled backwards in a lumbering attempt to catch it but smacked into something solid.

"Aaaah!"

A moment of silence followed the scream.

Then, *SQUELGGGCH.*

I closed my eyes in torment, the lizards momentarily forgotten. I shuffled around just in time to see Prince Lucastrian of Egloriem break the surface of the sewage pit.

CHAPTER FOUR
AN UNLIKELY PARCEL

"You!" The prince continued with some very unprincely curse words. "Wait until I get my hands on you!"

If that weren't bad enough, Alannah chose that moment to reappear.

"What the-"

She stared with her mouth open at the broken glass, then at the stewing, soiled prince, and finally at me.

"I didn't mean to," I insisted, my insides twisting with anxiety.

Alannah mumbled something under her breath.

"Right, come with me."

Aware she would most likely report me to Queenie and I'd be sent home in disgrace, I hung my head and hurried after her. I wondered if I should try to at least offer the prince some help, a tissue maybe, although it wouldn't do any good given the stench following us, but Alannah's quick pace suggested I was better off not being seen by him again.

Alannah led me behind the castle where the muck heap was giving only a slightly less pungent odour than the pit and the prince. When she turned to face me, I expected exasperation. I expected anger. I couldn't rule out threats or a minor strangulation. Choked laughter, however, was a surprise.

"That was brilliant," Alannah whispered, holding back her giggles. "I've wanted to do that to him for weeks, and worse. He's a complete whiner. I'll sort things out here, but you should go before he tries to behead you or something. This is my old orb. Take it back to Emil and say it needs cleansing first, okay?"

She held up a keychain with a rose pink orb dangling from it. I took it and put it secure in my pocket, not quite willing to believe this was apparently the bulk of the assignment completed already.

"Now, you have your own orb, right?" Alannah asked.

I nodded and pulled it out of my other pocket.

She smiled. "Good idea to keep them separate. You might be clumsy, but at least you're not dim. Okay, you know your troll's name?"

"Yes, Trevor." I nodded again. "Taz said he was the fastest-"

"Okay great. Just look at the orb, say his name and tell him you're ready to return to hub. That bit's important, always say 'Troll's name, I'm ready to return to hub'."

I lifted the orb and took a deep breath. Alannah nodded encouragement, her gaze flicking behind her as the prince's bellowed threats grew louder and more drastic.

"Trevor, I'm ready to return to hub."

Nothing happened.

I bit my lip as more voices were raised. The laughter of the crowd was being shouted at very loudly by the irate prince.

The air shivered in front of us. I clenched my fingers around my orb, the keychain digging into my index finger. A second later, I breathed a sigh of relief. I'd never been so glad to see a short, mossy-looking troll with bat-like ears and a rickshaw before.

"Hiya, Demi." Trevor beamed at me. "And Alannah, not seen you around in a long time. Assignment going okay?"

"As much as can be expected in Faerie," Alannah said as I clambered into the rickshaw.

"Okay, well, back we go." Trevor winked at me. "The young lad will be waiting for you. Had a good feeling about you, and my feelings are never wrong."

That warmed my insides somewhat and made me smile.

"Thanks." *I can't believe I actually did it.*

I sagged against the rickshaw seat, my satchel heavy on my lap, and lifted a hand in farewell to Alannah. As Trevor started running on the spot, I closed my eyes before I could see what exactly happened during realm-skipping. My stomach somersaulted as the rickshaw lurched forward. Air hit my face and pushed at my hair, but almost immediately the rushing sensation stopped and the rickshaw jolted. I tumbled chest-first into the front rail with a muffled "oof".

After a few uneven breaths, I raised my head to see a disapproving pair of green-blue eyes swimming in a sea of freckles.

"Thanks Trevor." Taz stepped back, arms folded.

I clambered out of the rickshaw with my limbs shaking. "Yeah, thanks Trevor, truly."

"My pleasure." Trevor beamed. "I'll be your transport now, any time you need to realm-skip. Just find me, or call me, and I'll come."

He ambled away with the rickshaw in tow before I could thank him any further. Still amazed I'd actually succeeded, albeit not smoothly, I glanced around at the suspended platform before I found the energy to face Taz.

"So, that went well." I grimaced.

Taz's eyes flashed like the Northern Lights. He turned toward the narrow platform and set off toward the lift at a blistering pace. I stared after him. I'd expected 'congratulations' or a quick 'well done' at least. Even bashful acceptance that I'd actually succeeded would have done.

I followed, cautious to stay in the middle of the walkway, and stepped into the lift beside Taz.

"I got what I went for," I tried.

As the lift zoomed downward, Taz frowned at me.

"You stink," he said. "You'll have to report in first though before anything else. They shouldn't have thrown you in like that on your first day, and without a mentor assigned to you. I was watching on the Ogle screen and- well, at least you got back okay."

Okay, it wasn't the most graceful way I could have handled things, but I got the job done.

My plummeting insides had nothing to do with the lift zooming downwards. I didn't dare comment on the assignment any further, choosing to dwell on something less embarrassing. I'd read about the Ogle of course, the enormous bank of screens that showed a view into every realm Arcanium had links to. I'd just not considered that people might be able to sit there watching it like a budget blooper reel.

"You know how lucky you are, right?" Taz said more quietly.

I nodded. "I know, it could have been so much worse. I don't try to screw things up, things just sort of happen."

"No- well, yes that was lucky, but I meant Trevor choosing you. Trolls don't just take the first fairy they give a lift to, you know."

I couldn't remember ever being chosen before. Not at school, not as someone's specific friend and certainly not in P.E. Except by Xavio, and he was odd by every single possible description. The cruel fingers of doubt threatened to creep in, but I shook them off, the memory of Trevor's compliment making me smile again.

"He did say he had a good feeling about me."

"Hmm." Taz looked me up and down, his brow quirked in disbelief. "I'd wipe that dopey grin off your face before you see Queenie either way. She hates smirkers."

The lift came to a stop, and I arranged my face in what I hoped was a suitably non-smirking expression of respect. As I followed Taz along the hall, I reassured myself that Queenie at least would have better things to do than watch me on the Ogle screen.

"Ah, there you are." Emil appeared in front of us.

I flinched. *I didn't even hear him open a door or anything.*

"I did the assignment," I explained. "Alannah gave me her old orb to bring back and said it needed cleaning first."

Emil smiled and held out his hand.

"Queenie's in a frightful mood," he said. "I need to see her anyway, so I'll hand it in for you. She'll only throw it back at me and tell me to process it. Better my head than yours!"

I reached into my pocket and pulled out the rose-pink orb. I handed it over, secretly relieved I wouldn't have to face Queenie after all. Emil pocketed the orb and wrinkled his nose.

"That was some landing by the way," he chortled. "Taz, find Fianna and get her to show Demi to her room, or Ace if he's about. After that, Demi, you can go through your induction."

Taz turned back to the lift as Emil set off toward Queenie's office. Even if he had been watching my less than graceful efforts, Emil didn't seem to think it was the end of my career here. I slipped my hand into my jeans pocket and moved my thumb along my fingertips, back and forth in a routine to calm my fluttering nerves as I hurried after Taz.

"Who's Ace and Fianna?" I asked as we got back in the lift.

Taz sighed. "A couple of qualified FDPs, or close enough to."

"Oh." I didn't know what to say to that. "So, um, Ace and Fianna, they're already taking on charges and assignments and things? Sorry for all the questions, but it's a bit overwhelming."

His expression softened then. "I imagine it'd be overwhelming without the random assignment, let alone with it. Ace is a mentee, but he's in his second year. Fianna just finished hers so she's fully qualified. We have mixed residence halls anyway, so we'll just find one or the other and they can take over showing you what's where and things. Then, when you're ready, they'll bring you down to the Ogle."

I could feel my eyes threatening to pop out by this point, the surprise at mixed residents' areas topped only by the prospect of ticking off a life goal.

"I get to see the Ogle? It's not authorised access only or anything?"

I almost forgot about the lurching in my stomach and the wind rushing up my trouser legs as the lift hurtled downwards. Taz gave me a weary look and I pulled the cuffs of my cardigan down over my hands, embarrassed at knowing so little.

"Not really. We're all authorised to go in, although most people don't bother unless they need to. The best place to hang out is the library or, failing that, the canteen."

When the lift stopped, Taz undid the gate but didn't get out.

"This is the residents' hall?" I asked, just in case.

Taz rolled his eyes. "Well done, brainiac. Just ask around for Ace or Fianna until you find one of them."

I nodded and stepped out, wringing the strap of my satchel in both hands. I turned back to thank him in time to see him jab one of the buttons.

"Thanks, Taz. I really appreciate-"

A whoosh of air from the lift and he was gone. I breathed deep, filling my insides with air to push down the sinking feeling that Taz probably didn't think very much of me at all.

Okay, it's okay. He's just one person you happened to meet first. I'm sure there are loads of really great people you're going to meet next.

I waited a few beats before inching forward, my legs quivering as I peered at the gaping hole where the lift floor had just been.

"I wouldn't get too close."

For the umpteenth time in as many hours, I jumped. I scrambled back on turbo feet to get away from the lift shaft.

"Sorry, did I startle you?" The voice sounded friendly enough.

I turned to see a tall, broad-shouldered boy around my age. With black boots laced up, fitted black jeans and a navy V-necked pullover, he looked really cool, like a younger John Boyega. I eyed the stylish hair and the dark eyes that were wide with good-natured amusement.

"Um, I'm looking for Ace or Fianna?" I squeaked.

The boy smiled to show perfect white teeth. "Fortune's smiling on you then, you found me. I'm Ace. Are you Demi? Fianna asked me to hang around and start your induction as she's got errands to run."

To his credit, Ace didn't once give me a funny look for my grimy clothing. The moment I nodded, he turned and set off along the hall. Much like the corridor to Queenie's office, the walls were panelled wood and the floor carpeted blue underfoot. I grimaced as the now dry mud flaked off me with every step.

"Okay so you're double lucky," Ace chuckled. "Not only did you find me on the first try, but you also get a room at the end of the corridor right next to the hall. It's close to the bathrooms, but also not so close to everyone else or the common area that you'll get all the rowdy noise."

I tried to fix the stream of information in my head, and focused on keeping up with my new guide.

It sounds too good to be true. It also sounds like Ace hasn't heard about my assignment either. Maybe nobody will say anything and I can just start fresh.

The corridor ended in a T-junction, with halls going left and right. Ace hooked left and opened a door at the end, standing aside to let me pass.

It was a box room with dark blue walls, an IKEA-style pine desk and a cubbyhole unit to put clothes in. I sagged in relief to see my suitcase sitting on the single bed in the corner. No windows, but then I knew Arcanium existed in some kind of random in-between-space that I hadn't quite figured out yet. It was one of the questions I had on my long list of things to ask once I'd settled in properly.

"Okay so, I'll leave you be for a few minutes." Ace checked his wristwatch. "No time for a shower so just change your clothes, then I can take you round for your induction."

"Thanks, Ace." I managed to dredge up a smile.

The moment Ace shut the door, I let out a tumbling sigh and unwound my shoulder muscles. I pulled my satchel over my head and dropped it on the bed, leaning over to open my suitcase. Picking a fresh t-shirt and my best dark blue jeans out, I put them aside and quickly sorted the rest of my things into the cubbyhole shelves.

I flipped the flap of my satchel open, trying to decide if I needed to take it with me, or at least a pen and paper to make induction notes.

The scream of alarm got stuck in my throat, which was probably a good thing.

I stared inside the satchel.

A pair of beady eyes blinked back.

I opened my mouth, but no words came out. Beneath the eyes, a wide pink mouth opened, and a long, brown tongue flicked out.

"I- You- Oh, *no*."

CHAPTER FIVE
AN ILL-TIMED INDUCTION

I groaned, even more horrified when the lizard peeking out of my satchel copied me with a much more satisfied little grumble of its own.

"Crud, crud, crud, you can't stay here," I muttered.

I reached in and scooped the animal out, looking around the room in panic.

It must have somehow snuck in when I knocked the tank over in the realm. What do I do now?

I couldn't just waltz out with it in my bag. I couldn't very well go and say to Ace, or Taz, or Emil, 'by the way, I kind of brought a stowaway back with me from my first assignment'. I could plead that nobody had actually given me any instructions, but even I knew creatures from Faerie had a reputation of being unexpected. Bringing one back would most definitely be on the no-no list.

It must have crept in when I was trying to pick the others up. I could run upstairs quick and ask Trevor to drop it back into the realm for me. I shook my head immediately. *I can't ask him to do that. He might not even be allowed to, or able. He might have to report me.*

I held the animal up to my face at a cautious distance. Knowing my luck, it would burp acid or something and fry my face off.

It blinked at me and, a moment later, a ripple passed over its scales. Where it had been a brownish grey, now it was a rich blue to match the room.

"You *are* a chameleon!" I murmured. Delight overtook my anxiety. "You shouldn't have hidden in my bag though, that wasn't sensible. What are you, a boy?" I took the quickest of underbelly peeks. "Yes, you are. Well, we'll have to be careful until I know what to do with you safely. I'll try to find a way to bring you something edible as well. Perhaps I shall startle everyone with my originality and call you Leo."

Leo the chameleon made an adoring murmur, and I copied it right back. He opened his mouth in a wide grin and relaxed against my fingers. Another reason my sisters tormented me was my alarming ability to replicate sounds, but here it might actually come in useful.

A smart tapping filled the room as someone knocked on the door. I looked around for a suitable hideaway. If I put Leo under the bed, he would climb out again. If I hid him in the satchel, someone might ask me for a tissue or something and expect me to open it.

"Demi?" Ace's voice floated through the door.

I pulled open one of the larger desk drawers. "Um, just finishing changing, one second."

I plonked Leo inside and pulled an apple from my satchel.

"There you go," I whispered. "And here, this will do for something to lie on. It's not a rock or a branch, but I'm never going to use it."

The ghastly knitted sweatshirt a distant aunt had given me a while back went into the drawer. I hadn't had the gall to bin it at home, but at least now it had some use. I shut the drawer most of the way, but left a crack for light to get in. Beginning to feel dizzy from all the upheaval, I toed off my shoes, changed my clothes quick and unearthed my spare trainers from the bottom of the suitcase.

I eyed the drawer one last time, but there were no sounds of distress and no signs of another daring escape attempt. I opened the door, hoping Ace wouldn't notice how flushed my cheeks were. He smiled at me normally enough, or at least as normally as he had been smiling before, and there were no shouts of 'watch out, behind you' or anything alarming.

"Ready for the grand tour?" he asked.

I nodded, closed the door behind me and checked it wouldn't open again. Ace grinned and held up a key.

"Meant to give you this before. Lock the door behind you if you're worried. Some do, but we're an honourable bunch generally."

I took the key and slid it into my pocket with one hand, pressing against the door to check it wouldn't swing open or anything by accident. The fact that Leo might be some mutant creature able to open doors occurred to me, but I brushed that aside and did my best to look unflustered despite my thundering pulse.

"Right, necessities first." Ace set off down the hall. "This is our bathroom. Rules are clear up after yourself, no using other people's stuff without permission and absolutely no non-students allowed up here, except for tutors and the odd member of staff."

I nodded. *Who would I even know to invite?*

Ace closed the bathroom door and carried on toward the lift.

"Laundry is every Friday evening so put your hamper outside your door if you want stuff washed."

I followed him into the lift and braced myself for the rush of air. Usually, the mass of events and information would have overwhelmed me, but fear of being found out and sent home was keeping my mind panic-sharp.

"What about animals?" I asked. "I suppose we aren't allowed to keep pets here."

"What kind of pet?" Ace frowned, shoving his hands in his

pockets as the lifted whistled downwards.

"Er... just wondered. I used to have goldfish, at home obviously," I bluffed.

Ace's brow wrinkled deeper. "No, not allowed pets. To be fair, I never asked, but haven't seen anyone with any. One of my friends at home though had a pinksie, one of those tiny creatures with all the quills, and he didn't realise eating Oia berries made them bloat and shed their quills at speed like darts. His mum was digging them out of the furniture for weeks."

His frown lifted as I laughed. Then I thought of the stowaway in my desk drawer and sought frantically for an alternative solution.

"I read that human phones don't work down here as well?" I tried.

"No, there's no signal as we're essentially beyond the reach of any network known to man." Ace grinned as the lift stopped. "Any communication that does work is all processed right here in the Ogle."

I followed him out and my jaw dropped open. The room reminded me of an aircraft hangar, except there were no open sides, just rows and rows of screens like library stacks, a window into every realm all at once, or an Aladdin's cave of potential charges. Desks ran beneath the screens, most of the padded office chairs empty.

"Welcome to the Ogle," Ace announced. "The Centre of Realm Surveillance and Knowledge."

I barely heard him. I didn't notice anyone else approaching either, too busy gawping.

"You said it was your life's goal to see it, right?" Taz's voice made me jump.

"Did I say that?" I murmured, stunned beyond thinking. "I wonder why they called it the 'Ogle'?"

"Because CoRSaK is an awful name," he suggested.

I wandered toward the nearest row of screens, staring in amazement. One showed a lady with a large hat reading in a garden. The next showed nine bulbous eyes and what looked like a bruise-coloured tentacle.

"There will be more explanations once you get to the classes of course," Ace insisted. "But I'll save you the spiel by giving you the gist now. Basically, we get told there's no referencing places, people or history from the human world."

Oops, I told the prince I was from Salisbury.

"Don't interfere with the flora and fauna." Taz joined in, grinning at me in an unsettling way.

Does knocking over lizards and throwing a prince in a sewage pit count? He definitely must have seen me do that on one of these screens.

"And obviously, don't bring anything back without permission."

I gulped. *So I've pretty much broken every rule already, great. There goes any hope of a job here if anyone finds Leo.*

"I'll leave you to it," Taz said. "I've got to finish up stuff, but no doubt Ace will give you his undivided attention."

He skulked off further into the rows of screens without waiting for us to say goodbye. I watched him go, relieved that he'd come across to talk to us when he didn't have to, so at least that was something. Ace rolled his eyes.

"Taz is alright, but he acts like he owns the place. Probably because he's been here so long. Anyway, we should have time to swing by the study floor."

With thoughts of Leo still lingering in my mind, I carried the anxious stone of guilt in my gut as Ace led the way back to the lift and upwards to see where the study floor was. The training hall and study rooms were shut for the night, all looking much like school classrooms with tables, chairs and, in the case of the training hall, a big empty space.

"Attend the training classes or have a good reason if you don't," Ace insisted as he herded me along the lamplit hall. "Arcanium likes to see willing and determination. Oh, and try to make friends with the mentors, as they choose you as their FDP when the time comes."

"Like the trolls?" I asked.

Ace's face lit up in admiration, so much so that I couldn't help blushing. Not often anyone looked my way positively, let alone with such enthusiasm.

"Exactly. People say being an FDP is a great honour, but actually it's the trolls and the mentors and the support staff that have the real power. We just get the glory, for what little that's worth."

I grinned then. "Sounds about right, I'm always getting the short end."

Ace laughed as he led the way down a curving staircase more fitting for an English manor house and along a corridor. I decided I would draw a map for myself when I got back to my room.

Although there might not be much point if people find out about Leo and I get kicked out for bringing him here. Or if he's escaped the room somehow and ends up doing something dangerous, like Ace's pinksie story.

"Now, we can get to the best bit." Ace strode faster. "The canteen. Guaranteed to make you feel more at home."

That gave me an idea.

"So, what do I do if I want to call home?" I asked.

I wondered if the RSPCA would come out for a potentially alien lizard. I could call them and say I found a chameleon on the beach, and just not mention the potentially alien part. Leo was most likely a normal lizard, and the experts could find him a good home.

"You have to go up to the arcade." Ace checked his watch and grimaced. "Doubt we'll have time for that tonight though. There's no actual curfew inside, but mentees aren't allowed up to the arcade or the human world after ten o'clock without approved clearance."

I slowed in surprise at the sound of no curfew inside the hub. Even my sisters, two and four years older than me, still had to be back by eleven-thirty in the evening at home before Mum bolted the front door.

"So, I could sit in the library studying until two am if I wanted?" I asked.

Ace laughed. "The library would be shut for the night but the study rooms and common area you could use 'til then if you really wanted yeah. But for tonight it's getting late so we'd best get you something to eat now then run back up."

My stomach growled in agreement as Ace pushed open the canteen door and a leftover waft of delicious smells flowed out.

"Obviously FDPs get a bit more leeway though about leaving the hub," Ace continued, standing aside to let me go through ahead of him. "I turned seventeen a couple of months ago and I heard they relax the rules when you become eighteen even if you're not qualified yet. I'm guessing you're the normal sixteen?"

I nodded. "Yeah, as of three days ago."

"Oh, well happy belated birthday then." Ace grinned as he led me toward the buffet counter.

"Thanks."

I beamed at him, so pleased he was being kind to me that I didn't see the figure sweeping toward us with a large cardboard box.

"Watch out!" Ace shouted, a fraction too late.

I collided face first with a wall of cardboard and stumbled back. Ace caught me with a heroic sweep of his arm as the box toppled to the floor.

As if this day couldn't get any worse.

I shuffled away from Ace with my cheeks burning and bent to help pick up the box. I grabbed it at the same time as its owner did. Mortified, I let go and stared up into a narrowed pair of steely grey eyes. With a pale pink cardigan and puffy curled blonde hair, the woman reminded me strangely of Miss Hattie from *Despicable Me.*

"Give that here." She snatched the box closer to her chest, glowering around the side of it. "Why don't you watch where you're going?"

"I'm sorry, I didn't mean to-"

The woman stormed off toward the exit, as the burning shame crept through my gut, into my chest and up over my shoulders. One more incident would definitely result in me bursting into tears.

"Wow," Ace muttered. "You must have caught her in a *really* bad mood. That's Sandra, the librarian."

I closed my eyes in torment. Libraries had always been a place of refuge for me, a safe space away from my sisters and their friends during lunchtime at school. Now I'd started on bad terms with the Arcanium librarian.

Ace might have noticed the shiny blush fighting the corners of my eyes, as he clapped a gentle hand to my shoulder. I flinched and wriggled away, so used to trying to evade my sisters that human contact was almost as alien as Leo might turn out to be. Ace's easy smile didn't waver.

"Come on, we'll get you some food. The Braunees are the best cooks in all of Faerie."

I blinked as we reached the buffet counter. Two faces popped up, a young woman with bright brown eyes and a twinkling smile, and an elderly man with the same eyes and expression. Where the girl's hair was also brown, his was greying, but they both seemed unexpectedly pleased to see us.

"This is Demi, Braunee." Ace introduced me, looking from one to the other so I couldn't tell which one he was addressing. "She got here this afternoon but was thrown on an assignment and we're just doing the induction now."

I noticed Ace's unimpressed look, but had no time to fathom if that was because of me or what had happened to me. The young woman tutted.

"Oh dear." She winked at me. "You must be famished. How about a nice club sandwich, and we have some crisps leftover. Oh, and take a muffin. There's a bottle of juice somewhere. Braunee, go find that apple juice for me."

Ace leaned close as both cooks scurried off into the kitchen behind the counter.

"They're both called Braunee, which can get confusing, but they're amazing at cooking the food and guessing what people like to eat. I'm guessing club sandwich with apple juice is your favourite?"

I nodded as the female Braunee came back. I wondered if I could ask for a salad and give the leaves to Leo, but didn't want to push my luck.

"Now, you look like a girl who likes her lettuce. Lots of lettuce, and cucumber too, why not."

I froze. "It's like you read my mind."

The older Braunee hurried back with a half-litre bottle of apple juice, a muffin and a packet of ready salted crisps.

"No time for reading minds." He grinned. "We just sense what people need for their bellies and their hearts to be full."

The joint twinkling grins weren't exactly reassuring, but I

took the bag of food they handed me with a huge smile.

"Thank you, that's really kind."

Both Braunees waved the gratitude aside, despite their identical pleased smiles and tinged cheeks.

"Now, it's almost nine o'clock," the older Braunee chided. "Off to your rooms."

I said goodbye and followed Ace out of the canteen toward the lift. I clung to the bag tangled around my fingers all the way up to the residents' floor and along to my bedroom, relieved to find I was getting used to the lift already at least.

"Thanks for showing me around, Ace." I managed a weary smile. "Hopefully tomorrow won't be so eventful."

Ace chuckled and took a step back.

"Don't count on it, this is Arcanium after all. I'll knock for you tomorrow morning so I can show you down to breakfast if you like. Nine a.m., okay?"

"Okay, thanks Ace."

Bemused that he was going out of his way to be so helpful now my induction was done, I mumbled further thanks and inched into my room. With the door shut, I let out a hefty sigh, dropped the bag of food onto the bed and rushed to check on Leo.

For a moment, I couldn't see anything, but then a flicker of movement stirred amid the orange wool. I pulled Leo out, amused to see the apple half-eaten and the wool shredded.

"You have been busy," I muttered. "You'll have to stay in there for now, but I got you some lettuce."

Aware I should be panicking instead of crooning, but finally too exhausted to be jittery, I fed Leo my crusts and smiled as he snapped them up.

I can't risk going upstairs, but tomorrow I'll need to call home anyway. If there's no way of getting Trevor to drop him off in the realm, or take me back so I can drop him off, then I'll go up and search for the nearest pet shop.

I looked down at Leo, now midway through a lettuce leaf and staring up at me.

"They'd be bound to look after you," I promised. "Then I can come back to start afresh with no more stupid mistakes."

Leo chomped through the leaf, his gaze never faltering.

"What?" I huffed with my eyelids threatening to close right there and then. "Don't you give me that disbelieving look!"

CHAPTER SIX
A CHASE AND A SECRET MEETING

I kept waking in the night because the mattress was softer than my one at home. I also couldn't believe I wasn't at risk of getting dive-bombed by one of my sisters either, or doused in cold water because they thought it was hilarious.

Mum had brought me a really nice pair of pyjamas as a going away gift, soft black pants and matching t-shirt with purple bows on, and I actually risked wearing them. Fear of my sisters had taught me to dress for bed as if I was sleeping outside, just in case they chose to torment me early in the morning. It only took the one incident of the neighbours seeing my ragged Star Wars pyjamas and I vowed never again.

Even the room, simple though it was, beat the alcove covered by a curtain that I called a bedroom at home.

I reached over and grabbed my mobile phone to check the time. *07:45*, but without a window I couldn't be sure it was still keeping proper time in the realm-bubble that was Arcanium. There was also an Arcanium-issue clock on the bedside table, which read *08:42*. So I guessed I now only had eighteen minutes to get ready. I sat up with a satisfied yawn.

Uh-oh.

The desk drawer was open. I scrambled across the room in a flurry of covers and dropped to crouch over the drawer, but Leo wasn't there. A cautious feel inside proved he wasn't camouflaging either.

He can't have escaped, surely. I stared around in growing horror. *What if he's not a chameleon at all? What if he's a mutant*

51

Fae lizard and has transported to the other side of Arcanium to eat people?

I checked all the drawers. I grappled around under the bed. Then I pulled out all the clothes I'd placed so neatly in the shelving unit the evening before.

Kneeling to sort through them, I cursed my horrible luck.

"Come on, Leo. You can't have gotten out of the room, so you must be here somewhere."

I found a stray bit of lettuce and waved it, as though that was somehow enough to summon an errant chameleon. Clothes flew as I did one last search, checking their weight for any clinging reptiles.

A knock on the door barely registered.

"Yes, I mean, no, wait-"

The door swung open to reveal Ace.

"Morning! I brought you some towels. Fianna is meant to be your hall buddy technically, but she's not feeling so good, so you get me instead."

Ace's broad smile faded.

"You subscribe to the chaos theory of unpacking then?" he asked, one eyebrow raised.

I clambered to my feet and spied a twitch near Ace's boots.

Leo!

I took a couple of steps forward as Leo ambled out of the room, hellbent on adventure, but Ace had no intention of unblocking the doorway.

"Whoa." He stood with one hand up, palm forward. "What's the rush? You might want to change out of your pjs first!"

I bit my lip, anxiety playing leap-lizard in my limbs. I had no hope of moving Ace bodily, and no time to come up with a ruse.

"Okay, I got back last night," I whispered, craning over Ace's shoulder to stare down the hall. "From the realm I mean, the assignment, and I found a chameleon in my bag. I was going to sneak up to the surface and drop him off somewhere safe."

Ace gasped. Leo paused halfway between the bedroom and the turning to the lift.

"Oh wow, that is not good." Ace rubbed the back of his head. "You can't take it up to the human world though. What if it grew wings or started breathing fire? You can't be sure with creatures from Faerie."

On some level I knew that, had known it from the start. I wrung my hands together as Leo set off again.

"So, where is it now?" Ace asked.

I grabbed my satchel and flung the strap over my head, pointing past Ace's shoulder.

"Um, you kind of let him out when you opened the door."

Ace whirled around, giving me just enough space to squeeze past him. I scanned the hall, not giving myself time to feel awkward about the close proximity to Ace or the waft of fresh linen smell that surrounded him.

I set off in pursuit with him right behind me. Leo, perhaps feeling the vibrations of two sets of feet approaching, scurried off in the direction of the lift.

"Leo," I hissed. "Come back!"

I skidded around the corner and stopped. The hall lay still, deceptively empty.

"Where is it?" Ace muttered.

I crouched low, changing my viewpoint until I spied a slight discolouration against the wall. I pointed, keeping my movements slow.

"By that side table with the pot plant on it."

"The ficus or the fern?"

"Er... the left one."

Ace gave me a weary look as I crept forward. The moment I

got close, all sign of Leo had vanished.

"He's gone again," I whispered, clenching my fists. "What if he gets into the lift shaft?"

I scanned the floor and the walls as Ace strode past to inspect gaping hole over the gate. Even the thought of it made my knees go funny.

"Can't see him." Ace turned his back on the lift and bit his lip. "You'd better have a plan."

I dropped to my hands and knees. "I have to find him first. If not, he'll end up squished, or someone else will find him first and I'll get kicked out for sure!"

"Who will end up squished?"

In the panic, neither of us had heard the quiet swoosh of the lift arriving. I shot up to my feet, my pulse starting to thunder.

Ace moved aside to reveal Taz still inside the lift with his arms crossed over the front of another *Demon Babies* t-shirt.

"Um…" I wracked my brains and scrambled to my feet.

Ace managed a guilty smile. "Would you believe us if we said we were playing hide and seek?"

Taz's scowl deepened.

I grabbed the strap of my satchel and squeezed. I had to say something, and Ace had done more than enough for me already.

"When I came back from the realm last night, I found a stowaway in my bag." I lifted the satchel as if that was proof enough. "He's a chameleon, but he got out just now. I was just trying to figure out what to do with him."

Taz's inhaled sharply, then huffed and shook his head.

"Where did you see it last?" he asked. "Actually, silly question. I doubt even you would be scrabbling in the hall on your hands and knees for the fun of it."

I ignored the 'even you', even though it hurt.

He doesn't know anything about me, or why I might do things.

Taz squinted, tilting his head from side to side, as if listening. I copied him, checking the hall for any signs of people coming toward them.

"A-ha." Taz pointed up at the lift's ceiling bars. "I spy a lizard."

I wondered if perhaps he'd been gifted with special sight but knew better than to ask.

Taz opened the gate a fraction, just as the lift pinged to warn us it was about to move. Before I could so much as think, let alone panic, Ace hauled the gate open and shoved me in, jostling behind me.

I wobbled, unsteady on my socked feet as the lift started downwards. My elbow shot outwards and hit two of the buttons. The lift jolted and slowed.

"Now what have you done?" Taz groaned.

The lift stopped for a mere moment before shooting upwards instead. Undeterred, I braced my hand on the gate railing and reached up. Leo clung on to the spindled metal, blinking down at my fingertips that couldn't quite reach. I bit my lip and pushed up onto my tiptoes. I curled my hand around the offending lizard and lifted him safely down.

"You are a horror," I muttered, relief tingling across my skin like bubbles.

Leo blinked at me and sagged, going limp and turning himself flesh-coloured. I settled him in the satchel with a small gap for fresh air and turned to Taz.

"He's not done anything Fae so far," I insisted. "I think he's a normal chameleon."

Taz eyed the bag warily. "You can't be sure of that. Honestly, I know we threw you in at the deep end-"

"Without any induction," Ace added helpfully.

"Yes, okay without an induction, but still." Taz's scowl

remained but his lips started twitching. "What do you plan to do with him? You can't keep him. You can't exactly let him loose on the human world either, just in case. He might be a baby about to grow into a T-Rex or something."

I peeked into the bag. Leo had his eyes closed and his mouth ever so slightly open, brown tongue poking out. He looked positively angelic.

"I don't know. Maybe I could find an excuse to go back to the realm and drop him off really quick."

Taz snorted. "You'd need a really good excuse, like an assignment or something. You can't just commandeer your troll and go realm-skipping whenever you feel like it. There's *protocol*."

The lift slid to a stop before I could find a suitable retort. Ace opened the gate, but Taz shot out a hand to stop him going any further.

"Don't," he said. "I don't think we're allowed on this floor."

I peered out, intrigued as Taz pressed one of the lift buttons. The corridor looked like any other with the wooden panels, but instead of carpet, there were worn, marked floorboards underfoot.

"Those look like classrooms." Ace pointed to the small rooms on either side of the hall with big windows on three sides. "Or interrogation rooms. I saw this film once where the Government had to interrogate all these people to find out if they were aliens, but the aliens ended up being the interrogators in disguise, looking for enemy aliens."

I shuddered. "Alien interrogators, no thanks. Why isn't the lift moving?"

"It must be a trigger floor." Taz sighed, tapping the button several times. "We have trigger floors, where the lift is forced to wait a certain length of time before being released and sent on its way."

Ace's eyes lit up. "Either that, or they're hiding valuables here. Imagine, stealing something and an alarm going off all around, you get to the lift and it refuses to move."

"Or it's a safety feature." I joined in. "If you had something dangerous up here. Imagine if it got loose, you'd want to know the lift would be waiting when you got here."

Taz rolled his eyes. "The most dangerous thing up here is probably that lizard."

Chastened, I checked on the slumbering Leo again, just in case. He definitely didn't look dangerous. Given the way Taz was eyeballing the bag though, he wasn't so convinced of Leo's innocence.

"Oh crud," Ace murmured. "There's people over there, look, you can see them through the glass."

"Are we going to get into trouble?" I asked.

"It's not like we're here on purpose." Taz didn't look so sure. "We're not snooping around or anything. Just stay here and wait. The lift will wake up in a minute."

The two figures moved out of sight and I stood waiting with my heart pounding, but none of us could avoid catching the voices that floated around the corner clear as a bell.

"It's taking too long," a strident male voice insisted. "The bond is weakening but any time we waste is time that they will use to strengthen it again! We can't let it continue."

"We cannot risk everything going wrong through foolish or rash action either," a higher voice replied, even more determined than the first. "We are all working to the same goal, but you must trust me when I say I'm almost there. A little longer, that's all."

"You've got one more week, then it's out of my hands. The old ways of Faerie must be reinstated, before the alliance gets too strong to overthrow. Arcanium is in chaos right now behind the scenes, and we can't let them reorganise themselves. If they do, it'll be on your head."

The higher voice huffed.

"Don't use that supercilious tone with me. The Forgotten will take control of Arcanium and install someone to run it who is more in line with our traditional Fae values. Now, wait for the next lift. We can't be seen together."

Panic swirled in my gut as I eyed Taz and Ace. Taz jabbed the lift buttons several times in random order, with no success.

"Look like we're deep in conversation," Ace hissed, then straightened up with a smile. "It's quite simple really. The game of chess isn't so much about knocking the next piece off the table, but going after the powerful pieces-"

"What are you three doing up here?"

I recognised the voice now, and the woman it belonged to. The puffy blonde hair was complimented by a pale purple cardigan, but Sandra the librarian's expression was nothing if not suspicious.

Inside the satchel, Leo began to wriggle. I clamped a hand over the flap, my fingers twitching ready to catch him if he made another mad dash.

"We must have pressed the wrong button." Ace slid smoothly into damage control mode. "Too busy discussing chess. But the lift doesn't seem to be going anywhere now."

"I thought this might be a trigger floor," Taz added, his wary expression matching Sandra's.

I clutched the strap of my bag. If Leo chose that moment to pop his head out, there would be more than trouble coming my way.

"Open the gate," Sandra demanded.

I shuddered. Something about her reminded me of my sister Jenny, the domineering tone perhaps, or the hostile face. If

Sandra got into the lift with us, if she interrogated us further, or if Leo made an appearance…

The lift pinged then, the buttons lighting up. Sandra made a grab for the gate, trying to pull it open. I panicked. I hadn't tried what I was about to do very often, but it was the only thing I could think of.

Without any time to take much of a breath, I made a small gap between my lips and threw my voice.

"Grrraaaarrrrouggghhh."

The snarl echoed behind Sandra's back, sounding every inch like a ferocious beast was right behind her.

Sandra jumped and whirled around. Ace slid the gate fully shut with his foot. As Sandra turned back, her face bright and livid, the lift dropped.

I breathed a sigh of relief and sagged over my bag, checking Leo was still safe inside.

"What was that noise?" Ace asked, staring upward as if something would come crashing down on top of the lift after us.

Taz looked at me. "That was you?"

"Yeah." I shrugged, staring at the gate as the brick whizzed by behind it. "It's nothing, I've just always been able to mimic sounds, and throw my voice."

"Wow." Ace grinned. "That's impressive. I thought we were about to get done for leaving her to be eaten."

"I think we should find a safe place to discuss all this," Taz muttered, turning to look at my satchel. "And *him*."

I bit my lip and breathed a tiny sigh of relief. Standing in my pyjamas with a potentially Fae lizard in my bag, I wasn't in any position to argue, but at least it almost sounded like Taz might be about to try and help me after all.

CHAPTER SEVEN
AN OMINOUS WARNING AND A MEGA SALAD

"We'll go down to the Ogle," Taz decided. "Say you're interested in finding out about it and I offered to show you around."

I straightened up. "I *am* interested. I have so many questions."

Taz grumbled something under his breath but didn't lower himself to commenting out loud. I guessed asking any of my questions now wouldn't get me a positive answer, given the moody scowl on his face.

"We can't tell anyone about what we just overheard," Ace said. "Whatever's going on, they wouldn't believe us blindly. We'd need proof."

The lift stopped at the Ogle floor and I stood aside so Taz could exit first. Once again, the sheer size of the vast room distracted me, the flicker of so many screens mesmerising.

Taz stalked away from the screens to the left corner of the room, where a bunch of old boxes were heaped in messy stacks. He leaned back against one and lifted a hand to flick his curly fringe out of his eyes, his gaze dropping down to my satchel as if Leo might come bursting out with fangs or something. I bit my lip and focused on the other issue before he could bring up lizard-gate instead.

"I get the feeling I should already know this," I began. "But why are traditional Fae values a bad thing?"

Ace and Taz exchanged a dubious look.

"You're not from a Fae family, are you?" Ace confirmed.

I stared down at my feet. "No, but I try to learn everything I can to make up for it. I know most people grew up with the stories and histories."

"It's not a bad thing." Ace hurried on. "It used to be that Faerie was just for the Fae, full-blooded. Then they started encroaching more into the human world."

"They always have," Taz interjected. "But humans became more interesting around the 1500s apparently."

Ace raised an eyebrow at Taz's dismissive tone before continuing.

"Sure. So then fairies were born, part-Fae and part-human."

I nodded. "I know that much, and that most fairies have a distant pure Fae relative to gift them something when they're young. Except me clearly, I have to work and earn any gifts the hard way through working in Faerie. I just don't understand why the old ways are meant to be so bad?"

I rubbed the back of my neck as Ace gave me a reassuring smile.

"Traditional values go beyond mischief and having to make ourselves tiny once upon a time," he said. "It's all about the power struggles of the ancient Fae families. They don't like having to tiptoe around the human world basically. That's why the full-blooded are called Fae and those with human-blood in them are called fairies."

"Yeah," Taz scoffed. "Nothing like keeping the terminology 'clean'. The group they mentioned, the Forgotten, they're nut-jobs, the lot of them. They say they want to close Faerie off from the human world and stop FDPs going between, but anyone with any sense knows they just want to turn it into their personal playground and eventually overthrow the Queen."

"Queenie?" I blinked in surprise.

"No, the Queen. The Fae monarch who holds the balance of

the realms of Faerie."

"Oh."

I had known about the Queen of Faerie, but the idea of Fae royalty was still firmly lodged in the 'story-book' part of my brain along with the rest of the Faerie I hadn't experienced yet.

I busied myself with checking on Leo to hide my burning cheeks. I could just imagine the withering looks passing between the other two.

I can't help it that they grew up with Fae families and have spent time here already, but at least they're still talking to me.

"There are those who think removing the Queen and electing a different monarch will change everything," Ace explained.

"A different kind of monarch," Taz muttered, his tone dark. "The sort that thinks our gifts solve everything and that the only way to succeed at anything is to be the most gifted. Unfortunately, that involves a lot of manipulation, spite and sitting on the "little people" to achieve what they want, whether that be humans, or fairies, goblins, trolls, and anyone that's not pure-blood court Fae."

I stared at him in alarm as all the carefully-squashed-in history of Faerie data leapt straight from my brain to my mouth.

"But what about all the non-Fae people that have done great things? Like Amana who helped lead the goblin uprising, or Jarvik taking on the Old King for the Queen, even though he was only a fairy-"

"*Don't* say 'only a fairy'," Taz growled, startling me into silence. "Fairies have some of the best traits, like compassion, humility, effort, dedication, and many other things that full Fae and the Queen's court know nothing about. Fae are the reason Faerie has so many wars in the first place, they see it as sport."

"Okay, that doesn't sound great," I agreed. "But what can we do now about what's happening here? As you said, Ace, nobody will believe us without proof."

Taz sighed. "Then we also have the Fae code to contend with. The Faerie code is-"

"-the boundaries all fairies must abide by," I interrupted. "It includes those of the Fae court, and outlines the rules of everything outside of magic law. You're thinking of rule 37 hyphen B slash 779, aren't you? That no Fae nor fairy can use eavesdropping for potential gain against any other Fae or fairy without obtaining prior proof, or without first obtaining approval from the Fae court, or regent, or elected representative, whichever should come first."

Taz blinked, his nose wrinkling. "Er, yeah, that one. Queenie is our elected representative, but we can't use what we heard against Sandra until we get proof, as we didn't get permission first. It's a ridiculous boundary, but it's there."

"It's there to make sure anyone who wants to spy on someone has to go higher to get permission," Ace added. "Going higher inevitably involves a price or a debt. It's all politics."

I snorted. "Everything's politics. Real morality is so rare these days, it's practically non-existent."

Aware the other two were eying me with identical wary frowns, I guessed that had come out more vehement than I intended.

Tone it down. You don't want them finding out about home and thinking you need pitying, or worse, want it.

Ace rubbed his chin. "There are kind people out there. Just way less than there should be, you're right. Still, doesn't sort out what we're going to do about this."

As he eyed the screens, I tried to avoid catching Taz's eye as his gaze flicked over my face. Before I could think of something to say, amid the quiet hum of the Ogle, my stomach gurgled loud enough to be heard three screen rows away. Ace grinned, which made me laugh, and even Taz managed a smile.

"So, what do we do?" I asked. "We can't just let it drop."

Taz opened his mouth to answer but his words were masked as a loud buzzing filled the air. Ace winced and covered his ears. I held one hand on my suddenly thrashing satchel and pulled my orb out of my pocket with the other.

A ghostly grey figure, hooked and cloaked, projected into the room as the buzzing dissipated, leaving a cacophony of silence behind. I only had time to notice a diamond-shaped charm just visible at the neckline of the cloak as a deep, female voice boomed around the cavernous room.

"This warning is going orb-wide. There are fairies and Arcanium insiders who want to bring us down, to bring down Faerie as it should be. The time must come soon. Trust nobody."

The vision disappeared without any farewell. Taz span around, looking back and forth in alarm.

"The only place anyone can beam orb-wide is in here," he muttered. "They might still be around!"

He sped off toward the rows of screens.

"That explains the buzzing then." Ace set off after him.

I secured my satchel against my hip with one hand and followed. Ace jogged along easily beside me, but I could already feel the impromptu exercise stealing my breath away. I was almost, *almost*, considering conceding that my sisters had a point with their whole relentless exercise regime.

As we ran past countless screens of images, my gaze snagged on numbers. They were in the two hundred's and going up.

So many screens, and realms. How on earth can anyone manage or keep track of all of this?

I focused ahead and saw that Taz was rows in front of us already. I put my head down and renewed my effort, trusting Ace to guide me left and right. Only when he came to an abrupt halt, did I double over and try to catch my breath again. Gazing at my bright orange Tigger socks, I realised that I was still in my pyjamas and hadn't yet brushed my hair. *Or my teeth. Oh god.*

Taz gave me a wearisome once over and I resisted the overwhelming urge to give him a shove.

"Right," he said. "Best we're not seen down here after that. This is the service lift, but we should be okay sneaking up in it and through the kitchens. The Braunees won't mind."

The metal doors of the service lift opened, looking very much like normal lift doors when compared to the golden gate of the normal one. I shuffled in as Taz jabbed a button.

Nobody said a word on the way up. I wasn't sure if that was because the others were deep in thought or afraid of being magically overheard somehow, but I took my lead from them anyway.

Mysterious cloaked figures sending warnings, a threatening librarian, and I still haven't figured out what to do about Leo.

This was meant to be my big opportunity, but I hadn't imagined this much adventure would hit me in the first twenty-four hours.

The lift doors opened onto the heated clash and clang at the rear of the canteen kitchen.

"After breakfast hours but not lunch-time yet thankfully," Taz said.

He strode out into the kitchen and cleared his throat. Both Braunees turned to face us, eyes wide with amusement.

"Visitors, Braunee," said male Braunee.

My stomach growled in reply and female Braunee grinned.

"Hungry looking visitors, Braunee," she agreed. "Wasting away all four of them."

I swung around to look behind me for a fourth person, Ace and Taz doing the same. Braunee's eyes drifted down to my middle, her grin never fading. I followed her gaze and saw a scaly nose.

"Leo," I groaned. "Why is this the one time you can't be bothered to camouflage yourself? You're going to get me into so much trouble."

Leo gave me a supremely bored look and mashed his gums a few times in reply.

"Don't think the Department of Inns, Restaurants, Taverns and Yeeteries would like us having visitors," male Braunee chuckled. "Especially reptilian ones."

"What's a Yeetery?" I asked.

Male Braunee waggled his bushy eyebrows. "You're too young to know. But they would give us a warning, I fear."

"They'd close the kitchen for decontamination." Female Braunee nodded. "Best we say no more about it, hmm? Now, how about an early lunch? Some sandwiches to take on your way, oh and we've got some lovely Oia berry loaf cake too, fresh fifteen minutes ago. How about a salad as well?"

I stared at them, amazed. I wasn't known for being lucky, or even getting my fair share of good fortune really, but it sounded like on the Leo front at least I was getting a break.

Taz sagged beside me with a huff of relief, and Ace was already grinning on my other side. Male Braunee paused and scratched his head.

"I know what you want." He flicked his eyes lightning-quick at the satchel. "Cricket salad! A delicacy. Been a long time since I've had the chance to make a proper cricket salad. Lettuce, tomatoes, some banana, perfect!"

I tried not to pull a face. "Um, yes please, that sounds lovely."

The Braunees laughed as they scurried around the kitchen in perfect harmony with each other. Even Taz managed a smirk, although I guessed it was caused more by the thought of me having to eat cricket salad than anything else.

He might make me eat it after the morning I've caused him. I shook the thought from my head.

A short while later, Ace took the hefty brown paper bag from female Braunee and I took the lettuce leaf she held out. The moment he saw it, Leo clamped his jaw around it and disappeared into the satchel.

"At least he's happy." Ace raised his eyebrows.

Male Braunee laughed. "Eat and so will you be. Off you go now."

We did as we were told, leaving thanks in our wake, and exited the canteen.

"Are we going to come up with a plan?" I asked as they reached the normal lift. "After what we overheard, then that message from the mysterious cloaked woman, we have to do something."

Ace pressed the button as Taz leaned closer to both of us, his turquoise eyes narrowing.

"It's simple," Taz said. "We raid Sandra's office of course."

CHAPTER EIGHT
THE GRUESOME TWOSOME

"You want to what her *what*?" I hissed. "What do you expect to find in her office? We could get into serious trouble for snooping around, even if she is part of the Forgotten group."

I stepped out of the lift onto the residents' floor and turned to face the others. The last thing I needed right now was more opportunity for trouble. But then, I couldn't just pretend we'd not overheard anything.

Taz scowled at me. "Keep your voice down!"

All three of us looked around, but the hall was deserted. Ruffled by his sarcastic attitude, I pulled a face. I hadn't exactly had the greatest morning and he wasn't helping.

"Why, are the walls listening then, or just the paintings?"

Ace pressed his lips together and took a step back, his meaning clear: *leave me out of whatever this is.*

Taz folded his arms. "You'd be surprised. You don't have to help or anything, if you're worried. Ace and I can handle this."

"Excuse me?" I snorted. "I heard what you heard, so I'm just as involved as you are. I can't just sit and do nothing now, not if there's something dangerous going on. I can't risk having to go back home."

I skipped over mentioning that we wouldn't even know about it had Leo not escaped, guessing that wasn't a positive thing to throw into an argument.

Taz refused to relent, his dismissive expression still directed at me and his pierced eyebrow arched to perfection.

He probably practices that in a mirror.

"You need to at least keep your voice down," he said.

"Because the walls have ears?" I glared back at him.

A smile curved at the edges of his mouth, widening as he leaned forward into the challenge, his face inches from mine.

"Maybe. We don't want anyone hearing us talk about the group by name, or they might think we're part of it. Besides, you've already proven you're destined to cause trouble, and you're a total newbie."

I matched him folded arms for folded arms.

"I may be a newbie, but I've already done my first assignment-"

"Oh yeah, marvellously, I remember."

"Screw you."

Ace's hand inched into the few feet of space between our faces.

"Um, less of the arguing please," he said. "We've got actual stuff to worry about here, not your egos. We still need to decide what to do about, the conversation."

I bit my lip and stepped back, keeping my arms folded as I gave Taz a dirty look. He had the gall to stick his tongue out at me.

Next time I'll pull it out and tie it to the lift railing or something.

I'd pegged him as someone who might be alright, but he was going to new lengths to annoy me now for some reason. Still, Ace was right. We had bigger things to worry about than Taz's ego.

"We raid her office." Taz lowered his voice to a whisper. "We look for clues, anything that might seem out of place. We watch her movements too. Follow her as much as we can. See who she speaks to. Once we have something concrete, we take it straight to Queenie."

I wisely decided not to comment, looking to Ace instead. He rubbed his chin.

"It's the only plan we've got," he conceded. "We should probably-"

"This looks cosy."

A voice made us all jump. I looked past Taz to see a girl and a boy standing a few metres away by the lift shaft. I marked out the expensive-looking brown boots the girl wore with tan tights and a knee-length black suede skirt, and her manicured hands. I couldn't remember the last time I'd stopped biting my nails, let alone painted them.

The boy stood a head taller than the girl did, and had much darker hair than her chocolate brown waterfall, but otherwise they were identical down to the dismissive expressions and perky noses. I glanced at the others, gauging their reaction. Taz's tense shoulders, hands shoved in his pockets, and Ace's tight, less-than-friendly smile told me all I needed to know.

"Taz, Ace, aren't you going to introduce us to your new friend?" the boy asked, his tone haughty.

I still had my arms folded and held his gaze.

"I'm Demi."

"Demi, as in 'half'?" The girl scoffed. "Fitting."

Yep, these definitely aren't people to be friends with.

Flashbacks of my sisters laughing in my face and calling me 'half-breed' swirled in my head. My insides bubbled. At least this sort of conversation I'd had plenty of practice with.

I gasped as if the girl had mortally wounded me.

"Oh no, I'm so hurt, I've like, so never heard that one before."

Their mocking smiles soured.

"Watch yourself," the girl said, eying me up and down. "We already have gifts between us, like glamour, speed and levitation, so you should choose your connections very carefully. You have no idea who you're messing with."

"Someone utterly terrifying, I'm sure." I faked a yawn behind my hand for good measure, a taunt which never failed to anger my sisters when they tried to threaten me.

The couple exchanged a dark look and turned in an identical lifting of haughty noses. I watched them glide toward the canteen doors. The anger settled as quick as it had flared, leaving anxious doubt roiling inside me like a snake pit. She'd baited me and I'd risen to it without much provocation, a kneejerk reaction from a lifetime of growing up on the defensive.

"Go on then," I said, not quite able to look at Ace or Taz yet. "Who am I messing with? I'm guessing they're important somehow."

Ace cleared his throat. "You could say that. Diana and Kainen are from the Hemlock family, one of the most influential Fae lineages."

"The 'traditional' kind," Taz said, still glaring at the canteen doors. "The sort that are gifted skills they haven't earned by fancy relatives who should know better."

I guessed this was one of those 'don't ask' moments and pressed a cold hand to my hot forehead. Somehow, in less two days, I'd managed to bring back an uninvited guest from Faerie, alienate the potentially hostile librarian and get on the wrong side an ancient Fae dynasty. Any more blunders, and I'd likely be back home before a week was up.

Ace's worried frown softened into a smile, as if he could tell exactly what I was thinking.

"How about we show you the library next?" he suggested. "After the morning we've had, you might need a pick-me-up. Also, we should probably do some observations there while we're finalising who's going to be doing what with Taz's plan."

I nodded. "Okay. I've heard Arcanium's got one of the

biggest collections in Faerie."

I expected some kind of withering retort from Taz as we started walking toward the lift, but he surprised me instead.

"A lot of Faerie history is here for safekeeping actually," he said. "As the main hub between Faerie and the human world, it doubles as an archive for artefacts. Even the original book of Faerie is here."

I gaped at him as we stopped to wait for the lift.

"The *actual* book of Faerie? Can we see it? As in, is it on display?"

Taz glanced at Ace and started to laugh, his surly expression finally lifting. When he smiled, I could see his freckles clearer, like a dusting of pollen across his nose and cheeks.

The lift arrived and I pulled the gate open, stepping inside first as if I belonged here with them. My sisters would usually make every effort to elbow me backwards, even if I was going into a room they didn't need to enter, but Taz and Ace merely followed me in.

"You have a lot to learn about fairies and Fae," Taz said as the lift shot downwards. "Heritage is everything. Lineage is everything. Both those things lead to power which is, of course-"

"-everything," Ace and I chorused.

Taz froze for a moment before laughing. "Yeah, okay so where do you think the most important book of Faerie would be?"

"On show somewhere for all to see?" I guessed.

"Bingo."

The lift stopped and Ace opened the gate directly onto the main chamber of the library. Both boys stood aside to let me leave first. I only made it two steps before coming to a stop again. I stared around, all the way up, then all the way down.

"Wow."

For some reason, I'd expected something similar to the library at school, like pale walls and dark floors of carpet matting, with metal shelving and the smell of old books. The smell was there alright, but the rest of the room was as far from my school library as a room full of books could get.

I managed a few more steps forward to clutch at the waist-high railing of curling black iron that ran around the edge of the vast room. Over the railing, the space dropped down. And down. And down.

Metal platforms formed several circular levels that climbed above and dropped below, and each level had green carpet running to gaping holes in the centre of the floor. My knees all but gave way at the mere thought of the gaping chasm yawning below. I gawked at the walkways crossing over vast nothingness in the centre of the great chamber, reminding me of the floating despatch platform upstairs.

All around the circular floors were uncountable bookshelves and doorways, all promising a treasury of knowledge waiting to be found.

"There are several floors spreading down from here," Ace explained. "Then many turns and tunnels leading out. There are parts as yet undiscovered, but we have other resources charting how far it spans. I heard that the Queen of Faerie herself helped design this place, modelled partly on the British library and in the decorative style of Trinity College."

"This is- wow," I whispered. "It must be a monster to clean."

Taz scoffed beside me, his elbow knocking mine.

"That's the first thing that you think of when you see this?" he asked.

A twinge of embarrassment tweaked in my chest, but I ignored him.

"It's really something isn't it?" Ace added. "What's worse, the students all have orb-readers and rarely end up in here now, but a prestigious institution must have a fearsome library. Come on, there's bound to be a reading nook free near the main desk."

He set off along the platform and I followed with one hand safe on the railing, just in case. My gaze drifted to the side and down into the gaping hole that fell to the base of the chamber.

I can't even see the bottom from here.

The platforms were wide enough to fit several rows of bookshelves from wall to railing, and space to move around them in groups, but it still made my knees go funny.

"Okay, this one will do."

Ace slid behind a row of shelves hidden between three bookcases set in a horseshoe shape.

"This is amazing," I insisted, twisting to look back at the library. "I didn't see the Book of Faerie though."

Taz appeared beside me and put a hand on my shoulder. I flinched at the touch out of habit, but he ignored that and pointed toward the nearest walkway crossing middle of the chamber.

"See that huge statue there on the pedestal?" he asked. I nodded, conscious of his fingers still curled close to my neck. "That's the Queen of Faerie, and the book she's holding is the Book of Faerie."

I stared up at him. He removed his hand and stepped back with a quirked frown.

"It's just there on show?" I asked. "No protection?"

He shrugged. "Who would dare steal it? There are all sorts of wards and enchantments on the place, and even the lift to the human world would ring alarms if anything other than orbs or normal objects tried to go up."

I left his side and started toward the statue. I guessed, given the amount of people walking across the walkways every day, that they were more than sturdy enough to hold me, but I still pressed my hand to the railing as I took that first step onto the nearest one.

The statue faced the lift entrance, double my height so the Book of Faerie in her hands was right at my eye-level. How I hadn't noticed it coming out of the lift, I didn't know, because up close the statue was breathtaking.

I lifted my hand and ran a finger over the marble of her arm, then snatched it back and waited for the alarms to start blaring.

"It's not cursed or anything." Taz appeared beside me.

I jumped. "You really do like sneaking up on people."

"Cool." He grinned. "At least I have one natural gift to my name then."

I turned my attention back to the statue. The Queen's face was tilted up slightly higher, her features delicately beautiful as much as a marble carving could show such a thing. But I took in the strong set of her shoulders, the slight press of her lips and narrowing of her eyes. I reckoned the real Queen of Faerie could probably pierce a person's soul with just one look, like Medusa without the head of snakes. I turned to mention this to Taz, but the words ebbed away when I saw him staring at it.

Like with the pictures in Queenie's hallway yesterday.

I assessed his wistful expression, eyes wide and glazed, mouth quirked by thoughts I didn't know.

Aware it seemed to be a private moment for him, I focused on the book itself instead. It looked much like my manual, except instead of leather binding with the Arcanium logo stamped on the front, this one looked like it was made from hide. I leaned closer to see.

"It's bound with vellum," Taz said. "Old way of covering books."

I asked the only question I could think of.

"What happens if I touch it?"

Taz glanced around and leaned closer. "Try and see."

Mischief danced on his face, right to the tiny dimple in his right cheek. I shook my head.

"Not with you grinning like that, something bad is bound to happen if I do."

Again Taz made a huge show of looking around to check nobody was watching us. Then with his index finger, he reached out and touched the book.

"Ouch!" He hissed.

I stared in horror as he clutched his finger to his chest.

"What, did it shock you? Bite you? What?"

"It's poisoned me I think," he groaned. "I've heard about *Daisiatus* before, but I didn't think it was true."

I reached out as Taz spun to face me with his finger held up. On the tip was a daisy, tiny and perfectly formed without the stem. I did the sensible thing and leaned closer.

The moment he flicked his finger toward my face, I yelped loud enough to carry three levels in all directions. He started laughing.

"It's just a glamour." He shook his finger and the daisy disappeared.

I folded my arms, digging my nails into my hoodie sleeves, sick of people making fun of me.

"Oh very funny. The new girl knows absolutely nothing, let's make a show of her like everyone else does. Really nice."

I turned away from him, refusing to accept that my eyes were burning as I gulped at the catch in my throat.

He's just a boy, and you barely even know him. I strode back across the walkway. *Who cares what Taz Elverhill thinks anyway? He's just like Jenny and the rest. Everyone is. Sooner you accept that the better.*

"Demi, wait!"

Taz hurried past and stopped in front of me to block my path. I could try pushing around him, but I had visions of one of us going splat into the yawning chasm below if he tried to stop me. I stared at his shoulder instead of meeting his eyes.

"I didn't mean to upset you," he said. "It was just a joke."

I scowled. "Everything's just a joke when you're the one doing it. How would you feel if you were always the one being picked on?"

He rubbed the back of his neck but I kept my focus away from his face, my insides twisting with nerves.

"You're right, I'm sorry. We don't know each other that well yet. Start again?"

Why does he even care? Is it because of Leo, and what we overheard?

I forced myself to glance at his face. He looked so sheepish, and I couldn't see any hint of mockery or trickery lingering there at all.

"Fine, fresh start." I nodded. "I take it Daisy-artis or whatever it was isn't a real thing?"

He shook his head. "No, just word-tangling. I didn't lie either, I don't know if you noticed that?"

"You said you'd heard of it before, but you didn't think it was true."

"Exactly. My sister used that one on me when I was a kid, so technically I had heard of it. And because it was historical, I could say it in past tense."

We all knew fairies and Fae couldn't lie without consequences, and I'd read all about word-tangling and practiced at fairy classes with Xavio, but this was the first real experience I'd had of someone using it to trick me.

As we started walking back toward Ace, who had taken a seat

and lost himself in a book already, I vowed to myself I'd get Taz back one day for the daisy thing. I wasn't used to people apologising to me though, and although the remnant of irritation remained, a tiny warm glow picked up inside me.

"I guess there's loads of stuff I have to learn that you already know from childhood," I admitted.

Taz shrugged. "Well, if you want to know anything about Arcanium or Faerie, just ask. I promise I'll give you a straight answer if I can."

I took a seat around the table as Ace looked up in alarm.

"That's a big thing to promise, Taz," he said.

I thought it through, a smile slowly beginning to creep across my face as Taz slid into the seat beside me.

"I'm guessing there will be a million reasons why you can't though, right? If it suits you?"

Taz chuckled. "Girl's a quick learner."

I shrugged over the happiness fluttering in my chest. He could have other motives, like an elaborate ploy to make a big joke of me, but my instincts suggested not. I just had to hope they were right.

I glanced over my shoulder at the statue and the book. Another issue was irking me now, and I had to ask.

"Can stuff come in?"

Taz frowned at me. "Eh?"

"You said before about the lift to the human world ringing alarms if magic stuff was taken up. But what about magic stuff being brought in?"

"You know, I never thought to ask. Even if you can't bring things in, there must be other exits and entrances that only Queenie and Emil or a select few know of."

I let him consider this for a few moments, before turning my attention to the more pressing matter.

"So, who's going to take the first watch for Operation Forgotten?"

CHAPTER NINE
AN IMPOSSIBLE THEFT

I woke the next morning with a buzzing excitement in my stomach. Taz had rushed off shortly after we'd decided on Operation Forgotten, otherwise known as 'The Plan', and Ace had given me a rambling tour of the library before taking me back to the canteen for dinner. But today was my first day of training classes, and I wanted to experience everything. I shot out of bed, checked Leo was still behaving himself in his drawer and stood in front of my meagre collection of clothing.

This is silly, I don't care what people think of my clothes. I stared at the shelves with my arms folded. *These are fairies though, and Fae. Appearances do matter to a lot of them.*

I pulled on my favourite purple t-shirt, my best black jeans and my black and white chequered trainers. With a zip-up woollen cardigan, I pulled my spilling dark curls back into a ponytail in front of the mirror.

As good as it's going to get without some of kind of fairy glamour. I pulled a face at my reflection. *I won't learn that until second year either. Still, here's a chance for me to get to know everyone and really make a good impression.*

Someone knocked on the door. Ace hadn't said he was going to come and get me for breakfast again, but he'd said 'see you tomorrow' after dinner last night.

"One second," I called.

I slung my satchel over my head and checked Leo one final time.

"You be good now," I whispered. "I've put enough lettuce to

last you a lifetime, and I'm going to lock the door."

Leo flicked his tongue out at me before closing his eyes. I left the drawer ajar, knowing he could push the gap wider if he wanted to, and opened my door.

"Oh, hi." I stared at Taz.

He frowned. "Hi yourself. Expecting someone else?"

I shook my head and shut the door behind me, turning to lock it.

"Who would I be expecting?" I asked, unable to admit outright that I'd been expecting Ace. "I was just on my way down to get breakfast."

Taz didn't look convinced, but he fell into step with me as we started down the hall toward the lift.

Silence swelled between us, although Taz nodded and grunted a greeting to the odd person in passing. Without Ace as a handy buffer, I had no idea what to say to him, other than to ask about Operation Forgotten, which nobody was supposed to know about, or mention Leo, who nobody was supposed to know about. I could ask Taz about himself, which would probably get me a withering retort or a non-committal answer. I couldn't even think of a single thing to ask about Arcanium, which was almost unheard of for a girl who usually had all the questions.

We stood side by side in the lift, with only the sound of the air rushing around us for company, until I couldn't stand it any longer.

"I still need to figure out what to do about Leo," I blurted out.

Taz turned to look at me. "I've been thinking, but it's not like it's a normal problem."

Surprised he was bothering to think about it, although he was technically complicit considering he hadn't turned me in straight away, I risked a smile.

"People don't often bring things back from realms by

accident I take it?"

"People never bring stuff back from realms, by accident or on purpose." He sounded completely serious. "Arcanium has such strict rules to stop invasions and attacks by ancient outcast clans, like the Forgotten, that it's almost impossible. But then, everything about your first day was unusual."

You're telling me.

I ignored the swoop of uneasiness in my stomach at being unusual as the lift came to a stop. Taz opened the gate, but I hesitated when he started laughing.

"What's so funny?"

He grinned at me. "I still can't believe you called him Leo."

"So?"

I strode out of the lift and toward the canteen, Taz keeping up with my disgruntled pace easily.

"Well it's not very original, is it? Cham-e-*leo*-n."

I pushed the doors to the canteen open and decided I was going to ignore him until he had something sensible to say. I continued ignoring him and his infuriating grin all the way to the buffet line and while I was waiting to get my cereal. Even when I found myself a seat and he plonked down opposite with a huge stack of toast and what looked like chocolate spread, I ate without acknowledging him. We were clearly going to need Ace around as a buffer after all, or I'd probably end up throttling him.

"Have you seen Ace this morning?" I asked eventually.

Taz looked up with half a slice of toast hanging from his mouth. He crunched the last bite with a frown.

"He's a year older than we are, so he won't be in our classes or anything. I think he gets up early and goes running or something. Why?"

Why? I don't actually know.

I shrugged as Taz checked a clock hanging on the wall above

82

the kitchens.

"We should get going anyway," he said. "You don't want to be late for your first class."

I followed his gaze and shot to my feet. "No, I don't."

I cleared my tray and fell into step with Taz and a tangle of other people leaving the canteen.

"This way." Taz nudged my elbow. "If we wait for the lift it'll take ages in this crowd."

I followed him toward the wide wooden staircase and weaved through the clustered bodies amid the heightened buzz of confident voices. Everyone else seemed to know exactly where they were, and who they were talking to. I had to press closer to Taz to ask him as the crowd crushed around us.

"How many new students are there?" I asked. "Is this your first class, or did you start early?"

Taz zigzagged through the crowd at the top of the stairs so fast that I thought he was trying to dodge me. Only when we reached a less cluttered hallway did he slow down and check I was still with him.

"I've been here since I was fourteen," he admitted. "My family wanted to send me to some Fae boarding school, but I refused to go so my mother pulled some strings and they took me here as a sort of apprentice instead. I've sat in on classes before loads of times, but this is the first as an official mentee."

"Wish I could have come here at fourteen instead," I said.

He laughed. "I can only imagine the trouble a fourteen-year-old you would have caused."

I rolled my eyes as we slowed down outside one of the classrooms. People were already seated inside, but Taz went straight for a double desk at the front. He sank into the chair then looked back at me hovering in the doorway.

The classroom looked much the same as any other, tables and

chairs, boards full of posters and data on the walls, and a huge whiteboard at the front. The effect looked odd against the wood-panelled walls and the blue carpet underfoot, but I was more overwhelmed by the way everyone else seemed to know each other already, clustered in groups or calling across to other people.

Taz caught my eye and slid a hand onto the desk next to him, tapping it once. Grateful for the invitation, I hurried between the desks.

"Thanks." I slid into the seat next to him, flinching as a shadow loomed over us.

"So glad you found a friend finally, Taz." Diana Hemlock appeared complete with a vicious smile. "Although you should have given the poor girl a chance to make some proper connections before saddling her with you."

I cast a doleful eye over her pale blue jeans, knitted sweatshirt and pristine trainers. Even her hair shone like a sunlit conker, plaited into an elegant bun and not a strand out of place. One look at the flawless skin and I was conscious of a spot lurking under my jaw. Suddenly, my attempt at dressing nicely earlier seemed laughable.

Taz dropped his gaze to where his hands lay on the table, his shoulders hunching over. Unsure why he didn't just tell her to bugger off, I glared at Diana, forcing myself to meet her gaze even though every instinct inside me screamed at me to back down. I'd been in this position so many times before, fight or flight, but it never got any less daunting.

She reminds me of Mary. I realised, recognising the similarities between Diana and my sister. *Vicious with her words, unlike Jenny who's just violent. Taz said Diana's family were 'traditional' so I bet she wouldn't like being compared to someone who's non-fairy.*

"Wow, I can't believe I was so wrong," I said. "I figured there couldn't possibly be bullies somewhere like this, but I guess you're just the same as the human ones I grew up with. Shame."

My sisters would have invented ultimate payback if I'd dared compare them to someone fairy or Fae. Diana's honey-coloured eyes flashed with pure venom as she assessed her next move. Even Taz lifted his head to stare at me. I slid my hands under the desk to hide the shaking.

"I already warned you to watch who you were talking to, *sweetie*." Diana's voice was treacherously smooth.

I shrugged, although my shoulders were stiff from tensing.

"No, warning would imply you care. You threatened me. And we both know you don't care, *love*."

I clenched my stomach muscles tight against the fear pounding through me and held Diana's gaze, refusing to back down. The anxiety was roaring in me, and the agony at having to stare straight into her eyes made it feel like my skin was peeling, but I refused to back down.

So absorbed in my staring match, I didn't notice anyone else come through the doorway.

"Di, you picked up my bag after breakfast." Her brother, Kainen, strode in, holding out a tan leather handbag.

The bag hanging from Diana's shoulder was a satchel version of the one Kainen was holding. I managed to hold in a snort at the idea of them having matching bags. As they swapped, I hoped Diana would just go on her way and leave me and Taz alone.

"Thank you, brother." She winked at him. "See you after class."

She hung her handbag over her forearm and turned back to face us. She opened her mouth, no doubt to resume insulting us, but a woman wheeled into the classroom before she could.

"Welcome to Legend and Lore class," the woman boomed.

Diana jumped in alarm, but still managed to give me a death-stare before sweeping past to go and sit near the back. I turned my attention to the woman now parked beside the desk. She was younger than I expected a teacher to be, with braided black hair, brown skin and sharp hazel eyes that assessed the class. I noticed the hint of a tattoo beneath the collar of her knitted sweatshirt.

"My name is Avril," she continued. "Please don't call me Miss, or Madam, you're no longer in school. This is serious stuff you're getting involved in now, and I won't accept any mucking about. I recognise some of you, and not others, but you'll have to get to know each other on your own time."

She clapped her hands, her energy levels spreading across the class as she grabbed an armful of books from the desk and moved forward to start throwing them in front of us.

As she went toward the back, Taz leaned closer.

"Thanks," he muttered. "Diana may have a point about you making better connections, depending on what alliances you want to make for your future in Faerie society, but thanks."

I shrugged. "I hate bullies no matter how up themselves they are. Besides, you've been decent to me so far, mostly. She hasn't."

"Mostly?" Taz pulled a face. "Ouch. But you're probably in the wrong place if you don't like bullies. Faerie is full of scheming, trickery and power-hungry people."

I forced the cold chill that threatened to steal over me away, and ignored the shudder that followed.

"Still beats home."

I focused on pulling the textbook toward me so I didn't have to see the inevitable pity on Taz's face. Luckily, Avril resumed her place in front of the class, which fell silent like magic.

"Now, on the subject of Legends and Lore, this is basically a history class. We focus on the difference between what we know to be real, and what people have theorised happened long ago."

As Avril paused to flick through her copy of the textbook, Taz slid his hand into the middle of the desk and tapped his forefinger. I glanced up at him.

"*Watch this*," he mouthed.

I stared as he put his hand up and cleared his throat. Avril looked up.

"Taz, you know you don't need to put your hand up." She sighed. "What is it?"

He put his hand down with a grin. "I was wondering if we could learn about the Forgotten first. I know it's technically myth rather than history, but you always tell that kind of stuff so well."

I almost snorted at the obvious flattery. I bit my lips together instead to hide my smile as Avril gave Taz a long, shrewd stare.

"It's not something that we usually discuss in this class, but I suppose it can't hurt." She rubbed the bridge of her nose. "I'll need an entirely different book for this."

Taz shot me a triumphant grin, and I had to smile back, amused at how happy the bit of minor manipulation had made him.

Fairies, easily pleased apparently.

The thought made me realise I'd never considered asking Taz if he was actually fairy or Fae.

Once Avril had the book she needed, she surveyed the class with a serious face.

"The Forgotten are a group of Fae who believed in the stereotypical view of Faerie." Her dark tone sent shivers over my shoulders. "Long ago, the Fae would blast through the human world, using it as their playground. It wasn't just stealing milk or snatching livestock either, but making deals with the desperate and tormenting those that dared to try and join in."

Taz's fingers curled into a fist, and he slid his hand under the desk. I watched him out of the corner of my eye, but he wouldn't look at me, his face now set in distant brooding.

"The Queen of Faerie, our Queen now although she wasn't then, started a rebellion," Avril continued. "The Old King refused to relent, vowed to tear the human world to the ground. The Queen wanted to create peace."

"Hardly peace if you have to start a rebellion for it," Diana said with a sniff. "Although I'm sure the Lore isn't always reflective of the reality."

I resisted the urge to twist in my seat with something to throw, not only because I had awful hand-eye coordination, but because Taz had started bouncing his knee up and down. Even though he'd asked for the story, something was seriously needling him now.

Avril held Diana's gaze for several silent moments.

"Lore is just that, oral folklore carried down over the ages, *well done*." Her voice was laced with sarcasm. "But behaviour is far more telling than tales. The Old King offered to marry the Queen in the name of peace, but intended to control her. Luckily, she was smarter."

"Smarter?" Diana seemed to have no off switch. "She killed him and took his crown by default. Or so I've heard."

Avril smiled wide then. "As you say, Lore isn't always reflective of reality."

I struggled to hold in my urge to laugh, making sure to keep my face forward. Unless there was someone who could teach me to conjure lightning bolts or something really cool, I had a feeling Avril was going to be my favourite teacher.

"No more interruptions?" Avril waited. "Okay, good. So, the Queen set about creating peace that we hold to this day, and Taz has sneakily moved us onto the topic of our first class: protection wardings."

I sat up with interest, but froze as everyone else in the room including Taz gave a hearty, collective groan. Avril laughed.

"Faerie lesson number one, there is always a price to be paid, even for stories! The only other thing I'll say about the Forgotten is that there are always going to be rumours. That doesn't necessarily mean they're true, or untrue, but words are easy, and Fae can spin them better than most. Now, we're going to practice our simple protection wardings."

Another chorus of groans filled the room.

"Yes, I know, I know." Avril grinned. "But needs must. So, I want everyone to pair up. If you don't have anyone, go with the person nearest to you."

Taz slouched in his seat as low murmurs filled the room. I resisted the urge to turn and see who was in the class, and who was pairing off with who, but Taz leaned in before I could.

"Protection wardings are easy," he murmured. "Most here will know how already. Have you connected yet?"

I nodded. My connection with my fairy side hadn't been the most easy or triumphant achievement, but I could find it at will now in quiet times. It had taken me months just to feel it nestled inside, waiting for me. It was like having a little voice that tingled inside my body, speaking with a fuzzy warm feeling instead of words. It only came when I tried to connect with it, but I loved knowing it was there.

"Okay." Taz looked more than a little relieved. "Just find your connection then, and visualise like a dome or a bubble of protection, whatever works best for you."

I'd never done anything more than try to connect before, and the thought of having to actually ask my fairy blood to do anything made me feel queasy. Fairy classes had always been about theory, like when the Science teacher at school spends the first class talking about exciting experiments but then you don't get to actually do any for three years.

What if I can't do it? I couldn't voice that to Taz. *What if I try and nothing happens, or the connection disappears because I'm not fairy enough for this after all?*

I took a breath and let my focus drift toward my body, as if I was scanning it for aches and pains. Usually I found the connection somewhere around my left elbow first, then it would spread everywhere.

Come on, come on, please.

"You don't have to do it first time or anything." Taz must have noticed my panicked face. "Nothing goes wrong if you don't manage it."

I resisted the urge to snap that he shouldn't have said about most people being able to do it already then, and continued trying to connect.

"Okay, Diana, Charley," Avril called out, reclaiming everyone's attention. "You can go first."

I had to turn in my seat and watch, despite knowing it would only make my fragile self-esteem worse.

The tall, raven-haired girl sitting next to Diana stood up. Swilling in laconic confidence, Diana picked up a pen and threw it at Charley's head. Charley didn't even flinch. The pen sailed toward her, but Charley flicked out a hand and the pen hit an invisible forcefield, bouncing backwards and clattering to the floor.

I took several deep breaths as Diana had her go, making it look just as easy as Charley had, and tried frantically to find my connection again.

A buzz twitched near my left elbow.

Phew.

I focused on it, feeling the tingle spread through my fingers then up my arm, soaking through me until I felt alive with the energy of a thousand coffees.

I'd been focusing so hard, that I hadn't noticed the whole class taking their turn.

"Taz? Demi?" Avril asked from her desk.

I almost lost my connection as Taz faced me and handed me a pencil. I chucked it underarm toward him and ignored the instinctive temptation to snatch it back before it hit him. Taz didn't flick his hand out, as Diana had done. The pencil simply sailed toward his chest, hit his invisible protection barrier and changed course in mid-air, zooming not to the floor but into Taz's waiting hand.

"Smooth," I muttered, my insides about to explode with nerves.

I took a deep breath as Taz stretched his hand out, ready to throw the pencil. I visualised a big glass dome around me and nodded.

Big glass dome. Glass dome like the one with the rose in the Beauty and the Beast. Taz threw the pencil. *Didn't that get smashed?*

In that split-second, I imagined the dome in shards on the floor. The pencil sailed right toward my forehead and past the barrier I'd visualised. Lightning quick, Taz's lips twitched. The pencil bounced away in the opposite direction centimetres from my face, and I knew that he'd saved me the indignity of the class seeing me fail.

I can't even do a simple protection warding. I sat forward with my face burning as Avril clapped her hands to reclaim the class's attention. *Now I probably owe Taz a favour, and either way he's going to pity me. What if I can't do this kind of stuff, ever? What if I'm just not good enough, or not 'fairy' enough?*

I missed whatever Avril said next, but I saw her head shoot

up as drumming feet filled the room. Everyone stared at the hall windows in time to see the blur of someone running past. Avril wheeled toward the door fast enough to give the Flash ego-issues.

"She has a speed gift," Taz murmured, leaning close. "Among others."

In all honesty, I was surprised he was still even bothering to speak to me after my failure. Out in the hall, Avril had caught up with the runner and was jostling the boy back toward the classroom with a hand on his wrist.

"Did you notice how she uses 'fairy' and 'Fae' differently?" Taz whispered.

I nodded. "I got the same vibe from snooty-knickers back there. Fairy as a dirty word is a traditional trait, clearly. Although, I'm thinking now perhaps she's got a point when it comes to me."

"Don't say that." Taz frowned. "Not many of us learn stuff on the first try, it's just that everyone here is probably on their hundredth go. You're plenty fairy, and I'll help you practice all this stuff."

I stared at him. His head was right beside mine, so close I could see a speck of sleep on his eyelashes.

"Why are you being so kind to me?" I had to ask.

He shrugged, inching back. "I don't know."

"Do I owe you a favour then for that little act of charity?"

"Of course not." His brow dipped into a scowl. "Not everything is about favours and stuff. Okay, a lot of stuff in Faerie is, but you were on my side earlier with Diana when you didn't have to be. Now I'm on yours, but not because I owe you, or you owe me."

He inhaled as if to say more, but never got the chance as Avril's voice drew attention back to the hall.

"Just tell me what's going on," she insisted. "What do you mean 'been taken'? What's been taken?"

The boy rubbed his hand over his face, his eyes wide and his limbs fidgeting.

"It's gone. The Book of Faerie has been stolen!"

CHAPTER TEN
A NICKNAME AMONG FRIENDS

Even I knew the situation was serious, but I wasn't prepared for the sheer level of mayhem that exploded. Students leapt from their desks, all clamouring to be heard. Several stampeded straight from the room toward the lift in a dramatic tangling of elegant limbs. Avril looked horrified, her hands on her head and her class forgotten.

I glanced at Taz. His cheeks were pale, his eyes wide with alarm.

"Should I ask?"

Taz shook his head. "That book should be all but untouchable. I mean, someone could easily lift it off the pedestal, but it shouldn't be able to leave the library, let alone Arcanium itself. This is huge. Let everyone have their theatrics before we leave. I need to process this."

Stuck for something to do now that the students were leaving and Avril had disappeared into the crowd, I reached into my satchel and pulled out the first thing my hand landed on. I tore the packet open and held it in front of Taz.

"Jelly Baby?"

He stared at the bag for a couple of seconds, before his shoulders sagged and he reached in to take a handful. I found myself a black one and a pink one before putting the bag back in my satchel.

"Is this all linked?" I asked.

Taz nodded, his handful of sweets already gone. "It has to be. Weird warnings going orb-wide, that conversation on the trigger floor, now the Book of Faerie has gone missing, which is almost impossible. All these things point to one thing."

"The Forgotten?"

Taz scraped his chair back and stood up. I followed him out of the classroom and along the now deserted hall. He headed toward the stairs, his head bowed.

"We can't talk about this out in the open," he muttered. "First, we find Ace, then we'll find somewhere to hole up. Classes will be cancelled."

"I imagine the library will be off-limits now as well," I added.

Taz stormed toward the lift and I had to jog to keep up. For someone only a head taller than me, he had extremely speedy legs.

"The library and the human world." He stopped outside the lift and jabbed the button. "They'll likely have locked us down already. Trolls will be the only way in or out now, and there will be searches for anyone using them."

The lift arrived and Taz waited for me to get in first. He rubbed his chin with a sigh.

"I don't know where's be best not to be overheard," he sighed. "We can't risk anyone listening to us, right or wrong."

"Then you go where the noise is," I suggested. "Talk in riddles that only we three can understand."

"When shall we three meet again?" Taz quoted. Catching my eye, he smiled, his rapid change in mood startling me. "Oh, Shakespeare was totally Fae."

I shook my head. "Learn something new every day. What I don't get is how everyone was so adamant the book couldn't be stolen, when clearly it can."

Taz ran a hand through his hair as the lift stopped. He opened the gate to the resident's hall and followed me out.

"There's a common area at the far end of the floor, basically just go to the opposite end from your room. If I find Ace, meet us there?"

I nodded. "I need to stop by my room anyway to check, stuff."

Taz's smile returned as we continued down the hall toward the rooms, his turquoise eyes crinkling at the corners.

"I knew you'd be trouble the moment you came into the arcade, all blinky and nervous. You didn't steal the book, did you?"

The question came straight out of nowhere, but I heard the serious undertone, along with an alarming sweep of desire inside my head, compelling me to answer him. I stopped and folded my arms.

"What a silly question. You're really asking me?"

Taz didn't answer, just stood waiting, stubborn but not quite able to meet my eyes. Everyone knew fairies couldn't lie without consequences, but I was still annoyed he'd asked.

"No, I didn't steal it. Did you?"

Taz huffed a laugh, but I stayed exactly where I was. If he refused to trust me, then the same applied to him.

"No." His face fell as he shook his head. "Sorry, but we tell you about the book, then it goes missing. I had to ask. You could be someone completely different sent to distract us, or glamouring somehow to find out information."

"Who would a newbie be able to distract exactly? And you say 'somehow' like just not anyone can glamour, but all the students learn it in second year, don't they?"

"They do, but people can't glamour to enter Arcanium, the way in wipes any enchantment. That's why I was sent to get you when you arrived, a pair of eyes to make sure nothing dodgy was going on. Not just you, lots of mentees are given fetching new arrivals as an errand."

"You said you were just passing through," I reminded him.

Taz nodded. "I was. We didn't know when you'd arrive, so I just kind of, passed through now and then during the day."

I pressed a hand to my forehead. "I really need to figure out how this place functions."

Taz looked up and down the hall. When he straightened up, his gaze fixed on the lift, I turned to see Ace hurrying toward them.

"There you are." He beamed with relief. "This is absolutely bonkers. Everyone's panicking. Half of the students are orbing home from the Ogle, and Emil's down there screaming about the wave-width not holding out forever."

"The common area should be empty," Taz suggested. "We need to get our heads around this."

Ace nodded. "Before we do, I need to ask. Diana Hemlock stormed past me and shouted that I should choose better friends before it's too late. Is that because of yesterday, or did I miss something? She looked furious."

I shrugged, but Taz started grinning.

"Demi went all sparky again and shot her down. I like that actually, I'm going to call you Sparky from now on."

Residual torment from being called many names by my sisters and other kids at school over the years wound tight around my throat. It took me several moments to realise Taz wasn't saying it to be cruel.

"You are not calling me Sparky," I muttered.

"You don't get to pick your nickname, your friends do."

I copied his raised eyebrow. "Oh, we're friends now?"

Taz froze. We stared at each other. Despite the conversation in the classroom, and his insistence that it wasn't just about favours, I hadn't considered that we were actual friends. After an excruciating pause, Ace patted us both on the shoulder.

"Of course we're friends," he said with a soothing tone. "Not sure how, I'll be honest, but Demi's as much one of us as either of us are now. Um, neither of you had anything to do with the book, did you?"

Somehow, when it was Ace asking with reluctant hesitation, I found it impossible to be grumpy with him.

"No, I didn't. I didn't even know it was here until yesterday, which Taz seems to think is super suspicious." I pulled a face at him. "I've got enough problems of my own to deal with anyway, without nicking the Faerie bible as well. I wouldn't even know how."

Ace smiled. "I didn't think you had, but everyone's asking everyone else, so it'd look weird we didn't at least ask each other. I didn't either. I was out running, then in training, so I didn't even have time for breakfast."

"Here." I burrowed into my satchel and produced the Jelly Babies. "Keep your sugar up."

Ace peered into the packet and carefully picked out one of each colour. I wondered if anyone had realised you could tell a lot about people by how they selected their sweets. Taz was very much a grab at random and shovel in the mouth kind of boy, moving quick and restless. Ace was cautious and always tried to be considerate and equal, to think things through, balanced and fair. I checked the bag and saw there were still a fair few pink ones.

Does that make me selfish, wanting just one colour? I wondered. *Or just liberated that there are still some left that my sisters haven't already hoovered. Oh well.*

I put the packet away as we walked along to the intersection, and turned left when the boys went right.

"I'm just going to-" I faltered. "I'll meet you in a minute."

I let myself into my room and shut the door behind me. A brief look in the wide open drawer suggested Leo was taking full advantage of his roaming privileges. I checked around then stood completely still by the clothing shelves.

"Leo," I called softly. "Want to go see the boys? I'll bring you some more crickets if you- *eeek*!"

Something solid dropped onto my shoulder. I flinched as Leo wound his tail around the base of my throat and made a crooning noise right in my ear. I lifted a finger to rub the top of his head.

"You're a horror. We still need to find a way of getting you back, but it's going to be even harder if the whole place is locked down on high alert."

I manhandled him into the satchel and found the remnant of a lettuce leaf to drop in with him.

"I can't believe you've eaten all that already. I'm going to have to start bringing up supplies at this rate. Maybe the Braunees will do me some kind of deal."

I opened the door and peeked out to check the coast was clear, then down to make sure Leo was properly hidden, stopping only to lock the door behind me. I ventured along the hall, noticing most of the doors had little name plaques on in various forms. Some were just pieces of paper stuck on with pretty lettering, while others were beautifully painted wood.

I didn't recognise any of the names, but wondered if I should make one for myself as well.

Assuming they don't find Leo and kick me out.

It didn't bear thinking about.

I found Taz and Ace at the very end of the hall, sitting in a widened area full of dark blue armchairs. A television hung on the wall and a couple of small, round tables were dotted about. Ace was sitting upright in one armchair, all neat and ready, but Taz had sprawled on the one next to him, his legs over the arm.

"Welcome to the common area." Taz waved his arm at the room. "We should be okay to talk here for a bit."

I took an armchair for myself that had its back to the hall and risked opening the satchel a bit on my lap. Leo stuck his head out, eyed Ace and Taz, then pressed his scaly head against my finger. I scratched his neck, amused when he started crooning gently.

"Okay." Taz sat up in one swift swing, leaning forward with his forearms resting on his knees. "If someone comes, I'll say I'm hungry, then you'll know to put him away."

I smiled. "Thanks. I know this isn't a great start and you guys have kind of been dragged into it."

"That's okay." Taz shrugged, his cheeks dusting pink. "We like to live dangerously. So, what do we know so far?"

Ace pulled out his mobile phone. When he caught Taz and I staring, he held it up.

"Safest place to keep notes," he explained. "Everyone uses orbs as phones don't work down here, and a lot of Fae don't even have one."

I frowned. "Weird nobody's thought to password-protect orbs. Although, I'm guessing there's some kind of magic to make them only respond to their owner."

Ace shook his head. "Surprisingly not. Anyone can use an orb, just like anyone could pick up an old phone and dial a number from an address book. As long as you know the person you're calling, it'll reach them."

"Crazy." I pulled my mobile out, a battered model that my sisters had long since neglected. "I'll write some stuff down as well, just in case."

I swiped the screen, soothed by the familiar action of my thumb tapping. Taz watched us, his mouth turned down. I guessed he was one of the fairies or Fae who didn't have human stuff, but I didn't dare ask.

I don't know anything about him or Ace really. I should find a way of asking without being rude. Taz mentioned his mum sending him here instead of Fae boarding school so I guess he must be full-blooded or close to, but apart from that they could be anyone.

Ace finished with his phone and looked up at me, as if he could read my mind.

"So, Demi," he asked with a grin. "How are you finding it? Not the start to your FDP career you imagined I bet."

I snorted. "Not *exactly* how I imagined, although I guess it's character building or something. Seems every time I try to prove myself, I end up making things worse."

Taz rolled his eyes, then his gaze returned to flicking between my phone and Ace's with undisguised curiosity.

"You don't have to keep proving yourself," he grumbled. "You're here to train up, not do the actual job. Sometimes it's okay to just be people."

"Oh yeah, and you'd have the monopoly on being 'just people'," Ace snickered.

I eyed them both as Taz sank lower in his seat with a moody scowl.

I've definitely missed something here.

"What do you mean by that?" I asked.

Ace opened his mouth, but Taz beat him to it.

"It's nothing. Leave it. Ace just thinks he's funny."

Ace shrugged, still grinning. I ran my fingertips over Leo's head, focusing on his crooning instead.

"Well, I'm an open book at least," Ace added, reminding me that I probably should have asked him about himself before now. "Half-Fae, and half-human on my mum's side. We live in London near my nan, and I have one sister. She's shown signs of being fairy too, which our parents are delighted about."

I forgot about Taz's sulking. "But you're not?"

"Nope." Ace shook his head. "She was always our aunt's favourite, so she got a small levitation gift and I got a book."

I bit my lip. "That's a bit unfair, unless it was a really cool book, like a grimoire full of real spells or something. Same with my family, although none of mine are apparently fairy or Fae at all. My mentor at fairy classes said it can happen, but it's rare."

Taz sat up. "So you've really got no known Fae or fairy lineage at all?"

"Not that I know of." I shrugged. "Both parents can trace their family back at least two generations and no sign of fairy activity. I'm also the only one out of my sisters, so they're convinced I'm adopted, but Mum's got all the baby pictures and my birth certificate and everything so I'm guessing not."

Taz watched me for a moment, long enough that I had to avert my gaze and stare down at Leo instead, my cheeks beginning to burn.

My sisters had used my odd-one-out-ness against me for as long as I could remember, all the way into secondary school. There were a few of us who'd sat together at lunch, mostly for protection from the hordes, but always doing our own thing and not exactly speaking to each other. Even many of the teachers seemed to find me irritating, and I often imagined them thinking *'why can't she just play like the normal kids, make life easier and stop wandering off on her own.'*

I'd considered several times that perhaps I wasn't a fairy at all, but Xavio had managed to dredge some skills out of me over the past few years, like the ability to find things or know information that I shouldn't, which apparently is key fairy 101 behaviour. I shook off the memories and glanced around at Ace and Taz instead.

Now these are the closest I've ever had to actual friends, and I need to prove I do belong here.

"Perhaps you had a powerful relative a few generations up," Taz suggested. "It does happen sometimes."

I shrugged again, not wanting to talk about my fairy lineage, or lack of it, anymore.

Ace cleared his throat and waved his phone.

"Right, note time. Taz, you lay out what we know so far."

I scratched Leo's chin and thumbed onto my phone's note app.

"We have Sandra talking about reinstating traditional Fae values with a mysterious stranger, and taking over Arcanium," Taz said.

Sandra – librarian to mysterious stranger - bring back traditional values to Arcanium.

Ace nodded. "And the orb-wide warning saying the enemy are inside the walls."

Orb-wide warning – enemy inside Arcanium.

I bit my lip. "Then the book that can't go missing goes missing. Question is, how?"

Book of Faerie stolen.

Taz sat back. Ace frowned. I stared at my notes.

"What if-" I shook my head. "Never mind."

Taz rolled his eyes. "Can't do that, Sparky. You can't just say something then not tell us."

I gave him a look but ignored the nickname, tapping my finger on the side of my phone.

"We can't do anything about the orb-wide warning, not without knowing who to speak to. There were no specifics. But there's one common theme with the other two."

Ace sat up with a loud click of his fingers. Leo snapped his head up in alarm, but quickly grumbled and retreated into the satchel.

"Sorry." Ace gave me a guilty grin. "You mean the library

connection? Sandra talking about restoring traditional Fae values, and the fact the book disappeared from her library?"

"Yeah, so there's got to be something in that. Too much to be a coincidence. For all we know, the book is hidden in her desk drawer or something, or it's a diversion to get everyone talking while something else nobody's expecting flies in under the radar. What do you think, Taz?"

He fidgeted in his seat, frowning at me.

"It makes sense. The book must be here still, unless there's another route out, but Queenie and Emil would know of those."

"Are you sure they're not in on it?" I asked, remembering my one less than fluffy encounter with Queenie, and the brief times I'd dealt with Emil.

Taz snorted, slumping back.

"Neither of them would turn traitor, I'm sure of that. I think we're onto the right track with the library connection, but what do we do about it?"

Ace shrugged, putting his phone away with a pensive frown. Taz stared up at the ceiling, one leg back over the arm of the chair and swinging idly.

I shouldn't be interfering. I'll be in enough trouble as it is if they ever find out about Leo, but the book going missing is criminal. We can't just sit back and do nothing.

I looked down at the soft sound of snuffling coming from my satchel, and around at the others.

I'm already destined for trouble, as Taz keeps telling me, so I might as well make the most of the adventure while I can.

"We go on with the plan," I announced. "Ace and I will keep watch when the library opens again, find out where she goes, and what she does."

Ace nodded. "I imagine they'll open it up again tomorrow."

I turned to Taz next only to find him grinning with alarming devilishness shining in his eyes.

"Are you still up for causing a diversion of some kind then?" I asked.

He actually winked at me.

"I am, Sparky, but only because you asked nicely."

CHAPTER ELEVEN
A TAZ DIVERSION

The library didn't reopen for five days following the Book of Faerie's disappearance. Everywhere I went, the halls were filled with hushed tones of intrigue and loud theories on what could have happened, always more fantastical the longer you listened. I tried to make the most of my first week of classes, but my mind constantly wandered back to the missing book and the hostile librarian.

Where was she when the book was stolen?

I also still had Leo to contend with, a lizard who ate an astronomical amount. The Braunees found it hilarious when I turned up each evening at their insistence to pick up bags of cricket salad. If it wasn't for the fact Arcanium was on full lockdown to students, I would have gone out to buy some lizard food from the human world, but that would no doubt cause some suspicious questions if I marched into the atrium with a huge bag of dried crickets.

The moment the library was announced as open, Ace and I went straight there. Sitting in the small nook I now thought of as ours, under the pretext of studying while actually attempting to chart Sandra's daily routine, I began feel at home. The nook was also conveniently two down from Sandra's office, which was extra handy for espionage.

"Hey, look at this." I moved the huge book I was reading across the table closer to Ace. "Chameleons turn darker when they're cold because dark colours absorb more heat. They shrink and enlarge their actual cells to change colour, how cool is that?"

"Very factual," Ace grumbled with a fond smile. "But I don't see how that's going to help me memorise the Fae dynasties from beginning to end, or to learn all the words to the *Ballad of Finding Your Way.*"

"Oh, that." I shrugged and pulled the book back in front of me. "The Ballad is easy once you learn the rhyming words."

Ace scratched his head. "Eh?"

"So, the first four lines are all about obscuring where you've come from. You know, *ask me my origin, I'll tell you no lies, but pass on specifics around all seeing eyes.* It basically means be vague about where you come from."

I looked up again to find Ace staring at me.

"How can you just remember all that?" he asked.

"I don't know, it just kind of goes in and sits there." I shrugged. "Not as useful as being able to intuit like you can, I'll never be able to do that."

Ace laughed. "But that's just people. It's literally just knowing what to say in what situation."

"Oh yeah, I'm clearly awesome at that." I pulled a face. "I can imagine it now if anyone ever gifts me powers to wield. Someone will ask for strength to face the days ahead and I'll end up giving them the ability to lift mountains or something. Then they'll accidentally drop the mountain on a town, and I'll be chased away in disgrace."

Ace might have said something reassuring, which seemed to be his standard response to both my self-deprecation and Taz's withering sarcasm, but he was staring out at the main part of the room.

"Oh no," he muttered. "Witches incoming."

I looked up. "What?"

"The Eastwick sisters. I don't think you've actually met them, but they're second-years like me and utterly relentless.

Apparently, their mum let them change their names officially when they turned fifteen. Nobody's even sure if Cheryl is actually a sister- hi, ladies!"

He straightened up all smiles, but I could see the tension in his shoulders as the three girls stopped at our table and sat down without being asked. They all had hair dyed wild colours - at least, I assumed it was either dyed or they had the ability to glamour already. The tallest one with dark purple hair tied back in a ponytail smiled wide.

"Hi, Ace." She looked up at him through lowered lashes. "Who's your friend?"

Ace turned to me, unusually flustered. "Oh, this is Demi. She's a first-year mentee. Demi, this is-"

"I'm Beryl," the girl said. "This is my sister, Cheryl." The girl beside her with green hair waved. "And this is Meryl."

Behind the deep blue curls, Meryl's smile was less beaming than the other two, and infinitely more sincere.

"Hi." I raised a hand and managed a toothy grin. "Are you FDPs already?"

Of course they're not, Ace literally just said they're second-years.

I winced at my own ineptitude but the girls eyed each other and giggled for several seconds longer than necessary.

"Oh no, not yet." Cheryl shook her head.

"Maybe not ever," Meryl agreed.

"We're thinking of starting a band instead," Beryl explained, her 'cat-lining-up-a-mouse' expression increasing. "You'll be our first groupie, right Ace?"

"Um." Ace hesitated. "I'm not-"

Full of sympathy for my friend, I jumped in.

"What instruments do you play?"

Three pairs of brown eyes blinked at me until Beryl leaned

forward.

"Excuse me?"

"Instruments." I panicked. "You know, you play them, and they make noise, like guitars, pianos?"

Beryl straightened up, her expression narrowing. On reflection, it did sound a lot like I was making fun of them.

"We're singers." Cheryl sniffed.

I curled my toes in my shoes against the leaping anxiety.

"I didn't mean anything horrible," I apologised. "Um, I'm not great with people. Sorry."

Meryl looked as though her cold expression might start thawing again, but Cheryl and Beryl still wore identical expressions of suspicion.

"At least you know when to take a hint, Demi." Taz appeared behind the three girls. "Unlike some."

Beryl looked over her shoulder and rolled her eyes at him.

"Aww, don't tell me you've made some actual friends at long last, Taz. Still, we have much more interesting things to be doing. Come on."

The Eastwick trio rose out of their seats in one joint motion and walked away with their chins in the air, although Meryl lowered hers almost immediately.

"Wow." Ace chuckled, relieved. "Thanks, Taz. You must have superpowers. I can never bring myself to be mean and brush them off. I am forever grateful to you."

He swept one arm across his chest and dipped his head and shoulders in a small bow. Taz scoffed with a grin. He sank into the middle chair that Cheryl had abandoned and leaned his elbows on the desk.

"Right, The Plan," he murmured. "I've figured out a diversion but you'll have to be quick. She won't have time to lock the office behind her as she usually does either. Demi, are you up to it?"

I nodded, although my insides started backflipping. "Better than I am running interference if we need to distract people."

"That would be my superpower." Ace grinned. "So, I'm the distraction in case the diversion doesn't take as long as we hope. Taz, you're the lookout, and Demi, you're doing the digging. I only have one more question."

I looked at him expectantly. Taz waved an irritable hand for him to hurry up.

"What *is* the diversion?" Ace asked.

"And how will we know when the time comes?" I chipped in.

Taz bit his lip. "Yeah, about that-"

A loud clamour of voices echoed from a set of double doors that led into a hall. Sandra, hawk-like at the semi-circular desk in front of her office, got up with a fearsome scowl. She stormed past our nook toward the exit. The moment she opened the doors, the shouts became clear.

"SPIDER!   SPIDER   IN   THE   HALL! HUGEGREATBIGEFF-"

The three of us looked at each other. Taz stared at me.

"Well? *GO!*"

I scrambled out of my chair, knocking it to the ground. I had no idea how Taz had managed to create a giant spider as a diversion, and wasn't sure I ever wanted to find out. I hared between tables toward Sandra's desk and straight through the office door.

Right, think logically. I headed straight for the wooden filing cabinet against the back wall. *You can't move anything out of place or she'll know someone's been in here.*

I couldn't see anywhere else in the room that would hide anything illicit, no desk with drawers, not even any paintings that might hide a safe. The many piles of books stacked up suggested

I wouldn't get much luck trying to peel the carpet back for loose floorboards or trapdoors either. I bent and twisted back and forth, scanning the piles for signs of the Book of Faerie, but of course she wouldn't just leave it out in plain sight.

I pulled open the cabinet's drawers, rifling through old library card inserts and overdue letter templates.

A-ha.

The bottom drawer refused to open. I hauled the cabinet away from the wall with a lot of grunting, using a series of tiny shunts. Glancing over my shoulder, I reached into my satchel's side pocket. Xavio had given me one present before I left to come to Arcanium. It wasn't a fairy gift, like I'd secretly been hoping for, but a swiss army knife was a kind thought as well, if a bit daunting. I had no idea why Xavio had thought it would be necessary, but decided not to knock it now that I had a use for the screwdriver attachment.

The screws holding the back of the cabinet gave way remarkably easily. I pocketed them and pulled the back panel off.

The moment I pushed the middle drawer forward to see the one underneath, my mouth dropped open. I grabbed the topmost item, an A4 sheet of paper with Queenie's signature squiggled over and over on it. I had seen that signature on my acceptance letter, and on the various copies of the codes of conduct hung on the walls. Given the varying stages of accuracy, Sandra was trying to copy Queenie's signature. Underneath, I found a silken black wig in a bag, along with a familiar-looking dress in purple velvet. There was even a pack of purple fake nails right at the bottom.

"DEMI!"

I jumped and banged my head on the side of the cabinet.

"Oww!" I straightened up to see Taz glaring at me from the door.

"Well?" he demanded.

"I know I can't take any of this but it's incriminating. Is there a way we can get a picture?"

I rummaged in my pocket for my phone, but Taz waved his arms.

"Oi, no time, just hurry up!"

I noticed something gleaming right at the bottom of the drawer and grimaced. Nestled in a see-through muslin bag, were three different coloured orbs, a dark green, a dusky rose pink one, and a white one similar to mine.

What would she be doing with these?

I pulled the middle drawer shut, almost removing two of my fingers. With no idea how long I had left, I replaced the backboard and screwed all four screws most of the way. With my face burning from the effort, I shunted the cabinet back into place, making sure there was no sign of the carpet indentation visible to give me away.

I dashed to the door just as a stream of people burst into the library in an orchestra of excitable chatter. Heart pounding, I dropped to my knees and crawled to the edge of the library desk.

Close call. I peeked out.

Sandra was facing the crowd in the library doorway, her arms up and waving in a desperate attempt to calm everyone, her voice completely lost in the hubbub.

"It had sixteen legs, at least!"

"Don't be stupid, it had four legs because the other four must have been knocked off in the scuffle. I saw it, but it definitely had a hundred eyes."

"And it was green! Who ever heard of a green spider!"

"No, it wasn't, it was dark blue like the carpet, *I* saw it."

"Er, that was because it changed colour? Idiot."

I joined Taz at the table just in time. Ace arrived moments

later and stood right beside me, leaning over with one hand braced on the top of the desk.

"Open your bag," he hissed.

I lifted the flap and gawped in horror as Ace dropped a very disgruntled looking Leo into it, complete with four hairy spider legs sprouting from his scales. I stared at Ace, then twisted round to find Taz looking rather rueful.

"It's just a glamour," he promised. "It'll wear off any minute."

A bewildering sensation curdled in my stomach. Resentment I was used to. The odd indulgent dream about sending my sisters far away to military camp or a remote island was almost every day. But this, it felt very much like actual fury.

"I can't believe you used him as a distraction." I clenched and released my fist around my satchel strap. "He could have been trampled!"

Taz frowned. "I made sure Ace knew to stop him from getting hurt."

"What if he hadn't though? What if someone had stepped on him, or he'd gotten scared and run off somewhere?"

Taz at least had the decency to stare at his fingernails. "But they didn't, and he didn't. He's fine. He shouldn't even be here anyway."

Don't answer that. First off, he's right. Second, he's helped you this far and he's still right.

"Fine." I unclenched my teeth. "We have stuff to report now though."

"We need to go straight to Queenie then," Ace insisted.

As the crowds started to disperse, Taz got up without a word and set off toward the lift. Sandra watched us leave, her gaze following us across the room. Nobody said a word in the lift, but I held my satchel close to me, just in case. Residual anger at

Taz's use of Leo thundered through me, but I didn't want to alienate the only friends I'd ever had either.

"How did you get into my room to pick up Leo, by the way?" I asked, assuming Ace had been in on it too. "I'm sure I locked my door this morning."

"I stole the key from your pocket at breakfast." Taz shrugged. He pulled a familiar metal key from his hoodie pocket and held it out to me. "Then I just glamoured myself into you and popped into your room."

The lift came to a halt and Taz strode out like a mutant spider-Leo was at his heels. Ace gave me a look as I burst out of the lift and set off after Taz. The key had been in my pocket, and I really didn't like the idea of his hand going fishing.

CHAPTER TWELVE
ACCUSATIONS

I charged down the hall after Taz toward the doors of Queenie's office. As I stormed along, I slowed down enough to peer into my bag. Leo slumbered with his tongue poking out, his spider legs now thankfully gone. Shaking my head, I hurried after Taz. There would be time to ask him how the glamour worked later. As a first-year, he shouldn't even know how to glamour yet, but perhaps he'd picked it up already.

"Whoa."

Emil appeared from a side corridor without warning, so suddenly that I almost collided into Taz in an attempt to stop. I stepped away from him just in time, still irritable that he'd been able to pickpocket my key from me.

"What's the rush?" Emil frowned. "Surely you're not planning on bursting into Queenie's office."

"We need to tell her, or someone, something." Ace hesitated. "It's important."

Emil folded his arms across his chest, planting his feet between us and the doors.

"She's in a mood," he sighed.

Taz rolled his eyes. "When isn't she? We overheard something, but couldn't act on it because of the proof rule, you know-"

"Rule 37 hyphen B slash 779," I offered.

Taz gave me a dirty look.

"I take it now you have proof though to come up here in such a flap?" Emil asked.

This time, Taz glared at me when I didn't answer.

I can't win with him.

"We overheard a plot to overthrow the Queen of Faerie and replace her," I explained. "It does sound nuts, but we did some digging and found things that could at least prove something suspicious is going on, if not exactly that."

Emil unfolded his arms, his stern stance settling.

"Have you told anyone else?" he asked.

We shook our heads.

"We came straight here," Taz insisted. "It's Sandra, Demi found some things in her office."

"Like what?" Emil slid a hand into his pocket, the other rubbing his forehead. "And when you say 'found', what exactly do you mean?"

I bit my lip, beginning to wonder how much trouble I was actually going to be in. Our intentions were honourable, so there was that, but breaking into the librarian's office had to be hovering near the naughty list category.

They can't send me home for this, surely.

I kept shaking fingers clamped around my satchel strap, the other pressed to the flap to avoid any unexpected Leo appearances.

"Her office wasn't locked or anything," I insisted. "The cabinet drawer technically was, but I replaced the back panel exactly the same way I found it, and I didn't take anything."

Emil raised his eyes skywards. "That is something I suppose. But what exactly did you find to warrant this?" He waved his hand at Queenie's door.

Aware Taz and Ace didn't know what I'd seen yet, I tried to be as clear and descriptive as possible.

"A black wig and purple dress, identical to those Queenie wears- not the wig, I'm guessing, but the same as her hair. Oh, and the same fake nails. Also a piece of paper where it looks like she's been practicing Queenie's signature. And three orbs, one dark green, one pink and one pale like mine."

Far from looking surprised or horrified, Emil just seemed weary, his shoulders slumping.

"Sandra," he paused, dismayed. "Okay, slowly this time, what did you say you found again, in her drawer was it?"

"Yes, the bottom drawer of her cabinet, in her office. It was a wig and outfit to make her look like Queenie, plus a sheet of Queenie's signatures and three orbs."

Emil moved aside and waved a hand at Queenie's door.

"Well, I suppose we should get to the bottom of this," he said. "Go and knock, but she's not going to take it well."

Taz marched past him, his fist making a muffled banging sound on the door moments later.

"*WHAT?*" Queenie didn't sound happy at all.

I shuffled in behind Ace, one hand on my satchel in case Leo woke again feeling curious. Queenie stood behind her desk, elongated by a fitted velvet dress, her nails clacking an uneven rhythm on the wooden tabletop. I curled my toes and tried not to focus on the irritating sound.

"Well?" Queenie snapped.

Taz explained, and I managed to babble my findings without hiccoughing or running out of breath halfway through a sentence.

"We must check this immediately." Queenie stared at us for a second. "Go on then, out! I'll join you down there."

I was the first out of the door, aware of Emil, Taz and Ace close behind me. We squeezed into the lift, none of us daring to say a word. Students stared and scattered in equal measure as we strode through the corridor and into the library. Sandra eyed us with carefully polite curiosity.

I took a breath and almost choked on it as Queenie appeared out of thin air. One moment nothing, then *poof* there she was.

"Whoa," I gasped.

I knew it was possible, but translocation was a rare gift to receive indeed, because it was supposed to involve some great sacrifice on the part of the fairy or Fae gifting it.

"Quite." Queenie gave me a disapproving look. "Now, Sandra, these three seem to think you have some questionable items in your drawers. Your office ones."

Sandra blinked, seemingly confused. She stood up and pulled a key from the depths of her cardigan.

"It is in rather a mess I'm afraid," she said. "But nothing I would call questionable."

She unlocked the door and made a show of opening each drawer, starting at the top. When she opened the bottom, I noticed the tiniest upward twitch of her mouth as Queenie and Emil crowded around to look.

"More library inserts," Sandra announced. "But yes, I suppose I should tidy them. One gets so busy there never seems to be the time. What questionable items were you expecting?"

I ignored the scandalised looks Ace and Taz were giving me, my gut beginning to churn. The glint in Sandra's eyes as she glanced over at us made me sure.

I know what I saw. Somehow, she's moved everything already.

"Clothing to impersonate me, apparently," Queenie said. "As well as a sheet with practiced copies of my signature and three orbs."

Sandra's hand shot to her chest, her eyes wide.

"Why on earth would I have such things? If I had confiscated them, I'd have reported it immediately."

But she didn't confiscate them, she stole them. Word-tangling and nobody's saying a damn thing about it!

"I know what I saw." I couldn't keep myself quiet. "We were only looking because-"

I turned to Taz and Ace, well aware they'd at least overheard what I had up on the trigger floor.

But none of us can say anything about it. Not now there's no proof. Surely though, Emil must know I can't lie, so what I told him was real?

My stomach sank as I looked over at him. He'd moved across the room and now stood blocking the door, the meaning behind his frown unreadable.

"I never thought the behaviour of students would come to this." Sandra looked as though she was about to cry big crocodile tears. "I'm sure you're not entirely spiteful children, but it's gone far enough now. I can't turn a blind eye to your antics anymore."

I hung my head. *Someone should have stayed behind to watch her. Instead we all went racing off. We've got nothing.*

"I have tried to keep the sanctity of librarian-student trust since my appointment here," Sandra sniffed loudly and dug out a tissue. "But no more. That girl there has brought a *creature* into Arcanium."

I froze. My fingers curled around the satchel strap, my heart pounding.

"Is this true?" Emil asked.

Sandra veered forward, her eyes now glinting with expectant glee.

"It is, I've seen it. Horrible scaly thing. I can prove it. She carries it around with her sometimes."

My knees went weak, my chest crunching as Emil eyed me.

"Is this true?" he asked.

I hesitated. If they searched my bag now, I'd be done for, but I couldn't lie either.

119

"I- sort of. He's not my pet, or he wasn't at first. That assignment I took on my first day, he snuck into my bag when I wasn't looking and ended up back here with me."

I tried not to focus on the astonished expressions of Queenie and Emil, or the malicious triumph on Sandra's face.

"I didn't find him until I got back to my room," I continued. "I wasn't sure what to do, then Arcanium was locked down, but he's a very normal chameleon it seems, he's not done anything magic or weird."

"Students aren't allowed pets," Queenie insisted.

To my surprise, Taz's hands flew to his hips.

"Why not?" he demanded. "It's not in any of the codes of conduct, or the Arcanium rules of residence. There's nothing to actually say we're not allowed pets, so you can't just make up rules."

"I am the Director-"

"That's right." Ace leapt in. "Isn't there meant to be a group of Arcanium elders or something that has to decide these things? I could understand if it was something people could be allergic to, if it was a cat or dog maybe."

"Rabbits," Taz piped up. "Oh, one of my sisters is supposed to be *deathly* allergic to horses. But we're talking about a lizard. One that has been here for days without anyone having the slightest idea until now."

"Still." Queenie hesitated. "The creature is from a Faerie realm. There's no telling what could happen until it's been investigated properly. It should at least be kept in quarantine for the time being while the matter is being decided."

Emil sighed, drawing everyone's attention.

"Nothing's happened since Demi returned. There haven't been any swelling heads or mad occurrences, other than whatever possessed you all to assume our librarian was somehow up to no good-"

"And break into my office!"

"-And break into her office," Emil continued. "While we need to deal with the severity of what's happened, we can't penalise Demi for having a pet when it's technically not breaking any rules. We do however need to deal with the fact it's not a pet, it's an unknown creature from Faerie. Where is the animal now?"

Taz placed a hand on my wrist before I could open my satchel.

"She leaves it in her room a lot of the time," he said. "It has a habit of escaping. We'll go get it."

I closed my eyes tight.

I know he's trying to help, but they're not likely to let me keep Leo if he tells them he's an escape artist.

"Right well," Queenie wiped her face. "Go fetch it, and we will take it into quarantine."

"I know what's happened before to the few creatures that have come through by accident." Taz's tone turned menacing. "You will make sure Demi gets him back safe if the elder council decides we're allowed pets?"

Queenie's smile stretched. "Sure."

I didn't believe one bit of it. Queenie would make sure now that she'd agreed to it, as fairies and Fae couldn't lie, but if some accident were to befall Leo, out of her control, she wouldn't care at all.

I dropped my head lower, my insides churning as we left the office and the library. Taz's words about what had happened to previous creatures in quarantine echoed like a death knell in my head, but I couldn't risk trusting Taz, or even Ace, with what I had to do next.

I just need to get up to the arcade. If I can find a passer-by to take Leo or someone in one of the shops, then at least he'll be safe. If I can't do that, I'll have to find somewhere to hide him. As we walked along the corridor, I assessed the likelihood of my plan working. *All those great ideas about making a name for myself here, about getting through to becoming an FDP and away from home. Can I really throw all that away by trying to fix this myself? I'll only make things worse.*

I fought to keep the burn of tears at bay as we shuffled into the lift and Taz jabbed a button. If he and Ace insisted on accompanying me back to Queenie's office with Leo, I didn't fancy my chances outrunning them or giving them the slip.

The lift whistled downwards.

"Right, you definitely have him on you?" Taz muttered out of the corner of his mouth.

I frowned. "Yes, why?"

"Because, idiot, you need to get Leo out of here. Remember I mentioned creatures from before? They don't kill them or return them to their finder. They send them away to be tested on."

My insides froze. *Not Leo. I can't be the reason something bad happens to him.*

Seeing he had my attention, Taz pounded his fist against his palm.

"Whatever you saw in that office, she's found a way to hide it," he hissed. "We should have left someone down there to watch her, but can't do anything about that now."

Ace nodded. "If she can get rid of a drawer of stuff that quick, then why not other stuff?"

"You're thinking the Book of Faerie? I thought that too."

"You both believe me?" I blinked at them.

Taz rolled his eyes. "Of course we do, but we need to get Leo to safety before anything else. We're going straight up to despatch. I'm going to owe Trevor so much after this, and you're going to owe me even more."

The lift slid to a halt at the despatch floor, but Ace already had the gate open. I opened my mouth to thank Taz, but he glared at me with his eyes sparking a storm.

"No time, go!"

I half-strode, half-stumbled as Taz gave my back a helpful shove out of the lift. I took a deep breath and forced myself not to look down as I wobbled along the suspended walkway toward the circular platform.

"What brings you three up to see me?" Trevor appeared, his expression wide.

"Hi, Trevor. I know we're not allowed to realm-skip without a purple slip." Taz bit his lip. "But I need a favour, a big one. I can repay it though."

Even I knew what that meant. A big favour wasn't something to be offered lightly, because going back on it brought the deepest of fairy penalties, ones that went right into the natural magic of Faerie. Taz had also suggested that I owed him big, but he'd purposefully not extracted any obligation from me first, which was a kindness that would plague me to the end of my days if I didn't find some way to repay him.

"I'll accept." Trevor's expression wrinkled. "It's nothing too awful, is it?"

"No." Taz shook his head. "Just take Demi here back into the same realm as last time. We don't technically have-"

Trevor held up a hand. "Less I know the better. You've told me I have a job." He turned to me with a curious expression. "Inside then please."

I clambered into the rickshaw on Bambi legs, but made sure to check I had my orb in my pocket and Leo in my satchel.

I can't risk screwing this up on top of everything else.

"You should literally just be able to drop him off," Taz

instructed. "Actually, don't even get out. Just drop him over the side and tell Trevor to return to hub."

I nodded and closed my hand around Leo's middle inside the bag. The responding murmur of affection didn't quell the twisting sensation in my chest any. Putting him back where he belonged was the safest thing for him right now, but the loss was already setting up camp and ballooning in my ribcage at the thought of being without him.

As Trevor took off at a speedy jog toward the sparkling wall, I clamped my eyes shut and, for the second time in as many weeks, hoped for the best.

CHAPTER THIRTEEN
ANOTHER BUMPY LANDING

I experienced a brief sensation of weightlessness as Trevor hit the wall and the rickshaw jolted. The air was still rushing past me, but I couldn't feel the seat underneath me anymore. Before I could open my eyes, everything inside me screaming at me not to risk it, I crashed sideways into something hard. My brain bounced inside my skull, the disorientation making my head spin.

After a few tentative moments, the sound of indignant squawking reached my ears. I blinked until I could make out three people, two sitting on high-backed chairs and one standing beside them, all tilted at a ninety degree angle.

"Ouch," I muttered, pushing myself up on one elbow.

A quick glance left and right told me that not only had I not broken any upper body bones, which was good, but that Trevor had disappeared, which wasn't part of the plan.

"She just, appeared, like magic!" I could now make out a familiar face wearing a scandalised expression. "Witchcraft! Alert the guards!"

Prince Lucastrian of Egloriem sat up in his seat, waving an indignant pointer finger in the air. Next to him, the duchess rolled her eyes at Alannah, who was too busy staring daggers at me to notice.

"Oh, do not be so tiresome," the duchess huffed. "Always calling for your guards. Why not do some real fighting, or better yet, some real work. Some happy ending this turned out to be, hah!"

I struggled to my feet and looked around the vast, draughty castle hall. Trevor was definitely nowhere to be seen. I was on my own.

Distracted, the prince turned to the duchess, his posture stiffening with royal indignation.

"Perhaps, my *dear*, it would be worth my doing some real work, if I had adequate encouragement from my wife!"

Alannah swept past both of them, grasped my wrist in a tight grip and dragged me toward the nearest door. I stumbled as she all but flung me through the doorway and closed the door behind us.

"What are you doing here?" Alannah hissed. "Is it about the warning?"

I shook my head and delved into my satchel. I dug out an unimpressed Leo, who decided the best first impression was to go limp and impersonate a stuffed toy.

"He somehow snuck back with me last time. They were going to quarantine him, but I wanted to bring him back."

Alannah pulled a rueful face, her anger fading.

"I see. Those poor quarantine creatures don't end up too well. The other lizards you, um, *liberated*, escaped into the forest. I'll keep this one here if you like, at least until he decides to leave by himself."

I blinked hard to hold back the sudden swell of tears. I rubbed my finger over Leo's back, earning myself a satisfied, preening stretch.

"He likes lettuce, if you have it here, and cucumber. He eats apples as well."

Alannah smiled and shook her head. "Don't be soft, I'll look after him. Now, I think there's just enough room for you to summon your ride home in here."

I had to ask, even though I knew it wasn't my place and most likely way over my head authority-wise.

I've come this far breaking the rules, so I might as well.

"The warning," I hesitated. "I guess you saw it too as it went realm-wide. We found some incriminating stuff somewhere, but when we told Emil and Queenie, it had all been cleared. I'm not sure how we can prove what we saw, but I think the person might be in on whatever's going on. Should we be worried?"

Alannah sighed and rubbed her forehead. "I suppose anything is possible. I won't ask, and you shouldn't tell me if you don't have any proof, but there have been plenty of new recruits drafted in by Queenie recently, so you never know."

I noticed that Alannah wasn't confirming or dismissing anything. I waited, just in case she might relent and confide something more. Alannah eyed me for several long moments, then reached forward to take Leo.

I forced my fingers to let go and took a step back. Leo grumbled but, luckily, he didn't put up any kind of struggle.

"Trust nobody, that would be my advice to you," Alannah continued after a pause. "Also, remember that there are bigger forces at work than Arcanium, or even the Elders. There is always a bigger fish behind the scenes to chase the smaller fish. Now, that's all I'll say about that."

A loud hammering came on the door.

Alannah grimaced. "You should call your ride. That will be the prince and he's not accustomed to being kept waiting. It's tiresome and I'm almost out of fake smiley faces. I swear, one day I'm going to agree to go hunting with him and put an arrow in his back."

I found a smirk at the thought of that and pulled my orb from my pocket.

"Thanks again," I said. "If they decide I am allowed to keep him after all then I'll come back, if that's okay. Hopefully Trevor can get the hang of not landing in the middle of a scene."

Alannah chuckled as the pounding continued on the door.

"Hopefully you'll learn some proper lessons, and fast. Your troll brings you to your realm, but you control the location. No doubt you've just been thinking and saying 'oh, take me to Alannah' and there you land. Next time, try asking to land somewhere discreet within reach of whatever you need to find, that should do it."

Embarrassed, I bit my lip. "I didn't realise that."

"Why would you?" Alannah winced as the door started shaking. "Nobody teaches you anything useful in that place these days, it's just one big political stewing pot. But the food is *amazing*."

I smiled and held up my orb. "I'll agree on that. Okay, Trevor, I'm ready to return to hub now."

I stepped back as the air between us shimmered. Where the gap had been, Trevor and his rickshaw materialised.

"Phew, there you are." Trevor beamed. "I thought it best to make myself scarce."

I hopped into the rickshaw. "Good thinking. Bye, Alannah. Please keep him safe for me if you can. Bye, Leo. Be good."

Trevor started jogging on the spot to build up speed and shaking the rickshaw behind him. I couldn't be sure, but as Leo turned to stare at me, I was sure I saw him wink.

Trevor launched forward, propelling me back against the seat. I had enough sense to close my hand tight around my orb as air battered my face, then came the inevitable jolt forward right into the rickshaw's front rail.

"Well." I recognised Taz's voice beside me. "That was smooth."

I clambered out of the rickshaw, my head spinning.

"Thanks, Trevor." I smiled wearily at the beaming troll. "I

didn't realise I had to give you directions, on the way into a realm I mean. Alannah told me I should be specific, so I'll try better next time."

Trevor's beam threatened to split his face. "It's part of the troll-code. We only deliver you and fetch you back, and it's not our place to decide for you the where's and how's. We're not allowed to assume your preferences either, you see, or ask for them. Not sure why but no doubt there'll be a reason for it somewhere."

My minimal store of social politeness beeped on empty after all the upheaval, and I took a step back.

"Well, thanks, I'll try to be more specific next time." I turned to find Ace and Taz staring at me. "It's done."

"We'll have to go down and say we couldn't find Leo," Ace insisted. "Perhaps they'll only put us on a warning."

Taz raised his brow in disbelief and stomped toward the lift. I barely noticed the huge drop on either side of the walkway this time, mired in misery. Leo was back where he belonged, but I couldn't dredge up any relief at all.

"If there's a punishment I'll take it, don't worry," I promised. "I'll say it was all my fault."

Taz sighed. "They won't put us on a warning. Then they'd have to follow procedures and it'd all be documented. If they suspect we're up to something, they'll be sneaky about it."

Ace nodded. "I was afraid of that. It is the Fae way to try and outwit the other side rather than confront them."

I rubbed my face as the lift shuttled downward, my satchel feeling depressingly light now.

"Then we need to be sneakier than they are," I said. "I know what I saw, and she didn't have to mention Leo, he had absolutely nothing to do with it!"

Taz and Ace gawped at me.

"He kind of did," Taz reminded me. "He was- you know what, never mind. There's still no excuse for her turning on him like that."

Taz's fingers disappeared inside the sleeves of his hoodie as Ace settled a hand on my shoulder.

"I'm glad to see you so fired up," he said. "But we still need to be careful, no doing anything rash."

Taz snorted. "So, what are you suggesting? An in-depth surveillance operation?"

Ace only shrugged as the lift came to a stop.

"Why not?" I asked. "It can't hurt. We just need to be ready this time, and not go dashing off if we find something. We think smart and we take her down."

Taz stared at me like I'd grown two heads. Even Ace looked a bit bewildered by my sudden vehemence, but losing Leo had given me a burning anger roiling in the pit of my stomach. I wasn't going to let Sandra get away with this.

Taz frowned. "Right. Well, let's see what damage we're in first, shall we? Then we'll know if we can risk anymore."

We ambled along the corridor toward Queenie's office, not in any hurry. I almost groaned out loud when Emil appeared from the side corridor as if he'd been waiting for us.

"He wasn't in the bedroom," Ace said immediately.

I searched Emil's face, hoping to see some sign that he wasn't about to interrogate us. I knew I couldn't lie, but word-tangling was exhausting.

When Ace looked to me for confirmation, I nodded and gave word-tangling my best shot.

"He was there this morning, but he's escaped before. I'll be honest, I don't always lock my door."

Not a single lie. I waited, my insides churning.

Emil might have smiled, just a little.

"It's getting late," he reminded us. "I'll explain it to Queenie and ask the night crew to keep an eye out. You just better hope people don't start exploding or anything."

Amazed that I didn't seem to be in any immediate trouble, I tried not to envision what kind of incidents might be attributed to the mysteriously missing Leo in the coming days. As Ace mentioned food and we turned back to the lift, I could only hope that Leo was going to be okay.

CHAPTER FOURTEEN
FIGHTING FIT GOES WRONG

Two days passed after the 'incident' as we referred to it. More students were talking about the phantom mutant spider outside the library than about anything that had happened inside it. The Book of Faerie still hadn't been found either and Taz insisted he'd overheard Emil saying they had no leads.

I tried to throw myself into studying, knowing I'd had a close escape from being kicked out and sent back home. But I missed Leo so much, and I think the others could tell.

I skipped breakfast that morning but had agreed to meet Taz in time for object training class. I wasn't entirely sure what object training was, but so far my imagination had stretched from levitation to maybe even learning some kind of transmutation of matter, which would have been so cool. Taz had asked me to meet him fifteen minutes early at the large training hall, but hadn't told me why.

The moment I joined him, he looked me up and down with a frown.

"Are you sleeping?" he asked.

No hi, no, 'how are you holding up?'

I shrugged. "Sometimes."

"You've not done object training before, have you." It wasn't a question.

"No, that obvious is it?"

He ignored my prickliness and clapped his hands together, peering through the windows. I followed his gaze, but could only see the large hall with wooden flooring and several metal cabinets lined up against the walls.

"It gives you good life skills, for those that are good at it."

"What is it?"

Unlike me, he was dressed in gym trousers and a loose-fitting grey t-shirt, his hair swept back behind his ears. He looked fresh-faced and ready for anything. I looked down at my faded jeans and baggy hoodie, knowing I hadn't even remembered to wipe my face properly that morning.

"We train in combat, mostly defensive." He drew out a bunch of keys and unlocked the hall door. "Then there's object training which tests your initiative."

He swung the door open and strode across to open one of the cabinets. I followed him and goggled at its contents.

"Wow, those are swords."

Taz laughed. "FDPs train in fencing of a sort, but with full blades. We use daggers too but most of our combat training is self-defence."

I stared at the swords, some stout and strong, others elegantly long, thin and lethal. I wasn't sure I wanted to do object training after all if it involved this kind of weaponry, not with my lack of grace.

I took a step back.

"My hand-eye coordination isn't the best," I admitted. "I wondered for a while if that's why my sisters found it so easy to pick on me, other than the whole fairy thing. But I guess you're good at this by now?"

"Oh, Taz loves object training." A disdainful voice echoed through the hall. "He's so resourceful."

We whirled around to see Diana standing in the doorway. Her hair was swept back in a high ponytail, and she of course looked impeccably bright-eyed. Even she was wearing gym-wear, flawless navy leggings and a matching hoodie made from what was no doubt the finest, most expensive sweat-wicking material.

Someone like her probably doesn't even lower themselves to something as normal as a bit of perspiration.

I expected Taz to say something withering, like he would to me or Ace, but to my horror he just dropped his chin to his chest and shoved his hands in his pockets.

Why isn't he snapping back?

Anger grew, the restlessness chasing through my limbs like fiery ants.

"You don't even know what object training is, do you?" Diana crowed at me.

I couldn't lie outright, but the word-tangling wouldn't come quick enough for me to sound believable either. I shrugged, earning me a wider smile of glee from her.

"Random objects are put into the room and we're set loose basically," she explained.

I folded my arms. "So, fight to the death with a toilet brush?"

"No, of course not," she scoffed. "If you really don't want to fight then you just need to cross your wrists in front of you, but it's considered bad form. I'm sure you wouldn't descend to such cowardice though. As I suggested before, alliances you make here can make or break your future, and you're not doing too well on that score, clearly."

"Okay." I lifted my chin in disgust. "So you can refuse to fight but you can't really. Got it. Thanks. You can go now."

Diana ignored my dismissal. "The best one was the rubber duck incident, wasn't it Taz?"

Taz mumbled something inaudible, his expression downcast, but I couldn't understand his disagreeable refusal to stand up for himself.

"I'll leave you to fill her in then, shall I?" Diana gave him a wink. "I'll be seeing you in class, Demi. Remember what I said as well. Alliances cast long ripples."

She turned on her heel and walked out of sight. I glanced at Taz.

"As you can probably tell, I'm not great at object training," he sighed. "My family have known Diana's for ages, and we were in the same youth club together. During object training, I was up against a boy called Harvey. He had a sharpened chair leg and all I had was a rubber duck.'

"What happened?"

Taz scowled more like the person I knew. "What do you think happened? I threw the duck at him and ran. As I'm sure you can guess, I can't throw well when I'm under pressure. I just lobbed it up and it went backwards. I turned to run and skidded on it. The boys called me Skids for ages and the girls laughed at me."

"That's horrible." I bit my lip. "Sounds like my sisters would fit in better with this lot than I do. So, object training is basically fighting with whatever you find to hand?"

Taz nodded and rubbed both hands over his face. "Yeah. I asked you to come here early because I wanted to explain it all, because today is time-trials."

"That doesn't sound good."

"Basically, it's object training one on one, rather than practice. It'll be fine, you're not allowed to hurt each other or anything." He eyed a large, gold clock high on the wall above the door. "I wanted to give you a chance to practice first, but don't think we have much time left now."

Touched at his thoughtfulness, I rolled my eyes to hide it.

"Sounds about right, don't worry about me. I'll manage somehow," I said. "Wouldn't be surprised if someone like Diana doesn't try to get me picked on purpose as an initiation or something."

Through the open windows, I could see the rest of our class

gathering in the corridor and peering in at us. Taz hurried to close the sword cabinets and ushered me toward the door.

"If you get called in today, just do your best," he murmured, rushing me outside. "If not, we'll have time for you to practice."

The corridor was filling up fast, and even though I recognised everyone around me now from classes, it still unnerved me that many of them had elements of the Fae-like perfection. They even started to form two neat queues along the hallway without prompting from any tutors, which I thought was taking things a bit far. Taz and I lined up, him standing behind me.

"It's like injection day at school," I whispered, eying the lines.

Taz was too busy blowing his nose on a huge tissue to answer. A man I didn't recognise strode toward us, frowning over a battered clipboard. He had a short crop of mousy brown hair over a wonky nose, and I got the impression from deep furrows in his face that his frown rarely disappeared entirely.

"Good morning, group." He had an Irish lilt to his voice.

"Who's he?" I turned to whisper to Taz.

"Donal, our practical arts tutor. He's fair, but he hates anyone crying off."

I nodded and kept my gaze fixed on Taz's shoulder as the clatter of feet filled the corridor around me.

Not like I was thinking of crying off somehow, no, not at all. Crap.

"Diana, front and centre. Good!" Donal's voice carried easily. "And you are?"

I turned around to see who he was talking to, the poor soul who had to go up against Diana, and saw him.

Right in front of me.

Staring right at me.

A quick glance backwards and I realised the feet moving

wasn't from the class going into the hall, but scurrying around to avoid being first in line.

I gulped. "Um, I'm Demi."

Donal frowned deeper as he scribbled on his clipboard. "Okay. In you go, both of you."

Diana shot me a triumphant leer and swept forward. Short of fleeing and hiding in my room for the rest of my life, and barricading the doors until I perished from hunger, I had no other option.

The moment I stepped into the hall, the crowd surged toward the windows.

I eyed the objects now spread out over the floor. How Donal had managed to do that in the few moments Taz and I had been standing in line I couldn't understand, but then perhaps he had a speed skill or something.

A girl's tank top that probably only fit a small child lay near my feet. A laptop with a broken screen. A plunger. A spoon. A bit of rope cut into so many pieces it was unusable, unless someone had matches and wanted to start a fire from the strands. One of the cabinets stood open to reveal rows of books, both old, leather-bound volumes and shiny new paperbacks.

"Are you both ready?" Donal asked.

I glanced around me one final time and faced Diana with my entire body shaking. Her lips stretched wider into a hungry grin.

"Begin!" Donal bellowed, the door slamming shut behind him.

I kept my eye on Diana. She stood as though we were about to have a friendly catch-up, but of all the people I could be stuck with in here, she was the furthest from friendly.

Taz said it was a time-trial. Play for time.

"So, is this like to the death or, how do we know when someone's won?" I asked.

Diana pushed one perfect conker brown strand behind her ear.

"Of course not." Her laughter tinkled through the open windows to the watching crowd. "We train against each other until one of us concedes or is unable to fight back."

I risked a sigh of relief.

This is training, Taz mentioned initiative. Keep her occupied.

Without warning, Diana dodged forward and back again, mimicking fencing footwork.

"Go on then, let's get this over with." I faked a sigh even though my insides were rioting. "Ready."

Diana took a couple of steps back. "Oh, come on, it'll be fun!"

I rolled my eyes and mirrored her with a couple of steps back and a shuffle sideways.

Diana didn't seem keen to fight hand-to-hand, but I couldn't see her edging toward any of the items either. Maybe the laptop, perhaps she was just going to throw it discus-style at my head. That gave me an idea.

I glanced sideways and spied a roll of thick black tape on the window-sill.

"Come at me then, Tinkerbell," I taunted.

It was possibly the worst retort I had ever come up with. Diana's face threatened to split as she started laughing.

"Oh, that's *so* clever. Beating you will be so easy it's not even going to be worth staying awake for."

She advanced toward me, her steps slow and considered.

I lunged to the window-sill for the tape. Diana's smile faded as I found the tab of the tape and peeled some back. I tore it with my teeth, holding her gaze the entire time.

She's wondering if I have a plan she's not thought of.

I reached for the shelf behind me, grabbed a book and taped the covers shut.

Diana raised one eyebrow. I took a breath and chucked the

book high into the air.

"Catch!"

Her instincts swelled, possibly some innate ability to be good at sports that no doubt dwelled in her very bone marrow. She focused her gaze and zoomed forward with startling speed.

"What happens next in your flawless strategy?" Diana sneered, dropping the book to the ground. "I have to admit, I'm not going to bother catching the next one."

"I'm going to wait for your move now," I said. "How long do these things usually last anyway? What if we're here all day and nobody else gets a turn, does it roll over into tomorrow?"

She smiled wide. "We have fifteen minutes, so I really do wish you'd get on with it and do something."

"You do something."

"As you wish."

Diana attacked so quickly, lunging forward to clamp a hand on my shoulder. I didn't even have time to twitch my fingers. Diana spun me round and pinned my arms behind my back.

"Concede?" Her mocking tone loud enough to reach the crowd outside.

She had to feel my body quaking as she tightened her grip. I shook my head. She might be superior in every way that I could think of to me in terms of skill, but I'd been raised with my sisters, and I could do defiant with the best of them.

"Nope, just smack me or whatever and get it over with."

Diana laughed, tossing her hair for the benefit of the crowd outside.

Only one thing for it.

I twisted and flung my head back, knocking Diana right in the nose.

She staggered, and I looked over my shoulder to see pale red blood tricking from one nostril. With a pained wail, she let me go and covered her face. Not content with causing one injury, I fell to my knees and twisted again, bringing my leg out against hers. It was enough to knock her to the floor.

Diana shot to her feet before I could coordinate myself.

"You're going to regret that," she hissed, her words muffled by her hand and the nose filling quickly with blood. "I will destroy you, and you'll never see it coming."

She dashed toward the door and I clambered up. Nobody outside was making a sound as the door swung open and crashed back against the wall. Only once Diana had disappeared past Donal did the whispers start rustling through the crowd.

"You did well." Donal nodded at me as I stepped into the corridor. "That, at least, is something."

I ignored him and found Taz's astonished face in the parting crowd. Several of them looked at me, then away. Clearly, I'd gone too far.

"I didn't mean to hurt her," I mumbled to Taz.

He nudged my shoulder with his. "You did great!"

"You don't have to sound so surprised," I said, even though me winning was a huge surprise to everyone, especially me. "I thought everyone would respect a bit of winning."

Taz chuckled. "They do. They're noticing you and they're not sure what to make of it. That's Fae respect."

I squished my shoulders up to my ears and shuffled away, his whispering making my nerves jitter.

"Not sure I want it," I admitted. "Diana's out for my blood now, she said as much."

I expected Taz to brush this off, but his mouth quirked sideways in trepidation.

"Well, it's not like you endeared yourself to her before though, is it?" he said after a long pause.

Oh that's reassuring. I scowled and folded my arms as the

140

line moved forward.

I turn my head to the window to watch the next two practice, and realised that at least I shouldn't have worried about dying or anything drastic. While Diana would have happily ended me, the two boys next in the hall both chose to fight openly without any improvised weapons. When Donal got irritated and called time, they ignored him. He ran in minus his clipboard, but one boy got the other in a headlock and off they went again.

"That's Hutch and Harvey Hutchinson." Taz rolled his eyes. "Or Harold and Harvey, but don't go calling him Harold to his face. They're hopeless."

I let my mind wander away from the comedy duo putting on a show, dwelling instead on Diana's threat.

Fae like her are obsessed with social standing, and she's not going to take a slight like that lying down.

I sagged as one of the Hutchinson brothers threw the other into one of the cabinets.

No matter what I did here at Arcanium, despite all my good intentions and efforts, I seemed to be a magnet for trouble.

CHAPTER FIFTEEN
AN ACCIDENTAL SKIP

Diana sent me evils every time I saw her after our 'sparring'. Her threat weighed on my mind, as did the fear that someone would come and have a quiet word about me almost breaking her nose. She'd had it fixed in a flash by the healers, who Taz had assured me were the best in Faerie, but I still had nightmares about being asked to leave. After a lifetime of having to be the defensive one against my sisters, being kicked out for violence really wasn't the reputation I wanted.

I drifted through my lessons, barely paying attention in Beasts and Baronies class when Gnat, the tutor, had been extolling the virtues of the different Barony regions of the Fae courts in Faerie. It still baffled me that tutors like Gnat (the G was silent), insisted on being referred to by their first name. It took all my strength not to call them 'Sir' or 'Miss'.

There was one thing that kept me focused, and that was our surveillance plan. Two days after object training class, I sat in the library pretending to read the copy Faerie Fables open in front of me on the table, one eye on the Librarian's desk.

The trouble with surveillance when they suspect you're doing it, is it's so much harder to pretend you're not.

Sandra kept squinting at me when she thought I wasn't looking. I could only hope she hadn't been gifted with mind-reading.

She looked down a couple of times in quick succession, assessing me afterwards. I kept my gaze on my book with dedicated intensity, resting my forehead on one hand and slouching as if half asleep.

The quickest glance up confirmed my worst fears. Sandra was nowhere to be seen.

She must be in her office. I hesitated. *If she found me listening this time...*

I got up and headed toward the desk, grabbing a random book that had been abandoned on a nearby table a while earlier.

"I can't, those infernal kids won't leave." Sandra's voice sounded sharper than usual. "There's always one or another here, or creeping about when I try to come up and meet you. You'll need to distract them, but how?"

I glanced up at the clock on the wall, which pointed to 10:03. I was late for Lore class. I stepped forward to put the book on the desk and the toe of my shoe clonked against the wood. A dull thud sounded out into the library. Sandra fell silent. I panicked.

"Leaving this book here for you," I said, in a perfect imitation of Beryl Eastwick.

Without waiting for Sandra to rush out of the office, I scarpered. I huffed into the lift and pressed the button for the study floor. Tapping my foot, an idea dawned on me.

What if she just said all that so I'd leave? Ace isn't due in the library until 10:15 from his Gift Management class.

I hurried along the empty corridor and peeked through the open doorway into my classroom.

"Not like you to be late, Demi." Avril raised her brow at me. "Take your seat and stop dithering."

My cheeks burned as about twenty pairs of eyes swivelled in my direction, and I hurried between the tables. Avril's class was my favourite as she made the Lore of Faerie subject come alive.

Taz flicked a wry look at me as I slouched in my seat beside him with my satchel on my lap.

"Now, as I was saying," Avril began. "The need to recite the

Way of Warding has become less over the many seasons-"

Taz leaned about a millimetre closer to me.

"Anything?" he muttered.

I nodded and pulled out a pencil.

'Knows we're watching,' I scribbled in tiny writing. *'Said can't meet who she was talking to. Said they have to distract us.'*

Taz grabbed his own pencil.

'Talk after, get rid of this.'

I went into my bag for my rubber, knowing with my luck it would be right at the bottom, or gone.

"I'm not sure what to think about this rebellious attitude, Demi." Avril's voice bounced around the silent classroom. She nodded to the note, her hand out. "Is there perhaps something you and Taz want to share with us?"

"No, Mis- um, Avril." I shook my head, mortified.

Avril sat with her hand still outstretched, waiting for me to stand up and pass the page over. I flinched as Taz tore the written corner of the paper off and leaned forward as if to get up. As he moved, his hand lifted lightning quick to his lips.

I thought at first that he'd eaten it, but he still had paper in his fingers. Avril took it, glanced over it and looked at me with wide eyes.

"Right." She crumpled the paper into a tiny ball and smashed her palms together. "Back to the Way of Warding."

I gave Taz a questioning look, but he shook his head and busied himself rather too studiously in his *Lore and Legacy* textbook.

The moment the class was over, I chased him down the corridor toward the lift, fighting through the crowds going the other way toward the stairs to the canteen.

"What did you do?" I insisted.

Taz waited until we were in the lift and whistling upwards

before enlightening me.

"I just did a simple glamour. It's very easy on non-changeable stuff like paper, and she only needed to see it for a few seconds."

I eyed the tiniest pink tinge in his cheeks as he stared at the lift railing.

"But what did you change it to? It wasn't something embarrassing, was it?"

Taz shrugged one shoulder. "Kind of. It just said 'will you go out with me' as I didn't exactly have time to think."

I pressed my hands to my face and groaned.

"I said no, by the way," he added helpfully.

I wasn't sure if that was meant to be better or worse, but it at least explained Avril's expression when she read it. Taz stared at the gate, his leg bouncing like it did when he was frustrated or uneasy.

"We should find Ace," I said before the excruciating awkwardness could swallow us whole. "He needs to know. About what I overheard, I mean, not-"

I stopped talking and focused on checking my satchel instead for nothing at all. It gave me a suitable distraction at least, but still reminded me of Leo. I'd thought about using my orb to call Alannah and ask how he was, but guessed that would be overstepping boundaries. The fact that I wasn't already on some kind of probation or watch list was still baffling me a fair bit after everything.

We found Ace just inside the library entrance, crouched down behind an enormous bronze statue of an elf.

"Are you playing hide and seek with Ethelred?" Taz asked.

Ace started in alarm and whacked his head on the Ethelred the elf's bronze knee. I frowned as Ace straightened up, one hand rubbing the sore spot, but Taz couldn't hide his smirking.

"Very funny," Ace retorted. "I thought it'd be safest to wait out here, see if she deigned to come out."

"And did she?" Taz pressed.

Ace glowered at him. "Yes, she literally just left a minute ago, and she had a brown sack slung over her shoulder. I couldn't follow her either, not without getting in the lift with her."

"Maybe she's Santa," I joked without thinking.

Taz snorted. "Maybe you're an idiot."

Ace pinched the bridge of his nose and sighed, loudly and pointedly.

"When you two are done? I took the liberty of going through her desk while she was gone, just in case, but all I found were discarded truffle wrappers, like *everywhere*."

"I almost forgot, I overheard her speaking to someone before." I remembered, skipping hastily over thoughts of Taz's mortifying note glamour. "She said she can't meet them because we're always lurking and that they'll have to distract us. I didn't hear anyone answer though. Are you sure there's no using phones here, or could they have been using orbs?"

Taz shook his head. "Definitely no human phones. Orbs are possible, but the only way to check that would be the records kept in Emil's office."

"Do you know how to access them?" I asked.

Taz gave me his trademark withering eyeroll.

"Orbs are projections, so they get transmitted on light waves and soundwaves, kind of like chatting on your human internet. They're captured live and stored in the Ogle, but only Emil has a screen for them."

"Not as much privacy these days," I decided.

Good thing I didn't orb Alannah about Leo after all.

Taz shook his head. "They only get monitored if they're made here though. There's no telling how many communications out there are going untracked."

"Pretty cool though, huh?" Ace grinned. "Could we ever have a reason to go to Emil's office when we know he's not there?"

Taz quirked one eyebrow. "We don't have a reason as such, but I can make one. Emil lets me sort some of the records for him, so I could say I remembered one I didn't get a chance to finish yet. Wouldn't explain why you two were up there, but perhaps I could say you just wouldn't leave me alone or something."

I remembered the note again and went bright red. Ace didn't seem to notice, his mischievous smile widening.

"I'm in."

"Worth a shot," I agreed. "I'm probably already on the red list here by now anyway so what's a little more trouble. Let's go get it over with."

Even Taz dredged up a proper smile at that.

What if Emil's in his office? I wondered as the lift whisked us up to Queenie's floor. *What if Queenie comes out? What if-*

The lift stopped and Taz opened the gate, striding down the corridor as if he belonged there. I hurried after him, glad at least that the carpet underfoot didn't announce our presence.

We veered right just before Queenie's office doors into a long, curving hallway.

"This one's Emil's," Taz whispered.

He tiptoed to the nearest door and pressed his ear to the edge. I couldn't hear any voices, but that didn't mean Emil wasn't working silently inside. I glanced up and down the hall, wondering what it held and how far it went.

A dark blot on the blue carpet caught my eye, right underneath a tall window.

"Should we knock?" Ace murmured.

Taz shrugged, but I crept over to inspect the carpet. I crouched over and passed my fingertips over the dark red sweet wrapper, nestled in the few inches between the window's wooden frame and the ground. I picked it up and found Taz and Ace involved in a hissed debate, completely oblivious to my discovery.

Something flickered in the corner of my vision. I squinted at the window, distracted by twitches of movement. Rather than a window looking outside, it was a painting covered by glass showing a rocky path passing between two rocky cliffs. I leaned closer.

Is it actually moving?

No doubt some kind of illusion or glamour effect, a narrow stream of water rushed between the cracks in the rock, barely enough to call it a stream although it moved with a white-capped fury.

I pressed my head closer, just enough to hear the subtle rushing sound, like putting an ear to the mouth of a seashell.

"It's too much." Emil's voice filled the hall. "Trust must be earned before privilege is given. I stand by it."

I flinched back from the window in time to see Taz and Ace swing around.

"If you say so." Queenie's dismissive tone joined in, growing louder. "But the numbers *are* down. The responsibilities don't hold the prestige they used to, so we need some kind of lure to keep the mentees engaged. But if you don't agree, on your head be it."

Taz grabbed Ace's sleeve, catching him by surprise. He dragged him toward me, and I held up the truffle wrapper as if it could somehow make us invisible.

"The window was making noises," I babbled in a hushed tone. "And I found one of those truffle wrappers Sandra always has on the floor right underneath."

Taz bit his lip. He grabbed my arm and ignored my instinctive flinching.

"Walk."

He gave both of us a solid yank forward. I lost my footing and stumbled sideways. Ace had infinitely better balance and steadied me as we both tumbled after Taz, straight into the window.

I closed my eyes on impact. Instead of smacking forehead first into cold glass, a familiar huff of air blasted past my face and sent my stomach into freefall.

My feet hit solid ground, and I bent my knees without thinking.

Third landing lucky.

Ace landed on his hands and knees beside me. Taz stood upright but was wiping his pale face.

"Did we just-?" I asked. "Was that a-? Are we in Faerie?"

Taz nodded and hugged his arms around his middle.

"I haven't ever realm-skipped through a border with other people before," he mumbled, clamping his mouth shut straight after.

Ace clambered to his feet and stretched his arms out wide, bouncing on the balls of his feet and twisting his head about.

"That was cool!" He grinned, recovering much faster than Taz. "Look, the window's totally disappeared."

"So, we're trapped here?" I squished my satchel strap in both hands.

"No." Taz shook his head with a tiny groan and pointed to a thin, withered tree trunk. "The skip-way is still there. We're in Faerie, so it just assumes the form of something that won't look out of place."

I frowned. "How do you know it's the tree though? What if it's that rock there, or that one, or-"

Taz's wan complexion started to fill with colour as he gave

me his best withering look.

"It's *not* any of the rocks, it's the tree. Can't you see it? The haze of nether?"

I squinted at the tree. For one moment, I thought I might have seen something, a slight pearlescent flicker around the outline of the gnarled bark, but Taz's resigned sigh distracted me. Rubbing above my eyebrows, I shook my head.

"Maybe I'm just not 'fairy' enough." I shrugged.

Ace settled a hand on my shoulder. "I can't see it either, don't worry."

I guessed he was just being kind and focused on the more immediate problem.

"How will we know when it's safe to go back through?" I asked. "If it's a tree, we can't exactly see through, unless you're telling me there's some mystic knot for a viewing hole."

Taz blinked. On reflection, I decided, it had sounded way more disparaging than I'd intended.

"I didn't mean-"

Taz pulled his sleeves over his hands and pointed the other way.

"It takes a lot of energy to cross a border like that," he insisted. "I took the weight of the skip going first, so I can't manage it again straight away."

"Can we go first instead?" I asked.

Taz shook his head. "You've never tried and it's hard to do on your own, let alone with others. You could get stuck halfway, or it'll be too much for you to handle and you'll keel over. Plus, it looks like it's going to rain. We're better off finding an overhang or a rock to perch under until I can take us back through."

We looked up at the dark blue clouds rolling in. I squinted at the terrain just in time for a shiver of movement to catch my eye.

High up in the rock, a small flash of mousy brown amid the grey.

I watched but the movement was gone. Further into the pass, still high up, another small brown creature appeared. The mongoose lifted its head, the beady eyes watching us. I'd never seen an actual mongoose close up before, but I'd read about them and imagined them smaller than the spaniel-sized one I was staring at now.

Then again these could be Faerie mongoose, able to do all sorts of random things.

I scanned the cliff, searching for more, until I spied a dip in the rockface.

"Over there." I pointed. "There's some rocks that look like they'll shelter us at least a bit."

A spot of rain the size of a football splattered on Taz's head. His screech echoed through the canyon, bouncing off the rocks.

"Good spot." Ace yelped and shuddered as the rain caught him next. "Come on, we'll rest up while we wait for a clear spell."

With our arms over our heads, we ran in an uncoordinated gaggle with me leading the way. The dip in the cliff, no bigger than the inside of a wardrobe, was hidden behind another crop of rocks which sheltered us from the worst of the rain now driving down. The huge raindrops made a drumming splat on the rocks, and I could see a more immediate problem than us staying dry.

"Um, how long do you think it'd take for the river to rise with rain like this?"

Ace scratched his head, perhaps trying to do a mental calculation for the answer. Taz folded his arms and went for the practical one.

"Not long."

"So, what do we do?" I asked. "Try the way back now, or try to get higher up?"

I peeked out and up at the unforgiving rock-face. Taz seemed to be having similar doubts, although he was looking at me rather than the cliff.

"*Could* you climb?" he asked, giving me a once over.

I scowled. "If I had to. What, you don't ask Ace that question as well?"

"He's stupidly sporty, he'd be fine. Besides, this is Faerie, anything could be lurking."

Ace gave me a mischievous smile.

"Okay, *Oakthorn*," he said. "We all know you're the resident Faerie expert."

I stared as Taz's cheeks went bright red. Every mocking retort and every time he'd called me Sparky flowed to the front of my mind.

"Oakthorn? What, is that a nickname?" I grinned.

Taz glared at Ace and shoved his hands in his pockets.

"It's my name, unfortunately, my real Fae name, which I wish I'd never mentioned now."

Ace gave a guilty smile, but I was determined to get my own back on Taz for generally teasing me come hell or high water, both of which were increasingly likely from one look out at the rain puddles growing ever larger around us.

"Where did Taz come from then?" I asked.

He shrugged, rolling the toe of his shoe over a loose stone.

"My sister started calling me Taz, because her favourite cat was called Topaz when I was tiny. It stuck."

Sisters, deciding the fates of kids since the beginning of time. At least his sister was doing it to be cute and not cruel, unlike mine.

"I'm going to call you Oaky," I decided. *Solid, strong, dependable.* "Stubborn as a plank of wood."

Taz glared at me but I couldn't help the laughter spilling out.

"Wait, there's someone coming!" Ace hissed.

I snared my giggles with a hand over my mouth, and we shuffled together as two figures came closer. I recognised Sandra but couldn't fathom how she and her mint green cardigan were still entirely dry when her companion's cloak and raised hood were dripping.

"Element imperviousness gift," Taz murmured, as if he was somehow psychic to my ignorance. "They're rare though, so rare."

"We need to get them to stop so we can listen," Ace said.

Without warning, he picked up a tiny stone and threw it. Whether he'd aimed to get it both out of the dip and over the rocks shielding us from view or not, he succeeded. The stone plinked down onto the ground, stopping both Sandra and her hooded companion.

"What was that?" Sandra looked back and forth.

"A dislodged stone, no doubt," her companion said, the voice muffled and masculine. He folded his arms and faced her. "Now that the Queen's hold is weakening, parts of Faerie are most likely starting to decline. Anyway, I have to be quick. What do you have?"

I recognised that voice, the same man Sandra had been talking to on the trigger floor. I stayed silent, not wanting to draw attention to us, but made a note to tell the others the moment the cost was clear.

If he's able to get in and out of Arcanium through the skip-way, who else might be lurking within the walls?

"I have obtained enough orbs now for a suitable sized group to enter," Sandra explained. "Cleansing them is more difficult, and I don't exactly get much freedom of time, or movement with my current *role*."

The hooded figure flicked a hand to indicate Sandra herself.

"I can't take you seriously like that. You'll be safe enough here to assume form."

Sandra hesitated, still for a long moment. Then she took a deep breath, raised her shoulders up to her ears and relaxed in one tumbling sigh.

I expected some kind of shudder, a ripple throughout the air, but there was only the transformation in front of us.

Sandra's sandy hair wriggled into long, dark locks, her figure growing taller as her eyes turned from honey brown to dark blue. The only thing recognisable now, other than her suddenly ill-fitting clothing, was the pinched expression on her face.

"That's better." The hooded figure took a step forward. "Now, Elvira, where have you put the remaining orbs? I can collect them and take them to our friends. They've finally found enough of the Forgotten to make use of them and it has to be soon. I can't keep the real Sandra where she is for much longer without raising suspicion."

I wrung my hands while Taz's fingers clenched into fists. I was sure Sandra-who-wasn't-Sandra and her friend would hear Taz's teeth grinding.

Click-clack-click

I froze. That definitely wasn't Taz's teeth.

Click-clack-click-clack.

It sounded like claws, and it sounded like their owner was right above us.

CHAPTER SIXTEEN
A WHOLE LOT OF RUNNING

The moment the beast launched itself over our heads and onto
the rock in front of us, I yelped. I clapped a hand to my mouth as
the creature paused, head up and thick, trunk-like tail flicking.
Ace leaned back to avoid the tail's tip. I tried to think of how to
find my connection, but couldn't even summon a protection if I
did find it.

With one final whip of the lethal tail, the animal skittered off
toward Elvira. I sagged, still fighting to keep my panicked
breathing quiet. The beast crawled on squat, leathery legs the
colour of ash, the belly a darker shade of charcoal. The two-tone
scales on the body gleamed like obsidian and grey rust but, as
the creature crept toward the couple, it turned its head and I saw
large, snake-like amber eyes. Two sets of vast, muscled wings
nestled against the beast's back and I struggled to keep my voice
to a whisper.

"And she had a problem with *Leo!*" I hissed.

Taz shot me an incredulous glare as Elvira turned to see the
creature sneaking toward her.

"Luchia, there you are," she crooned. "Where is Draven? Out
causing mischief, no doubt."

The beast wound around it's mistress' legs and hissed at the
hooded stranger for good measure.

"You should keep them confined," the stranger insisted,
taking a step back. "Oricadae are unpredictable."

I flinched as Taz gasped beside me.

"What?" I mouthed.

"Oricadae are a banned species in Faerie," he whispered. "They're made from tainted gift-magic of the olden days, crafted out of bones and dark sorcery. They're supposed to have the body of a lizard with wings like a dragon, and the fangs and claws of a lion."

I risked a look up as the rain started to lessen. In mere moments it had stopped, although the clouds hung heavy with the promise of another burst.

I knew nothing of dark sorcery, save a few scant mentions of old Fae magic in the dusty tomes Xavio kept at the top of his bookshelf. Fear I understood though, the all-encompassing quaking that filled souls right to the marrow, and this creature commanded it.

"We can't just wait for it to find us," I murmured. "What kind of bones were they made from, do you know?"

Two astonished faces gawped at me. Unnerved, I waited.

Ace rubbed his chin. "Snake bones, I think, wasn't it? I swear I read that in Beasts and Baronies, or was it Fables of Faerie class?"

Taz looked like he was about to throttle him, his eyes flashing stormy.

"This is not a field trip!" he hissed. "It doesn't matter what they're made from."

The hooded man took another step back.

"I've stayed too long already," he insisted. "Where will I find the remaining orbs? I'll have just enough time to get them wiped and out of the Arcanium hub."

Elvira stopped scratching her pet's neck and folded her arms. The beast hissed and whipped its thick tail from side to side. I flinched as its head turned, my insides pounding right through my skin, but its gaze didn't seem to catch us.

"I'll bring them to you," she said. "After what those

miscreants pulled, it might look strange if you start rifling through my desk or unlocking my office."

The stranger said nothing for a long, tense moment.

"Fine. Chain your pet and bring the orbs to me the moment you return. Then you need to keep to your routine exactly. When the time for action finally arrives, you can join us."

He turned on his heel and stalked off toward the tree. As if sensing the potential danger had shifted, Elvira's beast lifted its head. It flared its nostrils as it looked back and forth.

I froze. "Um, we might have company, like now. What do we do?"

"Oricadae don't give up once they've started hunting someone down, so I've read," Taz muttered. "Two of us will need to be the bait, draw it off. We can only hope she'll want to taunt us a bit before it eats us. Then the remaining one of us has to run back to the skip-way and get help. Demi, when you get back-"

"Wait, why am I going back?"

Taz glared at me.

"Because you," he jabbed his finger against my shoulder, "aren't the quickest runner and that," he pointed at the beast, "most likely is."

"Can't I call Trevor?" I tried.

"You're not on assignment, we shouldn't even be here. If you call him, it'll be logged and we'll be in serious trouble. Just run back to the skip-way. You should be okay travelling through on your own now. Find Queenie and tell her what's happened. Here."

Taz unearthed a small cloudy crystal from the depths of his hoodie and pulled its chain up over his head. He leaned close to hang it around my neck and shuffled back.

"It'll help you through the skip-way," he insisted. "Show it to

Queenie as well. That way she'll know you're telling the truth."

"Why-"

"Because I've given it to you." He silenced me with a look. "Ace, you ready to run for your life?"

Ace twisted his head from side to side as if limbering up for a fun-run and nodded.

"I knew this year was going to be interesting."

Without waiting for him, Taz whistled one loud note and ran for it. Without a single goodbye or backward look, Ace launched after him. The beast wheeled around, wings unfurling. With a low hiss, it launched into the air and swept after them.

My gut twisted as I watched my friends disappear into Faerie, chased by a ferocious beast and, after a long pause for the shock to subside, a furious Elvira.

I waited until the sounds of feet disappeared and darted out from behind the rocks. My trainers slapped an unsteady rhythm on the stone, and I had to hold my arms out to the sides to keep steady on slippery rocks, but the fear of what would happen to Taz and Ace if I hesitated sent me forwards.

The tree was right in front of me. I had no idea how to operate a skip-way but had to hope it would just swallow me whole. I stretched out my hands.

Something slammed my chest, jolting me backward. I stared at the tree as I staggered back, convinced it had repelled me. The pressure diagonal across my chest remained. I didn't dare look back as something, someone, attempted to drag me away from the tree by my satchel. I strained forward, legs screaming as I pitted all my strength against my assailant.

The pressure disappeared as my satchel fell away. The ring holding the strap to my bag flew sideways and pinged against a nearby rock. My attacker fell to the ground with a loud thud.

I glanced back, bereft at the thought of leaving my satchel

behind. It had seen me through so many encounters with my sisters, protecting my face or my stomach as they punched or kicked laughing all the while. It had the pockets exactly where I liked them. Leo had liked snoozing in it.

Elvira rolled onto her side with a furious grunt.

I can get another bag. I can ask for more books. I probably won't get another chance to make friends if Ace and Taz get eaten.

As Elvira got to her feet, I leapt forward and slammed my hands against the tree.

Through the tree.

The air rushed around my face. Unable to close my eyes in time, a swirl of grey mist drowned me until I emerged into a familiar hallway and bashed hands first into the opposite wall.

Now I understood why Taz had insisted he needed a rest after first going through the skip-way. Somehow, and I had no hope of knowing how, Taz had taken the brunt of the effort for all three of us on our way into the realm. Alone now, I'd taken the brunt of just myself and it slayed me. My limbs ached like mega-flu and my head swam. My stomach was still fighting its contents upwards. With barely any strength left to push myself upright again, I forced my legs to get going.

I stumbled the few metres to Emil's office, knocking as I turned the handle.

Locked. I rattled it just in case. *Where could he be?*

I bit my lip and hurried down the hall to Queenie's doors. I knocked and hesitated a second this time before pushing the door open.

"Excuse me?" I poked my head in.

The office was empty. I pulled the door shut and hurried toward the lift, hopping from foot to foot as I waited.

If I can't find them, if they've gone out, who could I go to?

Would Avril believe me? I got into the lift, almost forgetting to close the gate behind me. *Maybe even the Braunees might know someone I can speak to, or call.*

I had no idea where to start, but figured if people were in classes, I'd at least find someone to guide me. I yanked the gate open and hurried down the hall. Turning a corner, I crashed straight into someone coming the other way.

"Watch where you're going!" Beryl Eastwick snapped.

Cheryl glared at me, but Meryl seemed to be frowning at me in more of a considered way.

"I need to find Queenie, or Emil, someone," I gasped.

"Why?" Beryl asked.

I hesitated. They wouldn't believe me.

"I can't say, but it's urgent. Please."

"It's okay," Meryl rubbed her lip with a forefinger, her tone gentle compared to the other two. "Just try to breathe and tell us what happened. If Emil's not here then we can help."

"Emergency, Taz, Ace-"

Beryl had been in the process of turning away, but she snapped back to face me now.

"What's that?" she demanded.

I doubled over my knees. "I need to find Queenie or Emil. There's a skip-way, we went through kind of by accident. Ace and Taz were distracting an Oricadae so I could come back and get help."

I lifted my head in time to see silent communication pass between the three girls.

"Come on, show us the way."

Beryl grabbed my shoulder to straighten me up and march me toward the lift, but when I flinched in alarm she let go as if I'd scalded her.

"Sorry," she muttered.

Meryl gave me a soft smile. "Show us where. You might not be able to find anyone in charge, and there's safety in numbers. We're not just pretty faces you know."

I had the strangest urge to smile, which wasn't at all appropriate when my friends were in mortal peril.

"Come on." Cheryl joined in. "It's us or nothing. After all the rumours about what you've done so far, bringing giant spiders into the library and accusing the librarian of being a super-villain, you'll need witnesses if this is true."

I bit my lip and nodded. "It's on Queenie's floor, by Emil's office."

Beryl set off toward the lift, Cheryl following behind. Meryl held an arm out to guide me after them. I stood in the lift, trying to occupy the smallest amount of space possible.

"What are we up against?" Beryl asked. "What kind of place is it? Busy? Cold, or hot?"

"Rocky, just a pass between two cliffs. Big rain, like football-sized raindrops. You won't believe me if I tell you, but Sandra appeared with someone hooded, I didn't see his face. They talked about having enough orbs and enough Fae, then the creature turned up. When the hooded man left, the beast was sniffing us out. Taz and Ace just dashed off to draw it away, but Sandra, although she doesn't look like Sandra because I think she glamoured, almost caught me. Sorry, I know I'm not making much sense, and I think I've just broken rule 37 hyphen B slash 779. Oh, hell."

The lift stopped on Queenie's floor and Beryl steamed out.

"I wouldn't worry." She turned back with a frighteningly eager grin. "Besides, if you are telling the truth, we could do with someone good-looking like Ace being in our debt."

I stumbled to a halt. "I can't let Ace bear a debt when he hasn't agreed to it. I'll take it, the debt I mean, I just need to help them."

Beryl assessed me, perhaps taking in what were no doubt shiny, blinking eyes and my lips clamped tight to hide the quivering.

"Well, we'll see," she decided. "I suppose, for the moment, a debt from you will have to do. Now, where is this skip-way?"

Owing someone a debt was never a good thing. Depending on the severity, they could call in a similar or equal request without you being able to refuse.

It's the least I can do to save Taz and Ace after all they've done for me.

I took the lead along the hall and past Emil's office. With the Eastwick sisters right behind me, I stood in front of the window and put my hand toward it.

"If you're able to go through," Meryl said, making me hesitate. "We might need to link up to go with you. If we put a hand each on your elbow, and shoulder?"

I gulped and nodded. Meryl placed her hand on my elbow and Cheryl hers on my other side. When Beryl's hand settled on my shoulder, the touch was firm but featherlight.

What if I can't carry any of them through and we get stuck? What if the skip-way doesn't work, if it's locked itself somehow-

I stepped forward, the girls moving with me in one cohesive unit. I almost sighed in relief when the air hit my face, but not when our feet hit the ground on the other side. Meryl and Cheryl dropped down, weighing on my arms. Beryl had no such grace and tumbled into the back of me, sending the lot of us sprawling.

"Ouch," Cheryl grumbled from somewhere nearby. "That was graceful."

"Sorry, I haven't got the hang of that yet," I muttered, lights flashing in front of my eyes.

Cheryl tutted. "Not you, Ballerina Beryl back there. She's

always knocking us over."

I managed to blink enough times to quell the glittering in my vision, but my skin rippled with flu-like chills and every part of me felt bruised.

"Oh, you are so funny." Beryl moved her withering look from her sister to the area around us. "Well, I suppose you were telling the truth about this. Where are the others? Is it far?"

I struggled to my feet, swaying back and forth as I eyed the water level. The rocks were still slick with rain, but I had no idea if I'd missed another torrent or just been away mere minutes.

"I have no idea how much time passes from place to place." I pointed to the rocks ahead. "But it was raining just before I left, and they were running from that crop of rock there, so hopefully not long."

"Right, eyes sharp and stick together." Beryl took charge and set off along the pass with Cheryl right behind her.

Meryl smiled as she started striding alongside me. I forced myself to ignore the weakness in my legs and the dry burning in my chest, powering on. I lifted my head for a quick glance around, my insides twisting when my satchel was nowhere to be seen.

"Time in Faerie passes much the same now," Meryl said. "It's part of the conjoining of Faerie with the human world, because the Queen is part of the two worlds. Much of Faerie is influenced by her. Of course, she can't change the weather everywhere at once, but rumour has it that if she's in a bad mood at home, it storms in the neighbouring realm."

"So, if it's ten o'clock in London, it's ten o'clock everywhere in Faerie?"

I focused on the buzzing in my brain that often came from trying to step with concentrated caution through the web of social interaction. Taz and Ace were used to me and my basic questions now, but the Eastwick sisters were a fearsome trio. Despite Meryl seeming like the most approachable, I doubted even she would see my awkwardness as endearing.

Meryl chuckled. "Not quite. The times are different, like time zones, but the time passes the same. A minute is still a minute. There are those who can do true skipping through Faerie, like the Fae royalty are fabled to be able to do."

"What's true skipping?" I forgot my intention to be careful.

"It means they can enter different times, so they might leave at noontime in one part of Faerie and arrive at dinnertime in another, but it's only the blink of an eye to them. Imagine if a plane ride only took you one second when you got on, because it's kind of like an in-between zone, timeless."

I nodded. "That makes sense I think."

"There are those who want to break all those similarities," Meryl continued, her tone darkening. "They want take Faerie back to the old ways, where the human world is a playground."

"Like traditional Fae court families, like the Forgotten?"

Meryl eyed me. "You could say that."

Before my curiosity could run away with me, the sound of voices echoed ahead. I couldn't see any variation in the rock, but up ahead the pass veered sharply left. Beryl and Cheryl edged to one side of the rock, peering around the bend. Meryl and I joined them, and I inched around to see past.

"You're doing it all wrong," Taz's strident voice echoed off the cliffs. "You're supposed to say, 'hahaha, I have you now', then we say 'you won't get away with this'. I'd ask if you stole the Book of Faerie as well, but I'm wondering now if you're even that clever."

Some metres away, in a shallow pit, Ace and Taz stood with their hands bound. Elvira was at the lip of the pit looking down, with her Oricadae circling the edge. Given the rigid set of

Elvira's shoulders and the fidgety way she paced a few steps from side to side, Taz was doing a wonderful job of being a total pain. I eyed the beast.

Beasts. There are two of them. A second reptile, larger with a lighter, silver belly scuttled around. *What would the plural be? I bet it's still Oricadae.*

"You stupid boy." Elvira sighed. "Do you think these childish taunts and tricks are going to provoke me into trapping myself? I was weaving word-tangles before you were even a thought in your family's lineage. As for that book going missing, why would I need to steal a list of silly new laws when the traditional ways are about to be reborn as they should be?"

Beryl turned, drawing Cheryl and Meryl to face her without a word. I shuffled closer to the huddle, just in case I was still included. I half expected Beryl to give me a weary look and ask me to give them some space, but she didn't.

"Right, this is going to be tough," Cheryl said. "Defensive first, divide and conquer. If we can get the whole lot, all the better. You two go in for Ace and Taz, one of you distract her the other aim for rescue. I'll stick with Demi and we'll be ready to step in and protect when needed. First opportunity to distract, take it and switch accordingly. All agreed?"

I had no idea what I was agreeing to, but I nodded anyway.

Beryl frowned, eying her sister. "Are you sure?"

I glanced at Cheryl, who grimaced.

"Yeah, no time to stress about it now, go on."

After one more moment of hesitation, Beryl straightened up, her shoulders squaring. Without weapons or anything to defend themselves with, she and Meryl walked out into the open.

"Whoa, are you playing banks and robbers?" she called. "Cool! Can we play?"

"What are *you* doing here?" Elvira snapped.

Her beasts kept circling the pit, but their gazes fixed on the newest threat to their mistress. I couldn't work out if it was the shock of relief on Taz's face, or just incredulous fury that I hadn't even managed to bring the right person back with me.

"How fast can you run?" Cheryl asked me.

I blinked. "Um, not very, I'm not great at sports and things. It's why my sisters pick on me so much at home I suppose, but I can't help it."

Cheryl gave me a rueful quirk of her mouth and grabbed my hand.

"Well, try your best."

Without warning, she dragged me toward the pit at a spritely run.

CHAPTER SEVENTEEN
DEFEAT BY EASTWICK SISTERS

I stumbled after Cheryl, very aware of her fingers strong and dry around my sweaty ones.

"I knew you'd be lurking around here somewhere," Elvira's lip curled when she saw me. "Typical human half-breed. That's the trouble with fairies, always in the wrong place at the wrong time. Well, whatever pathetic intervention you're trying to stage, it's pointless now. Luchia, see them on their way."

I pulled my hand away from Cheryl's as the smaller Oricadae turned toward us with her snake-like mouth and bright, hungry eyes. Something Taz said earlier danced into my mind, about them being made from snake bones. It gave me a vague, very stupid idea.

"Stay back," I squeaked.

Cheryl flicked a wary sideways glance at me. "What are you going to do?"

I appreciated that the question had been phrased as a general one, rather than with the tone of 'what are *YOU* going to do'.

I clenched my fists. "I have a plan."

To my astonishment, she obeyed me. While Elvira turned back Beryl and Meryl, now trying to guide her into forgetting about Taz and Ace stuck in the pit, Cheryl stepped back.

Luchia crawled toward me on her squat, powerful legs, her yellow eyes locked on mine. I gulped, my mouth and throat entirely dry. My plan, impromptu at best, was an awful one, but I still had to try. Luchia stopped and lifted her scaly head, the unusually large nostrils flaring.

With my heart pounding and queasiness turning my stomach, I took a deep breath and turned away from her, as if I'd heard something.

The giggling noise wasn't one of my best performances. I frowned and tried again, taking a breath and throwing my voice out toward the rocks in a high-pitched chatter that sounded like the gathering of several small, furry creatures. It wasn't quite the accuracy I'd been aiming for, definitely not a great impression of an Indian Grey Mongoose, but I'd only heard them once on a nature programme. I took a quick look back and saw Luchia had frozen.

Elvira's scowl was fixed on me now, but behind her Beryl and Cheryl were taking full advantage and sliding into the pit.

I made the noise one more time, putting every ounce of my effort into it. I didn't dare look back as several patches of rock began to rumble behind me. Luchia's head shot up and the wide wings unfurled. The other Oricadae, Draven, hissed a warning. The rumbling grew and a shaking in the cliffs caused small stones and debris to start plinking down to the ground.

An entire camp of mongoose tumbled down the rocks, leaping like mountain goats. I sagged, relieved and extremely out of breath. Cheryl was beside me in seconds, her eyes on stalks and her mouth wide open.

"Well done!" she whispered. "How did you know to do that? How did you even *do* that?"

I didn't have time to tell her that I read a lot, and had excessive amounts of time to watch documentaries on YouTube at home, what with having no friends. We twisted around, stepping close together as the pack of Mongoose charged past us. Luchia took flight, her companion too, and they wheeled away from the group.

"It's just vermin, you stupid creatures!" Elvira cursed.

"Luchia! Draven! Come back here!"

As the mongoose pack surged past her ankles, she squealed and jumped up on a nearby rock. Before she could recover, her Oricadae were haring off along the pass with the mongoose in pursuit. Ace cupped his hands under several eager feet as Beryl, Meryl, then Taz, scrambled out of the pit.

Cheryl strode forward to join her sisters and I hurried after her. Elvira eyed us, her mouth twisted with fury as she surveyed six teenagers standing strong together.

"We'll handle this," Beryl muttered.

Elvira laughed a mocking tinkle. "Oh, will you now? How? I have gifts and Fae court blood. I could strike you down without a second thought."

"But you won't." Cheryl joined in, her voice low and menacing. "Six missing kids won't look too good, especially as you're not who you say you are."

I could try another sound, but I don't think there would be anything Elvira would fear. I wracked my brain anyway. *Queenie maybe? Or Emil? Some kind of beast? It's hopeless. All I've learned so far is a load of theoretical stuff and a protection warding, and I can't even do that.*

Elvira threw out a hand so quick that I barely had time to notice. Taz yelped as his chest lurched forward like an invisible fishhook had caught his t-shirt. It dragged him through the air with his feet dangling, right into Elvira's waiting grip. She twisted him around with his wrists pinned in one hand and the other pressing a blade to his throat. I never even saw her draw it from anywhere.

I started forward but Cheryl had a hand around my arm before I could take more than a few steps.

"No further, children," Elvira said. "I'm sure you wouldn't risk his life for yours, being the upstanding *fairy*-minded people you are."

I tried to think of something I could do, anything. The mongoose trick wouldn't work again with no Oricadae left to scare off. Even if one of us did throw up a protection warding, it wouldn't protect Taz from Elvira unless she let go of him first.

"Your problem is that you're too afraid to embrace your roots." Elvira lifted the blade from Taz's skin and waved it at us instead.

Taz caught my eye. In a stunning display of agility, he dodged away from the blade, twisted his body and sank his teeth into her hand. She screamed, the sound bouncing off the rocks as the knife clattered to the ground.

Taz struggled against her grip on his wrists, wrenching himself free. He stumbled away from her, but she swung her foot out and caught his ankle. Taz smashed to his hands and knees.

Elvira advanced toward him, dipping to pick up the knife as she moved. I couldn't understand why the others were just standing there, or if they were just as useless as I was.

"Oh dear," Elvira sang, her voice laced with vengeance. "That wasn't very nice."

She kicked out again as Taz tried to stand, and sent him tumbling onto his side. I growled and pulled forward, but Cheryl had a tight hold on me still.

Elvira stood in front of Taz before he could get himself up again. Without a word, she pulled her leg back and swung. The sole of her foot smashed into Taz's face. He curled into a ball, but didn't make a sound.

"She's distracted," Beryl whispered. "Cheryl, Demi, cast a protection over him. We'll try to take her."

I can't!

I opened my mouth to tell Cheryl, but her gaze was already fixed on Taz.

He was still curled over as I searched frantically for my connection. I could see the blood on his face as Elvira lifted her foot back.

Anger burst into my chest, roaring at me to do something, anything, even if it was tearing at her with my hands until she killed me dead.

My connection surged through me, strong and potent. I visualised a shining white light drenching around Taz and laced it with all the colours of the rainbow.

Elvira swung her foot toward his back this time and I made the white strands of light around him pulse. Nobody else could see it besides me, but she sure as hell felt it. Her foot smashed into our warding and she veered backwards, arms windmilling as she tried to get her balance again.

"Keep it up you two," Beryl yelled.

I couldn't risk looking at her, or taking any of my attention off Taz, but I heard Cheryl beside me.

"Demi's doing it all herself!"

I ignored that, guessing she was just being kind.

Taz managed to get to his feet and spun in a pained circle. I gasped to see his face drenched in blood. He saw me and Cheryl and started toward us, even though the others had the larger group and were closer to him. I kept the warding around him as he moved, glad he was going slow because keeping my concentration was taking all my effort.

The moment Taz reached us, I visualised the warding gathering us together as a protected trio. He came to a stop right in front of me as I grabbed his hand and the three of us stood together. The others joined us seconds later and I sagged as I dropped the warding.

"Link hands," Beryl said.

Elvira laughed, but I saw a pinch around the corners of her

eyes as she regarded us.

I flinched as a hot wave of prickling swept over my skin, the way I imagined a thousand tattoo needles would feel, but Cheryl's laughter filled the pass.

"A memory-wipe?" she taunted. "On six of us at once? Have you really been outcast so long that you've forgotten the fundamentals? Even if our gifts were minimal, and believe me some of them are not, we are six standing together against one."

I had no idea what she meant, but I'd never been so glad to have to hold someone's hand before.

Elvira watched us for several excruciating moments. I wondered if she was judging who best to attack first and assumed that it would no doubt be me.

Elvira darted sideways, but Beryl lifted her head.

"*NO.*"

A jolt rippled through our joined hands, the force of her gift gathering strength from each of us. The sound ricocheted against the rocks, echoing once as a large chunk of rock broke free and crashed to block the pass. Beryl sagged and heaved a breath, her cheeks pink and sweaty with the effort.

"If she can fly, we're done for," Taz muttered, his words muffled by his bloodied nose.

I restrained myself from suggesting he do something more helpful than being the voice of doom, as Cheryl squeezed my fingers.

"Go back to the skip-way, find Queenie," she insisted. "It has to be her, okay? Not Emil, not the tutors, only her."

Meryl stepped forward as Elvira made a mad dash the other way, back toward the tree.

"Do you have anything metal on you?" Her voice took on a dark, sing-song quality.

Elvira stopped running but didn't turn back. Beryl and Cheryl exchanged doubtful glances.

"I'm going to give you a chance to come back and wait with us," Meryl offered. "We can't let you go, but perhaps you can try your luck at talking your way free of your situation, I'm sure you're good at that."

In the very fibre of sound coming from Meryl's mouth, I heard the dark, silken notes of olden days gone by. Times when Fae would roam the human world to wreck crops for fun, or steal cattle, or bewitch people. Or much, much worse.

Cheryl nudged me. "You three get to the skip-way and keep hold of each other until you're through. Go find Queenie as quick as you can."

I hesitated, but Taz rolled his eyes and grabbed my hand, threading his fingers tight around mine. He grabbed Ace's hand too and set off, dragging us behind him. I righted myself and broke into a jog to keep up.

"Oh, a talisman to ward against gifts," Meryl said, keeping Elvira with her back to us. "But unfortunately, my little trickery isn't a just a gift. Does that burn?"

I turned my head as we passed, in time to see the side of Elvira's face. Her eyes pinched in discomfort, her mouth pressed thin, and I wondered how Meryl could possibly be burning her while standing six feet away.

The tree was right in front of us when Taz kicked up a stone. It pinged off a nearby rock.

"DUCK!" Beryl roared.

Whether her voice power made us comply, or more likely Taz just had lightning quick reflexes and hauled me and Ace to the ground, I couldn't tell.

I managed to get an elbow out to break my fall and received a jagged gash on my other palm for my trouble. A searing heat blasted our faces.

"No!"

I froze as Taz's anguished voice filled the air. I lifted my head to see the tree ablaze and a shimmering haze around it dimming. Taz scrambled to his feet and put his hand forward, but flinched back immediately as the flames flickered away on the wind, leaving a charred black husk behind.

"It's gone," Taz cursed. "The skip-way is gone."

I clambered to my feet, seething at the sting in my palm.

"Gone where?" I asked, without thinking.

Taz rounded on me as if the imminent danger behind us, the evil outcast Fae still currently held by Meryl's power, wasn't there at all.

"Gone! Dead! No more skip-way. We're stuck in Faerie. Anywhere we can get to now will just be more Faerie."

I looked around the pass, more at a loss for what to do than to see if anything had changed.

No skip-way, no way back.

"That was unwise," Meryl said, her gaze still fixed on Elvira's now hunched form. "You may have destroyed our way back, but you're just as stuck here as we are."

Elvira looked up as a dark shadow swooped over them. I squeaked and covered my head, but Draven flew past us straight toward his mistress. Elvira reached up, her face still contorted in pain as Meryl tried to hold her with burning, and Draven grabbed her wrists in his claws.

The pair launched upward, sailing over the top of the cliff and out of sight before anyone could react. Meryl reached her arms up, her entire body shaking, then she collapsed to her hands and knees.

I forgot the others and hurried to her side.

"Are you okay?" I asked.

Meryl blinked, the subtle scent of heat and copper around her fading.

"I- I think so. Don't touch me or anything for a bit, okay? I tend to make things kind of melt. I'm still learning how to control it, but she was trying to hurt us and I panicked."

She hung her head, but I knew there was one thing I was very experienced in, and that was not wanting people touching me. I clasped my hands behind my back.

"I understand," I said. "That is a very useful gift though, once you learn how it works. I imagine you've not been training it long though, like except on your own?"

Meryl bit her lip. "Pretty much since last year."

"So, you're still new to it then." I forged on in an ill-advised attempt to comfort her. "It'll get better."

Meryl didn't look convinced, but at least she wasn't bursting into tears or yelling.

Beryl folded her arms and faced me. "She didn't help herself by pretending to everyone it didn't exist until last year either. So, come on then. Are you going to tell people?"

I blinked. "Um, I have to surely? We need to tell someone she got away, we can't just-"

"Not that." Beryl nodded to Meryl, who clambered to her feet with flushed cheeks and her gaze fixed on the ground. "An elemental gift like that is highly sought after in some circles, so we're keeping it a secret. Are you going to tell?"

I frowned. "Of course not. It's none of my business what your gifts are."

Before Beryl could answer, Meryl lifted her head, her face still slicked with sweat.

"What Beryl means, none too subtly, is are you going to hold it against us as a bargain? We did raise a debt on you for our help."

Baffled, I looked at Ace and Taz for guidance. Ace gave me

175

a tiny shrug, but Taz was staring at me wide-eyed like I'd grown two heads.

Does he think I'm mad for not considering using it against them?

Either way, I was apparently navigating this situation without any help from my friends.

"Why would I do that?" I asked. "You came to help me when you didn't have to. Last thing I'd do is repay you by twisting that against you."

I could see the others looking just as confused as I felt.

"Most Fae and fairies would use it to their advantage, a trade to save for later," Meryl explained.

"Oh." I hadn't considered that. "Well, I'm not doing so great at the whole 'succeeding as a fairy' thing, clearly, so don't worry about it."

Beryl's brow threw off a couple of creases, lightening the atmosphere somewhat. Meryl gave me a grateful, hesitant smile and glanced at her sisters. Both nodded.

"Well, thanks," she said. "Consider your debt paid in kind then. That was a cool diversion though, with the critters. Are you an animal-whisperer or something?"

I shook my head.

"Not really. I can just throw my voice places and imitate noises. Ace mentioned the Oricadae were like old magic made from snake bones, and there's the thing about snakes being scared of mongoose because they're resistant to their venom or something. I wasn't sure it would work though, and I have no idea what I said to them. It could have been the mongoose equivalent of 'bubble monkey pigeon poop' or something."

That earned me a small smile all round, even from Beryl. With two of the Eastwick sisters looking weary and worse for wear, I knew we couldn't risk inviting another fight like that.

"Nothing we've got is going to help us get out of here though." Taz reminded us.

I winced the moment I looked at his face. "We need to get you cleaned up. She took my satchel though so I've got nothing useful at all."

Ace folded his arms and looked around.

"No idea what's nearby? I could probably climb up a fair way and go for help."

Everyone shook their heads, Meryl still flushed and Beryl looking decidedly weary. I clasped my hands to my chest before realising my satchel wasn't there anymore. I slid my hands into my pockets instead. In the right pocket I had Xavio's penknife. And in my left…

My fingers closed around a small sphere, cool to the touch. I pulled it out with a gasp.

"I could call Trevor." I looked at Taz for confirmation. "Couldn't I? We're beyond not getting in trouble now surely, considering what we have to tell when we get back."

"Yes!" His eyes lit up. "Why didn't I think of that? Breaking another rule can't do much damage."

Beryl straightened up somewhat. "Who's Trevor?"

I opened my mouth, but Taz beat me to it.

"Demi got given that assignment on her first day, so she's been accepted for transport."

Three similar faces dropped in awe.

"You've been chosen by one of the trolls already?" Cheryl asked.

I nodded. "Yes, but I'm sure lots of people have as well?"

Cheryl shook her head, regarding me with a disbelieving head tilt.

"Students don't get chosen. Even a lot of first year FDPs don't, not for a long while. They have to make friendships, alliances to borrow someone else's transport until they earn their own."

Alliances cast long ripples. Diana's previous taunt circled my mind.

I bit my lip. I knew a few people in class had been whispering about me getting an assignment on my first day, speculating on whether I bribed for it or just had influential family. I was used to being held at arm's length by my peers, always the odd one at normal school and the teacher's pet in Xavio's fairy lessons but, with Ace and Taz as new friends, I'd not worried too much about it here. Until now.

"No wonder people in class don't like me much."

Meryl managed a smile. "Ah, you're alright really."

I blushed. From one of the Eastwick sisters, it was like a glowing badge of honour.

"Yeah, this was fun." Beryl hesitated. "Okay, not fun so much, but still, good to get out occasionally."

I tried not to look directly at Taz or Ace, but I could see their stunned faces out of the corner of my eye. As the sky darkened, threatening more rain, I held the orb up.

Knowing my luck it won't work now.

"Hi, Trevor, I'm ready to go back to hub now, but we've got a lot of extra-"

The air shivered in front of us, a simple haze. One moment there was rock, the next there was rock and a very amused troll with a very wide six-seater rickshaw.

"I knew you'd be fun." He grinned. "Been *ages* since I got to use the wide-carrier. The others are right jealous. I get a sense when you're elsewhere, so I guessed I might need to be on call. All aboard!"

I let Beryl, Cheryl and Meryl go first, noticing that they got into the back row of three seats with intrigued expressions of awe. I got in the front with Taz beside me and Ace on the far end.

"Hold onto something, or each other, and brace," I muttered over my shoulder. Remembering what Alannah had told me, I leaned forward. "Trevor, is there any way of reappearing on the platform slowly, like not with a huge jolt into the front?"

Trevor chuckled and started to run. "You only have to ask."

I noticed Taz had closed his eyes and Ace was grinning in anticipation. As air hit my face, I squinted out most of the filmy grey haze. A few seconds later, the air settled and I opened my eyes in surprise as the rickshaw glided gracefully to a gradual halt.

"Wow, thanks!" I got out and beamed at Trevor. "If there's ever anything I can do in return, and I'm able to, just ask."

I didn't expect Trevor's face to settle quite so furtively, but I'd offered and couldn't take it back now. I just hoped whatever he was inevitably about to ask of me could wait until we'd sorted Taz's face, and I'd had a shower and a sleep.

"Well, now you mention it, us trolls can't go outside into the human world, you see," Trevor said bashfully. "My last FDP, before he retired, used to bring me a pack of these human sweets now and then, Jelly Babies they're called. Just, you know, if you ever had time."

I started grinning. "Is that all?"

"My little one likes them," Trevor explained. "Although the wife says they're full of stuff that makes her hyper. It's worth the sleepless night to see her little face light up though."

Realising I'd asked next to nothing about Trevor or his life, mainly because asking questions made me feel like I was prying where I shouldn't, I nodded. I'd lost my other packet of Jelly Babies along with my satchel, but I'd find a way of getting him some sweets if it was the last thing I did.

"I will definitely bring you Jelly Babies," I promised. "As

soon as I can get out to the human world."

Thanks." Trevor started reversing his rickshaw. "I knew I had a good feeling about you!"

I chuckled as Trevor hurried off. Even though so many things were still uncertain, the relief of being back and the knowledge that I'd done something right, at least a little, made me giddy. The elation lasted all of a few seconds until I turned around to face the lift.

The other five stood in a huddle right in front of me, but over their shoulders I could see two figures blocking the walkway to the lift with thunderous expressions.

Well, at least Emil and Queenie are happy to see us. Not.

CHAPTER EIGHTEEN
THE WORST THING TO SAY TO TEENAGERS

"What on earth do you think you're doing, all of you?" Emil demanded. "Taz, why are you all beaten up?"

He stood in a wide stance with his arms folded, his expression clamped down tight. Queenie stood beside him with haughty stiffness, her normal uniform of purple velvet exchanged for black.

"Well?" Emil shook his head at us. "Go and wait in my office then, and I'll deal with you individually."

He moved to stand aside, and everyone started a woeful shuffle forward.

"Hold it." Queenie stopped us in our tracks. "No. I will hear it from them now."

Emil frowned. "I should remind-"

"I am still Director of Arcanium, am I not?" She eyed the trolls, all cleaning their rickshaws with avid dedication and not at all eavesdropping on the drama in their domain. "Everyone disperse, consider this a break."

Amid the grumbling of trolls who started vanishing on the spot, I was sure I saw Trevor tip me a lightning-quick wink.

I have to remember to ask him if trolls can vanish everywhere, or if it's just here at Arcanium. Assuming I'm here long enough to see him again.

"Now," Queenie continued, drawing my attention back. "We can talk without being overheard. Tell me honestly what you've seen."

Several moments of silence passed until I realised everyone was looking expectantly at me, and Queenie had asked for honesty. That at least bypassed the no telling without proof rule. I gulped.

"Um, well, I truly did find those orbs in Sandra's desk, and the outfit and things. Anyway, we were going up to your floor-" I paused as Queenie made a disbelieving 'hmm' before waving for me to continue. "We sort of accidentally found a skip-way into Faerie. When we got there, we overheard Sandra talking to someone about collecting orbs and the time having to be now. Then she changed form, like her glamour lifted, and she had these two Oricadae pets, but anyway-"

Taz gave me a weary look for rambling, which didn't have the usual weight considering he was covered in drying blood.

"*Anyway,*" he sighed. "Sandra became someone called Elvira. They didn't talk for much longer and whoever it was left straight after, but Elvira's Oricadae sniffed us out, so Ace and I ran to give Demi a shot of coming back for help. I told her to find you, but next thing I know she's back with Beryl, Meryl and Cheryl."

"You're welcome, Elverhill," Beryl muttered. "Remind me not to save your arse again."

I tried not to smirk, knowing we were in deep trouble still. Ace had no such qualms and smiled soothingly as he took up the story.

"We would have been in serious trouble if they hadn't turned up. It took a bit of gifted management, but we were able to get rid of her beasts and trap her. She destroyed the skip-way though and fled, so we had to get Demi to call Trevor to bring us back, so we could come and find you to give a proper report."

I was sure Queenie would insist we were lying somehow or at least fabricating manipulations, but it was Emil who spoke first.

"Right, that's quite enough."

Queenie silenced him with a another quick look.

"If what you say is true, this is worrying," she admitted. "There is one known to us who goes by Elvira, but she is said to be part of a band of outcast Fae without loyalty."

I recalled Cheryl taunting Elvira for being outcast, which I'd thought was a bit harsh at the time, but now I realised it meant something serious in Faerie.

"You mean the Forgotten?" I blurted out.

Queenie gave me a sharp look. "Yes. She can also apparently glamour at will, which you've mentioned, and has reportedly been gifted with the ability to lie without feeling it."

"How can that be possible?" Taz asked, perhaps forgetting who he was talking to.

Queenie looked him up and down with a sniff.

"It will be her undoing," Emil joined in. "The lies will still tangle her mind, but she won't feel it happening and won't notice the damage until it is too late. The price paid is a high one for power."

"The first step in their plan must be to take over Arcanium," Cheryl suggested. "If she's been posing as Sandra and waiting for a chance to impersonate you. She could make all sorts of changes here to rules and things while pretending to be you."

Emil shook his head. "The Forgotten will wait until a suitable moment crops up. The most popular plan will be to strike when Arcanium is weak, in the hope they can use it as a hub to hit various other strategic locations in Faerie. This isn't the first time someone has tried to overthrow things, so I would advise you not to overreact."

"I'm not willing to take that chance. Call a council meeting." Queen shook her head as Emil turned on his heel and stalked off toward the lift. "You six go and get something to eat. You can miss your remaining classes for the day, in case we need to ask any more questions."

Queenie headed after Emil who was already in the lift with the gate shut and no intention of waiting for her.

"Oh, I forgot." I called after Queenie. She turned, her frown weary rather than displeased. "I don't know if it means anything, but Elvira and her friend were talking about the orbs, saying they had collected enough and there were enough Fae now gathered to make use of them."

Queenie drew her shoulders tall. "Such a feat might have taken a very long time to achieve, as orbs are not loosely lost, nor broken. This may well be their way of communicating outside of the Ogle's tracking. But it's not for any of you to worry about now, your task is done. Taz, go and see the healing team immediately. And the rest of you, off you go. We grown-ups will handle it from here."

I didn't pride myself on my ability to understand people, but even I knew that last statement was the worst possible thing Queenie could have said to six wilful teenagers.

"Come on." Beryl sniffed and wiped her nose with her sleeve, making Taz grimace in disgust. "Let's get some food."

I followed the others past Queenie and squished into the lift. Although it barely held the six of us, the lift showed no signs of struggling as it shot downward.

"So, what can we do?" Ace asked.

Cheryl sighed. "Well, we can't leave it to the adults."

"No," Taz agreed. "You know what they're like. They'll insist on having meetings and agendas."

"They'll have to consult each other," Meryl added. "Then they'll argue over who gets to do what."

Ace shuddered. "They'll have to take meeting minutes. Then, when the time comes to actually *do* something, they'll suggest sleeping on it."

"And decide to call another meeting," I joined in.

Before anyone could add anything further, Ace's stomach growled so loud that Beryl started giggling. The relief at being back in relative safety set off a chain reaction and soon we were all laughing.

"We should probably do the sensible thing and eat first," I suggested. "We can discuss everything over sandwiches and whatever else the Braunees have to offer."

Beryl snorted. "Sandwiches? I'm asking for a roast dinner after all that!"

The canteen was empty when we arrived, except for female Braunee just visible behind the buffet counter.

"My, my." She surveyed us with twinkling eyes. "You lot must be famished! Take seats and we'll fix you up something proper. I'll get the healing team to pop in as well."

"Who's on duty tonight?" Taz asked.

"Melvin."

He shook his head gently. "Um, then no, it's okay. I'm sure nothing's broken, just a clean-up job."

Braunee laughed but didn't reply. I had no idea who Melvin was, but each time I looked at Taz's face all crusted with blood, my stomach went queasy.

"Have you got tissue and water?" I asked.

Braunee nodded and hurried off. Taz threw me a thankful look.

"Who's Melvin?" I asked.

Taz grimaced. "Leprechaun healer."

The others drifted to the nearest bench, but Taz waited with me as Braunee brought over a big jug of water and an industrial roll of blue tissue. We sat down with me on the end furthest from the doors, and I wet the tissue before dabbling at Taz's cheek.

185

"I can do it, if you want," he offered.

"Do you have a mirror?"

"No."

"Can you magically see where the blood is?"

"No."

"Then stop making a fuss."

He sat obediently as I mopped up the worst of the blood, but flinched as the doors to the canteen banged shut.

"Ouch." He twisted to face the doors. "Oh no."

A young man walked toward us, thin and lithe with a boiler suit much like the ones Emil occasionally wore. His black hair fell like a waterfall over his forehead and, as he drew closer, the greenish hue to his skin became noticeable.

I leaned forward. "That's a leprechaun?"

"Yeah." Taz turned his head back to whisper back to me. "Forget all the human fairy tales. We used to refer to their healing as liquid gold, but it got twisted into riches by the stories over time."

"I thought they were meant to be small, like the stories."

Taz flicked an unimpressed look at me. "Humans thought the same of fairies. Leprechauns are just like you or I."

I flinched as the man appeared in front of us, towering over Taz.

"With infinitely better hearing," he said. "We leprechauns are no more little green men fighting over gold than fairies are tiny and live in flowers. Unless you count a symposium on metaphysical anatomy as fighting, which I guess can get a little fraught once the mead's flowing."

I flushed and looked down at the table. I'd never thought much about leprechauns, so the tales had just sort of settled in my brain unchallenged, but I should have known better than to assume.

"Ah, now Taz." The man shook his head. "What have you done this time?"

"Hi, Melvin. I fell afoul of a Fae," he muttered, groping around behind him.

"Yeah, well I'm afraid healing hurts." Melvin held his hands toward Taz's face.

Taz's fingers found mine and I realised he wanted something to grip onto. I gritted my teeth as he began to squeeze, and Melvin closed his eyes.

Ace leaned across the table before Taz could do me any damage, tugging Taz's hand from mine and clenching it in his much stronger one. Taz winced and Ace winked at me when he wasn't looking.

Melvin's hands started to glow, a bright white-green light. It flickered multi-coloured faster and faster until it was pulsing pale golden. Tendrils started to separate and reach out from Melvin's fingertips. They inched toward Taz's face and he grunted as one drifted up his nose. His face contorted in pain and Ace looked less certain as he stared at their hands clenched on top of the table.

"All done." Melvin opened his eyes.

The tendrils drifted back to his fingers and he shook the golden light away. I almost reached out to see if I could catch some of the lingering glow, but guessed it wouldn't do me any favours. Taz opened his eyes with a weak smile.

"Thanks, Melvin."

Melvin nodded. "Your nose wasn't broken luckily, much more painful to fix if it was, but you should be more careful who you pick a fight with. Watch where the bruising appears over the next few days and you'll see where you could have burst an eyeball."

Taz shuddered and my stomach threatened to flip its contents like a pancake. Luckily, it had no contents to flip.

Taz slid his hands under the table, but I gave his shoulder a reassuring bump with mine before slumping my arms on the top. The gap between me and the edge felt weird, my legs already too light in the absence of Leo, but now my satchel was gone too.

I probably won't ever see that again.

"So, we all know what's really going on," Taz whispered. "How can anyone get into Arcanium using an orb? The trolls wouldn't betray this place. It's not in their nature or their creed."

He seemed to be gaining enthusiasm now his nose was fixed, but I didn't ask if it was the healing or just the relief that it hadn't hurt worse. When Beryl sniffed, he wrinkled his nose and passed her a tissue with a determined look.

"No, it won't be via the trolls," Cheryl agreed as Beryl blew her nose with a loud hoot.

Ace drummed his fingertips on the tabletop. I tried to settle myself with the noise, finding a sort of rhythm in it that took the irritating edge off.

"What about through other skip-ways?" he suggested. "We found one by accident, so who knows how many more there are. *She* clearly knew of it."

"But how would we ever find them?" Taz countered.

"It may sound stupid," I started, ignoring Taz's resigned eyebrow quirk. "What about just using the front door?" Everyone looked at me. "When I arrived, Taz you were there to greet me and show me the way, but if others knew where the entrance was, couldn't they just make their way down? Who's going to question them if they've got an orb hanging from their belt? Do you recognise every single face here, all the time? That entrance might keep humans out, but what about other fairies, does it keep them out too?"

Beryl rubbed her forehead. "No, I don't think so. We trust

that only people who've been invited are told where it is, I suppose. Never really thought about it."

"What if they're in disguise like *she* was, able to glamour or be glamoured?" My anxiety was warming up now. "What if they're already here?"

Everyone looked around at the deserted canteen, and the only sound around them came from the Braunees humming as they worked.

I went for overkill. "What if it's someone on the inside even, like Queenie, or Gnat, or Emil?"

Taz laughed then, his shoulders relaxing. His laughter seemed to ease the communal mood and the others started chuckling too.

"Emil's no traitor," Taz insisted. "But you have a point, especially after Sandra. I hope they find the real Sandra soon. No, people can't come down with a glamour, but there's nothing stopping them coming in amid a crowd of others and glamouring once they're inside. We're going to have to be really careful. Trust nobody except each other."

"Should we have a secret sign?" Meryl asked.

Ace nodded. "Good idea, we could do something discreet like pinch our bottom lips or something."

"How about tapping your fore and middle fingers three times on your lips." Beryl suggested. "As if you're thinking."

"You'll struggle with that then, not much practice," Cheryl retorted with a gleeful smile.

Everyone started laughing again as Beryl shoved her sister's shoulder.

"So, we watch, and we wait." Taz concluded, a little glumly.

"Not quite." I shook my head, my stomach rumbling in anticipation as the Braunees beckoned us over to the counter. "First, we eat."

CHAPTER NINETEEN
THE COUNCIL IS SUMMONED

Another week passed, during which I realised I hadn't thought about my family once. After a bout of inevitable guilt at not contacting Mum more often, I reminded myself that at least my sisters would be pleased. I studied hard in lessons and even earned myself a wry smile from Avril, once I'd answered enough questions to get back into her good books and also recited the Way of Warding from memory.

Beryl, Cheryl and Meryl hung around with us now and then in the library, or sat with us at mealtimes, but with them being in the second year like Ace, I only had Taz for company during classes. Even though I finally had the bewildering realisation that these were perhaps my friends, the feeling was tainted by the knowledge that it could get ripped away at any moment.

I caught myself constantly eying faces in the crowds between classes, or in the canteen. The library was being overseen by Gnat since Sandra's 'mysterious' disappearance, but now I couldn't help looking at him in a different way, with a 'what if he's one of the opposite side Fae waiting to take over' sort of worry.

But even with all of that rattling around in my head, I was adamant I wouldn't forget one thing, and that was Trevor.

I stood with the busy thrum of the Atrium washing over me. Although it was a Friday and technically time for Lore class, Avril had let me be late when I explained about my errand. Whether she would have done that for any student, or she had taken a liking to me, I took the opportunity and scarpered.

Now, I wasn't even sure if what I planned to do was possible. With a deep breath, I strode across marble floor toward the reception desk.

"Um, excuse me?" I asked the man behind the counter.

If it hadn't been for the busy buzz of the Atrium creating noise, I would have sworn I heard the spry old man groan quietly.

He eyed me over. "You are?"

I cleared my throat. "Demi Darcy, sir. I'm a mentee."

"No need to call me sir," he said with a frown. "Call me Henry. What can I do for you? Oh, now who's moved my pencil?"

Henry turned away to search the reception desk.

Something prodded my elbow and I flinched to find one of the Hutchinson brothers grinning right beside me. We hadn't actually ever spoken to each other before, and I checked over my shoulder just in case.

Nope, definitely me he's smiling at.

I blinked and stared at his hair instead of having to make eye contact. Normally it was brown, or at least, it had been the last time I'd passed him in the hall. Now it was the exact same shade of green as Cheryl's hair always was.

"Whatever you do," he whispered, "do *not* call him Henry. One unfortunate FDP made that mistake once."

"What happened?" I murmured back.

His expression darkened. "Let's just say you really don't want to end up with any stationery items installed anywhere unpleasant."

I nodded, alarmed. I could see now that the man had his pencil tucked in his ear, and also a stapler hanging, for some unknown reason, from his belt. I flinched as Beryl Eastwick appeared on my other side.

"Demi, I've been looking for you. Hutch, what the hell have

you done to your hair?" She frowned past me.

Hutch only grinned wider. "Imitation is the most blatant type of flattery. Look out for Harvey, his hair looks like yours."

He winked at her and walked off before she could comment, or possibly threaten to strangle him.

"Idiot," she muttered. "Their family is well known in Fae circles, and they love to torment everyone, but Cheryl gets on really well with them."

I wasn't sure what to say to that, so I nodded instead. Unlike her usual wardrobe of neat sweatshirts, today Beryl was just wearing a plain black hoodie and ragged jeans. I glanced down at my black and grey t-shirt, realising it needed washing and that I didn't exactly look much smarter.

It's laundry day, I reminded myself. *Don't mention anything about clothes or appearances.*

Call-me-Henry appeared in front of us, having found his pencil at last. I noticed his tie's pattern was made entirely of rulers and decided that flattery couldn't hurt.

"That's a nice tie," I said. "I just need to ask a quick question, sir."

Call-Me-Henry straightened the aforementioned tie and put on his most courteous smile.

"We are here to help, Demi," he said. "And call me Henry."

"Um, sure." I hurried on. "Is it possible for me to order something to be delivered here from the world outside, the human one I mean?"

Call-Me-Henry whipped out a small yellow pad from somewhere inside his knitted cardigan at lightning speed.

"Of course," he said. "We are here to facilitate the simple things so that you don't have to. What would you like to have delivered, and to who?"

I beamed, relieved. "I want one large bag of Jelly Babies to be delivered here every week for one of the trolls, Trevor, um I don't know his last- do trolls have last names?"

If Call-Me-Henry thought the request was weird, he didn't show it. I didn't dare look at Beryl.

"And how will you be paying for one bag of Jelly Babies each week?"

I blinked, thrown by the question. In my enthusiastic good will, I hadn't thought the logistics through. I knew FDP mentees were paid, but the meagre pittance got put into my account and I hadn't gone up to the human world to use my bank card since arriving. It still amazed me that I had four hundred and seventy-five pounds to my name already, and that it could be converted into Faerie currency as well as human. My mum didn't believe in pocket money, so I'd never had any. My sisters and I had always relied on the kindness of the adults to buy our sweets or books or toys. Or in my case, I had to rely on adults as well as hoping my sisters didn't nick whatever I got straight after.

"She can use her savings account, surely?" Beryl asked, her arms folded across her chest. "If you like, I'll take Demi up to the human machine, but we're still locked down. I'm sure nobody would mind letting the first week slide by, or you could dock it from her pay."

Call-Me-Henry stared at her for several seconds. I held my breath.

"I suppose that would be acceptable." He gave us a warning look. "Just this once, mind. I'll have the delivery set up each week for you, Demi, and have them sent up to Trevor on your behalf. I believe we have someone popping out on errands this afternoon as luck would have it."

I beamed and lifted my hand in farewell. "Thanks Ca-He- Sir. It was really nice to meet you."

Beryl didn't mention the Jelly Babies order as we made our

way to the lift. I thought about starting some kind of conversation once we were on our way downwards, but had no idea what to say. When Beryl prodded my arm with three, sharp jabs, I stared in alarm.

Beryl glared at me and tapped her fore and middle fingers very slowly and obviously against her mouth three times.

"Sorry, did you want to see me, or...?" I shrugged, confused as the lift stopped.

Beryl shook her head in disgust. "Come on, idiot."

Oh, good. Glad Taz's other nickname for me is catching on with the others. At least they're not all calling me Sparky.

I sighed and followed Beryl out of the lift and into the library, stumbling to a halt when she stopped immediately.

"Okay, we can talk here. Emil has sent Taz on an errand."

"Emil sent Taz on an errand?" I frowned. "Now?"

Beryl nodded. "It's not unusual for him to send Taz, but as you know all skip-ways in and out of Arcanium have been blocked. Nobody's allowed in or out without permission from Queenie."

I knew all of this but wasn't sure why Beryl had collared me about it. For the thousandth time, my hands went to my ribs, but I had no satchel strap left to fiddle with.

"So, you want me to tell the tutors Taz won't be in class?"

Beryl mushed her fists against her eyes, her knuckles cloaked by long hoodie sleeves.

"No, I'm saying it's unusual. I haven't seen Ace either since breakfast. Again, not unusual, but you generally do. He didn't come down to lunch?"

I shook my head, dismayed. "No, I didn't even think to be honest. He mentioned needing to speak to Gnat about interning at the end of the summer."

"Which is?" Beryl paused with wide eyes, waiting for me to

catch on.

"Unusual." I realised it then. "Why would he need to speak to Gnat about it?"

"Exactly. He's top in almost every question round in his classes. Something is going on."

"Why send Taz on an errand though? I mean, I know he's probably one of the most trusted mentees, and Ace said once that he barely ever leaves. But what could it be?"

Beryl regarded me for a moment, then shrugged one shoulder.

"Not sure, but we're going to find out."

She set off back toward the lift and it took me a moment to realise exactly what that meant.

"What, now?"

"Yes, now." Beryl got back into the lift and pointed to the floor, ordering me in beside her. "Why, did you want time to pack?"

She was clearly fired up in a foul mood today and I had no intention of arguing. I got into the lift and closed the gate.

It beats sitting around worrying.

"What exactly are we going to do to find out?" I asked.

Beryl lifted a hand and ticked points off on her fingers.

"Ace has disappeared. Taz has been told to go into a realm on an errand when nobody else is allowed to go in or out. The Elder council is meant to be meeting today in Queenie's office, in case you'd forgotten."

Oops.

I decided to ignore the forgetting of the council meeting. After a busy week of classes, my days were becoming blurred.

Why would Ace and Taz be sent out of the way? Unless...

"You think Taz and Ace have something to do with what's going on?"

"Possibly. They grounded the trolls last night as a precaution and stopped the lifts going up to the arcade, so it must have happened yesterday. Maybe something's about to happen, and they wanted them safe, or one of them might even be involved."

The lift stopped and I could see Queenie's floor. Beryl opened the gate but didn't move to get out.

"Who told you Taz had been sent on an errand?" I asked.

"I was there when Emil made the request. I think he cares about his safety, he's been like a personal mentor since Taz came here two years ago. I don't think Taz's disappearance is the one to worry about."

I frowned, saddened. "You think Ace is? You think something's happened to him?"

"Can't be sure." Beryl hesitated. "How well do you know him?"

"I don't, not really, only since I've been here, I mean you've known him longer, so you tell me. He was kind enough to show me around, explain things to me, and he was the first one to properly try and make friends, *with me.*"

Flashbacks from school filled my head. Nobody wanted to be my friend normally, unless they wanted help with homework or directions. Nobody in Xavio's fairy lessons had talked to me out of choice. Realisation dawned.

"Oh. You think Ace is somehow part of the enemy instead, and that's why he's been so nice to us? I can't believe that."

I shook my head even as doubt crept in.

"I could be wrong." Beryl shrugged, a strain of awkwardness passing over her face. "Maybe he's still in here somewhere, on some errand for Gnat or something. Just be careful who you trust, okay?"

I nodded, the sinking feeling in my gut now halfway down to the Atrium and still sinking. I'd never considered why Ace was so content to be my friend, as he seemed popular with other students from his own classes. I dragged my mind from the more depressing thoughts to the present.

"So, what are we doing here then?"

Beryl smiled. "We're going to creep into the council meeting and find out what they're planning to do. Then, if the answer is basically nothing, we're going to come up with a plan ourselves."

I hurried out of the lift as Beryl set off along the corridor.

"But how are we going to get into an elder council meeting? Is it actually in Queenie's office?"

Beryl nodded. "Sort of. She has to go to welcome them in when they arrive, so her office will be empty."

"How are we going to hide in there though? It's just her desk and loads of mirrors."

Beryl pressed her ear to the office door and waited. I glanced up and down the hall, convinced someone would come and find them snooping. Emil's door was shut, and the entire floor was silent.

"It sounds clear," Beryl whispered.

She pushed the door handle and swung the door open. I tensed and waited for indignant shouting, but none came. Beryl peered inside, just as the sound of the lift arriving echoed behind us.

Beryl backed up and pulled the door shut, darting down the hall toward Emil's office instead.

"Come on, quick, before they catch us and send us away!" Beryl hissed.

I followed as she hurried toward a tall mirror on the wall and stepped up beside it. And vanished. I gawped and rushed toward mirror.

"Beryl, where are-"

A hand came out and grabbed the front of my t-shirt, pulling me into a thin crevice behind the mirror. It was barely big enough for us both, but being squished up with Beryl Eastwick was better than being discovered by Queenie and a council of Elder Fae. Marginally.

I pressed myself against the wall to avoid awkward brushing of arms and legs. The tiny alcove behind the back of the mirror shrouded us in gloom, with only a person-sized slice of light as an exit. An exit that Beryl was now blocking. My chest started a sickening pounding.

It's okay, she'll move in a second once the hall is clear.

I pressed my hand behind my back and started tapping my thumb back and forth across my fingertips. *You can get out any time you like. You're not trapped.*

I tried to breathe, to calm myself, but the jitters hit my limbs and the breath that went in never seemed to quite reach my lungs.

It's just fear, it's not real.

My body wouldn't listen, the memories swirling of being locked in cupboards that were full of my sisters' laughter, knowing Mum wouldn't be home for hours.

"Welcome." Queenie's strident voice filled the hall, giving me an anchor to focus on. "Please go into the office and be seated."

I forced my mind to recall the visual of Queenie's office but could only remember the desk with the one chair behind it. No doubt such issues as an absence of chairs were easily fixed if you were the Director of Arcanium.

"What do we do?" I whispered. "Do you have some kind of fairy listening device?"

Beryl scoffed quietly. "No, we listen at the door, of course. Honestly, who ever heard of a fairy listening device?"

I brushed aside the desire to invent a fairy listening device just to spite her.

Beryl peeked out around the edge of the mirror and beckoned

me to follow. I bashed my elbow hard on the wall as I burst into the hall, taking deep huffs of the large space.

"What do you call a gathering of FDP elders?" Beryl whispered.

"Er, a gathering?"

Beryl shook her head with a sniff. "No, a complete pain in the arse."

I managed a weak grimace in place of a smile as Beryl pulled a tissue from her pocket and wiped her nose.

Taz's hygiene habits must have rubbed off on her somehow.

I followed Beryl as she crept back toward the office door, just in time to hear Queenie's strident voice booming loud and clear.

"We've received alarming reports, which have been told in truth by mentee fairies and Fae, that the Forgotten are once again trying to take Arcanium."

A brief swell of muttering rose. It fell just as quickly, and I could envision Queenie giving everyone assembled one of her disparaging looks.

"They have apparently been collecting orbs," she continued. "Although we aren't sure why. The attack is thought to be imminent. We need to decide how best to handle this, and to quell any invasion once and for all."

"Do you have any idea when they might strike?" A strong male voice with a northern twang asked.

"Only that it's coming soon and that they are ready. We all know what the Forgotten are capable of, and what they seek to achieve. Some of us have seen their handiwork first-hand. We believe they're the ones that have somehow stolen the Book of Faerie, but we cannot allow them to take the hub."

Another round of muttering that lasted longer. I glanced over my shoulder, but the hall remained empty.

"How could they steal it?" someone else asked. "It should

have been impossible."

"Improbable," Queenie corrected. "Nothing is impossible for Fae. One minute it was there, then it was gone, and we have witnesses to that."

A low hum of divided conversations took over.

I frowned, keeping my voice to a whisper. "Could someone have invisibility?"

Beryl shook her head. "It's one of the only gifts Arcanium lifts everywhere, for security. More likely to be someone with speed, misdirection or charm gifts."

"Speed, like Avril?"

Beryl nodded. "She wouldn't though, she's openly pro-human. But Elvira I don't think has speed, after what we saw in Faerie. Not saying it rules her out though."

We turned our attention back to Queenie's office as the conversation resumed.

"It's clear what we must do," said someone else. "We need to close the door to the human world permanently, for the most at least."

"What about the students?" Queenie asked.

"We should evacuate, quietly." I was sure I recognised Emil's voice that time. "We have to get as many out as we can if a fight is coming."

"What about the FDPs in the field?" Another female voice asked, her tone acidic.

"I know what you're thinking, Petra, but there's nothing else to be done," Emil sighed. "Getting everyone back from the realms without mass panic or economic carnage would take ages. All we can do is let them know to bunk down and be safe."

"What, even any mentees?"

Silence reigned for a few moments. I looked anxiously around the hall.

"Yes, all of them," Emil said.

My skin rippled with chills as I realised the reason for Emil's hesitation.

"Taz's still out there, isn't he?" I whispered.

Before Beryl could say anything, I wheeled around and set off toward the lift.

CHAPTER TWENTY
AN UNLIKELY IMPOSTER

"Wait!"

Beryl hissed behind me, but I was already charging along the hall.

Emil's planning to leave Taz out there to fend for himself. Trolls are grounded, but I can still get somewhere safe to orb and warn him. Emil must have given him an orb to go on an assignment.

I'd almost reached the lift when Beryl's hand landed on my sleeve and hauled me to a stop.

"Wait," she huffed. "Taz knows what he's doing, and he knew this might happen. If you don't trust anything else, trust that. It's cute that you want to look out for him, but he never does anything without knowing the risks. We, on the other hand, need to act."

I glanced back to Queenie's office, torn.

"They're going to panic and start evacuating the students pretty quick," Beryl insisted. "If we can find a suitable place to hide until after they've locked down all the exits, then we can use that time to make sure everyone is okay."

I bit my lip. "What can we do to help though?"

Beryl jostled me into the lift, slid the gate closed and pressed a button.

"The adults will be fine defending the place, but they never listen to us properly. Like there's a secret skip-way loop in one of the classrooms that some students use to sneak about. Have they done anything about it? No. There might well be skip-ways opened by enemy Fae who are inside the hub already, pretending to be on our side. So it's down to us to muck in."

I stared at the golden gate in front of me.

Two choices. Stay here and help or go home. I thought of going back home to my sisters making my life a misery. *Not really a choice though, is it?*

"What exactly do we have to do?" I asked. "Keep watch? I don't have any gifts if a load of Fae do come through."

The lift stopped and Beryl opened the gate to the classroom corridor.

"We're going to use the skip-way in the classroom to hide. We just have to be seen once for headcount and hope they don't check more than once. After the hub is sealed, we can emerge and be ready to defend it. If all else fails, you can trip people and I can tie them up."

I shook my head in despair, but couldn't do anything except follow her out of the lift.

The corridor was empty, but the classrooms were full. I wondered how much trouble I was in, considering I'd pretty much missed Avril's entire lesson now on top of all the planned skulduggery. Beryl headed toward the store-room where extra textbooks and a few chairs were kept. As her fingers landed on the handle, a vibration shook my pocket. I pulled out my orb just in time for the pearlescent grey face of Queenie to be magnified in all her glaring glory.

"Due to need for precautionary measures, Arcanium is now under evacuation. Students are to report to their nearest tutor or Arcanium member of staff. Once you have evacuated, a brief meeting will be held in the human world to assist you in making your way home."

Beryl snorted. "Oh sure, because that's not going to cause total mayhem."

"Once you have seen a member of staff, go quietly to the atrium and assemble to be sent up to the human world. Anyone who needs assistance getting home should wait on the beach outside the arcade and you will be seen to. Your things will be sent on to you – I repeat, do not try to retrieve any belongings. Now go calmly, and we will send further communication in due course."

Silence reigned for several moments after Queenie's face disappeared. Then a cacophonous rumbling started in the classrooms nearby.

Avril sat in the nearest one, her expression grave as the class started chattering and panicking.

"I have an idea," I muttered to Beryl. "Follow me."

I threw open the door to Avril's classroom and dashed in without waiting.

"We've just overheard Emil," I said, knowing it technically wasn't a lie. "If you tutors get the rest of the students down to the Atrium, we'll make sure nobody's left behind here."

I gave Avril my best, earnest 'trusted by teachers all the time' look. Technically, it would be easy for me to make sure nobody was left behind here, in the classroom.

Avril didn't even hesitate.

"Brilliant thanks, Demi." She smiled gratefully. "Faerie knows what this is all about but make sure you're down in the Atrium with the others in fifteen minutes, okay?"

I nodded, knowing, or at least hoping, she would quickly forget about us in the evacuation mayhem.

Does nodding count as a lie if I have no intention to do it?

It was too late to worry about that now as Avril rushed out of the room.

Beryl watched the crowds surging past the classroom window, pretending to look around until the corridor outside was deserted.

"Right, so we need to wait here," she explained. "If someone comes, I can glamour but you'll have jump into the skip-way. It should hopefully bring you out on the residents' hall."

I frowned. "Um, have you tried it before? Just worried it's some kind of trick, or they've fixed it recently and I get hurled into some kind of abyss."

Beryl's mouth twisted ruefully. "You know, I never considered that. Well, there's a cupboard there that's empty, but I doubt they'll even do a second sweep."

No cupboards. I skated over that possibility.

"And if the enemy come?" I asked. "The Forgotten? I don't have any gifts or anything to face them with."

"Well, there's a lot of books. Maybe try throwing them at their heads?"

"Helpful."

I pulled a face and perched against a desk, wondering if she'd seen or heard about me throwing a book at Diana during my first object training session.

Beryl grinned. "I do try."

I pushed myself off the desk straight away and started pacing instead. Beryl stood by the classroom window to keep an eye on the hall, but I had a sneaking feeling that if a battle did come, it would probably pass us by completely.

Either that or there won't be any battle and I'll just be in trouble for disobeying orders. Again. I bet my chances of them letting me come back for my second year are already slim, if not non-existent.

The thoughts twirled round and round in my mind as I paced, giving me no peace at all.

"Someone's coming," Beryl hissed.

I looked up but she was already in front of me, one hand on

my shoulder. I stumbled back as she pushed.

"What are you- Wait, hang on." I looked over my shoulder to see a door and a small space behind it looming. "Stop, wait a minute."

Beryl didn't listen. "It's just for a second. Quick, or whoever it is will send you upstairs with the other mentees. Is that what you want?"

My ankle hit the edge of the cupboard. I pressed my hands behind me to steady my weight, my skin beginning to bead with perspiration. I tried to catch a breath but Beryl's jostling had my foot stepping up to keep my balance, and I was in the cupboard before I could gather my senses.

"Just for a sec, okay? Trust me."

I blinked. *Just for a second. A minute at the most. I don't want to be sent home, anything but that. Beryl isn't my sisters.*

I nodded and closed my eyes as the cupboard door swung shut on me. A scraping sound crept through, like wooden legs on flooring. I flinched as something rattled outside, then silence.

"Ah, hi, Petra." I could hear Beryl's voice, muffled but audible.

"You're not normally this respectful, Beryl," another voice commented drily. "What are you doing hanging about in here?"

"I heard about this skip-way in here, behind the whiteboard," Beryl explained, her tone chastened in a way I'd never heard before. "I thought, well, when a few people tried to tell the staff it was here, they were told to stop making a fuss. I figured they didn't believe it existed."

"And you thought that FDPs still on base, even the ones who might have been using that secret skip-way only a few years ago as mentees themselves, would automatically forget it existed?"

Silence filled the air for a few excruciating moments.

"Didn't think, sorry."

"Hmm." Petra didn't sound convinced. "Okay, if you can finish off checking there are no *other* mentees lingering on this floor, I'll go and make sure the Braunees have the kitchen secure."

Footsteps echoed, but I couldn't tell if they were one pair or two.

Beryl might have gone outside to pretend to Petra she's doing a search.

I pushed the door.

Thud.

I pushed harder. A clonking suggested it was hitting against something placed right outside.

I slammed both hands against it, but whatever was blocking the door held firm.

She wouldn't. Please, no.

I pushed against the door with my shoulder, the sting of tears irrelevant in the darkness.

"BERYL," I screamed.

No answer.

Memories of old fears swarmed up, clawing at my skin and sewing the panic deep inside my head. I hammered my fists against the wood, my insides threatening to claw out of my skin. I gripped my hair with both hands and leaned back against the cupboard, smashing my foot against the door.

The door swung open before my foot could connect again, and I burst out into the classroom. I shoved past a startled Beryl and headed for the door.

"Whoa!"

Her hands landed on my shoulders from behind, but restraining me was the worst thing she could do right now. I fought against her, tears soaking my cheeks.

"Demi, what's the matter? Orbs alive, you're shaking."

She let go and I turned to face her, arms and hair flying like a demented banshee.

"I hate being confined!" I had to stumble over a couple of breaths before I could continue.

She stared at me, her mouth open in horror.

"What's wrong?"

"My sisters used to lock me in cupboards because they knew I was afraid of it. Why did you lock me in? Why?"

I wiped at my eyes, the realisation I was out in the open again beginning to trickle to the front of my mind. I eyed the door, the various windows that were smashable if needed, the many things that could be used in self-defence.

She won't understand.

"I had no idea," Beryl said, her eyes wide. "The door just swings open unless you pin it shut, and I didn't want Petra to see you and send you upstairs to be evacuated. Sorry, Dem, if I'd known."

She'd never called me Dem before, although no doubt she'd probably heard Taz use it in passing. I took that tiny gesture of familiarity and used it to stay put rather than flinch away or run as she came toward me.

Her arms wound around my shoulders, tight and reassuring. Every instinct screamed at me to struggle, that she'd use the hold to pull or push me back into the small space, but she didn't. She just held on, and somehow it was enough. The words flowed out, an explanation I'd never given to anyone before streaming past my lips.

"I was only six and really scared of the dark." I sniffed and stepped back, avoiding Beryl's gaze. "My sisters thought it would be funny to tell me a monster lived in the airing cupboard because the boiler gurgled a lot. They said that one day it would throw its tentacle out as I went past and pull me into the darkness, never to be seen again. Then they shut me in the cupboard and barred the door."

I flicked the quickest of glances up, my fingers tapping over each other in a frenzy as I tried to calm myself down. Beryl probably already thought I was ridiculous, so displaying the whole awful truth that was me, including my weird coping mechanisms, wouldn't matter now.

"I knew Mum wasn't due back for hours, so I drove myself frantic trying to get out. Towels turned into fingers in my hair. Sheets were arms trying to smother me. I thought the hoover cord was the tentacle trying to pull me into the darkness. Mum came home eventually and found me, but then the nightmares began. Even now I have the same nightmares when I'm stressed or tired, of being smothered and dragged into this suffocating darkness. That's why I can't stand small spaces. It feels like being buried alive."

Beryl wiped a hand over her face with a heavy sigh.

"I never would have asked you to do that if I'd known," she said. "We'd have brazened it out another way, somehow. Sorry."

I sniffed, aware of my hoodie sleeve now soaked in nose gunk and tears, and Beryl's shoulder that I'd cried on wasn't much cleaner.

Before I could reassure her, the sound of footsteps echoed in the corridor. A lot of footsteps, moving fast. Beryl pushed me aside, moving slightly in front as if she meant to defend me.

"Someone's coming," she whispered. "Get down!"

I quelled the urge to mutter 'and boogie', knowing it was the worst time for my sense of humour to appear. I ducked behind one of the desks as a head and shoulders appeared in the window. I popped up again.

"It's Ace. Ace!"

He turned and saw me. A huge grin spread across his face and he hurried back to open the classroom door. Now I was looking closely, I realised he had rather a lot of people backing up behind him.

"Thank god I found you!" Ace wove through the desks and I moved forward to meet him. "Meryl cornered me this morning, said there was a plot going on. Everyone was worried that the council would decide to evacuate Arcanium and that would leave it outnumbered."

"They've been clearing out the mentees," I admitted. "But everyone else is still here. That's a lot of people you've got."

Ace pointed back over his shoulder. "Well, I have a few family connections. We guessed something like this would happen after the Elders' meeting, so I said I'd sneak home to bring some reinforcements and caught the train straight after breakfast."

A girl strode forward before I could go and join Ace. She eyed me up and down, arms folded across her chest. Her dark hair was long and pinned back, her black pinafore dress and the flowery short sleeves underneath somehow at odds with the sharp gaze and tense, ready stance.

"I see you've been hiding a first year," she said.

I eyed Beryl and gawped to see her looking sheepish and downcast, her hands fidgeting behind her back and her eyes fixed on the floor.

"Yeah, sorry Petra, but needs must."

I recalled a Petra being spoken to at the Elder council meeting, and coming across Beryl while I'd been stuffed in the cupboard. Either way, I guessed her finding us wasn't going to go down well at all. Apparently, Beryl needed a distraction as she turned to Ace with a deep frown on her face.

"How did you get in?" she demanded. "Or out? They closed everything down last night."

"I left through the service entrance the Braunees use. We came in that way as well. It's basically a huge dumbwaiter delivery chute that Cheryl said they would most likely be keeping open in case anyone needed to flee. I thought she'd have told you. Where are the other two anyway? I don't think I've ever seen you without each other before."

I froze, my mind whirring as I remembered Beryl's distrust of Ace earlier.

Why wouldn't Meryl have told Beryl she was going to speak to Ace? Why wouldn't Beryl have known about the kitchen chute if Cheryl did? And where are Cheryl and Meryl, if the three sisters never do anything without each other?

A rumble shook the room before I could ask Ace, the chair legs rattling against the wooden floor. A prickling sensation, like very faint pins and needles, crept through my skin right to my bones. I shook myself to clear it, aware of everyone else shuddering around me, and turned to Beryl.

"Are you okay?" I asked.

She had her fists clenched and her face scrunched like she was struggling with some intense, invisible pain.

Did that rumble set something off for her?

I hastened forward, just in time to see her hair wavering. The vivid purple paled like petals turning brown in autumn, the previously straight strands shrinking as they crimped themselves into curls.

Her eyes widened, the brown colour flashing a familiar greenish blue. Freckles burst over her nose, which wasn't her nose anymore, and her shoulders widened.

I gawped in amazement at the boy now standing where Beryl had just been.

"Taz?"

I couldn't help asking, even though it was clearly him now

standing in front of me.

He looked down over his jeans and ragged hoodie, bringing his hands up to swipe back strands of curly hair.

"Yeah, don't get too excited," he retorted. "I know, I've got some explaining to do."

"What was that feeling?" Ace asked.

He'd been gathering his group into the classroom, most of them teenagers of varying ages. A blonde girl in a checkered shirt and denim skirt who looked about eighteen glanced up at the ceiling with a wary expression.

"They've done a glamour-lift," she announced. "That's no simple trickery."

I faced Taz, refusing to get distracted. He saw my face and aimed for a sheepish grin.

"I tried to hold onto my Beryl disguise but glamour-lifts are almost impossible to beat. I didn't want to startle you."

I folded my arms.

"Mission failed then. Why were you glamouring as Beryl. Also, where is she?"

"Right here!"

CHAPTER TWENTY ONE
THEY'RE HERE

The booming voice of the real Beryl Eastwick, I hoped, bounced around the classroom. I turned to face the doorway, aware of Taz now hovering at my side.

Behind Beryl, I could see Meryl and Cheryl and a crew of random people filling the corridor.

"How many do you think we're up against?" One of Beryl's lot asked.

"No way of knowing," said a young man from Ace's group, grinning at the thought.

Taz slunk across to stand beside me.

"Those are all active FDPs with Beryl," he explained quietly. "I'm sorry I couldn't tell you first, but Emil called me into his office last night and said he knows I see this as home so he couldn't trust me to leave if we were evacuated."

I said nothing, still bewildered by all the changes and even more so by all the people crowded around. Ace's friends were all young adults but the FDPs ranged from young to middle-aged. All I could think was that it was Taz who had locked me in the cupboard, Taz who had comforted me afterwards.

Taz who had called me cute for wanting to warn him.

Throughout the weeks we'd known each other, he'd been right beside me, from keeping Leo a secret, to saving him from the quarantine situation, and always helping me in classes.

It was something I'd thought of before, that he was a trustworthy friend to have, but now it hit me in the emotional parts with unerring clarity.

Taz is someone I can trust completely.

"I couldn't risk coming to your room to warn you," he continued. "He insisted on seeing me off himself, but Meryl distracted him while Beryl and I hatched a plan."

I folded my arms and perched against the nearest desk. I might trust him, but that didn't mean I would let him off the hook easy.

"What plan?"

"I glamoured into Beryl and she glamoured into me while Emil wasn't looking. The moment he packed her off thinking she was me, she re-glamoured as someone different and came back in through the lift from the human world. Then Trevor took her to the nearest realm where her cousin is the FDP and the message spread from there. I didn't know that Meryl spoke to Ace though, that wasn't part of the plan."

I considered this as Taz fidgeted with the cuffs of his hoodie and refused to look at me.

"Good thing she did by the looks of it. He's brought at least fifteen people."

Taz frowned. "We don't know those people though. Calling active FDPs home is one thing, but these are strangers. They could be anyone. They didn't come in by troll either, so there's no guarantee now that the way out has been left safe if we need it still."

I shrugged, still nursing my hurt at being left out. Even though Taz might not have had time to warn me, Meryl had gone straight to Ace over me.

Of course she would. I'm just a newbie, and Ace is a second-year who clearly knows loads of fairies. I don't even have any friends at home, let alone fairy ones. Who could I have gone to fetch back here even if she did tell me?

But Trevor was meant to be my troll, and now he was

apparently giving lifts to everyone at the drop of a hat.

"Sounds like trolls aren't too safe an entry either," I retorted. "If anyone can go in and out that way like Beryl did."

This time Taz did look at me, his turquoise eyes wide and beseeching.

"No, don't say that, please. I couldn't see any other way to raise the alarm and the council would have left this place completely undermanned. Orbs are tracked and anyone could be listening, even the enemy if there are spies inside Arcanium itself. Beryl had to tell Trevor you'd approved it, that you'd given her permission."

I eyed Beryl in bowed-headed discussion with her sisters, her eyes dull and her posture weary.

"She lied?" I pressed a hand to my mouth as the enormity of it hit me.

Taz nodded. "She must have done, a small one. Either that or offered a favour, but it would have to be a huge one for Trevor to go without your say so. Even Emil would have to ask your permission to realm-skip with Trevor now, that's how seriously these alliances are taken."

I rubbed my face with both hands. The crowd showed no sign of racing off, but I could see huddles forming to discuss potential tactics.

"I'll take it from her, if she has, the favour I mean. She was only doing what you asked her. But why did you have to glamour?"

This time Taz rolled his eyes more like his normal self.

"Use your head, Sparky. You don't think Emil would wonder why I'm wandering the halls after he sent me away? Or someone might wonder why Beryl was missing when they did headcount?"

I nodded. "Fair point."

"Arcanium is my home." His eyes flashed as he looked at me. "And I won't be packed off like some errant child."

I assessed the crowd in the classroom again. Even if Taz didn't trust Ace's friends, Petra and some of the other FDPs clearly did. Either that or the whole lot were amazing actors which, with fairies and Fae, was unnervingly possible.

"So, now we wait?" I asked, fidgeting with the cuff of my sleeve. "I don't have many uses if there is a fight. I could worry at them I suppose."

"Don't be dim." Taz huffed. "You're not as useless as you think you are. You chased off the Oricadae, didn't you? You managed to get help when we were in trouble, even after that *cow* went racing after you. You even managed to befriend the infamous Eastwick sisters, and that's almost unheard of."

I snorted a laugh and tried to think of a fitting reply, but after a few moments I settled for turning bright red instead.

"Why were you suspicious of Ace then?" I had to ask. "He's our friend."

Taz shoved his hands in his pockets and scuffed one shoe back and forth, refusing to meet my eyes.

"Beryl and I hatched the plan, but then I found out he'd disappeared. Now I know why, but I couldn't be sure. He's always been friendly to everyone before, but especially when you came along. I wasn't sure- I didn't know if you-"

He hesitated. I folded my arms across my chest and glared at him.

"You thought I was in on it somehow, that I was part of the Forgotten? That Ace was what, my mate on the inside?"

Taz rubbed the back of his neck, his cheeks pink.

"I guessed you weren't, but come on. You come in and get an assignment on your first day, you get a troll to pick you along with it, and you're the one who found the skip-way to Faerie.

216

Then Ace is suddenly really chummy with you. I figured either he fancied you, or there was something more underhanded going on. It just seemed-"

"What?"

"Unlikely." He sighed. "I'm sorry, okay? I'm not used to trusting people."

That I can understand. I kept my arms folded, even though I'd already forgiven him. *How do you let someone off the hook without giving them freedom to be an arse to you going forward?*

"I guess I can understand," I said. "But I'm not doing anything underhanded, or anything 'Fae'. I'm barely even a fairy yet."

Taz smiled then. "You're way more fairy than you think you are, don't worry."

Another rumble shook the room. I slammed a hand onto the nearest desk as Taz swore. With no prickling sensation, I couldn't be sure if it was another charm or the foundations being shook to their core by some kind of explosion.

"Think we're missing the battle," Ace announced.

Petra strode toward the door and swung it open wide. "Well then, let's go have some fun."

In her black dress and floral sleeves, she looked more suited to attending a poetry reading, except I could see a look on her face that would probably frighten off even the most fearsome Oricadae.

"Go up in the lift in groups of as many as can fit," she instructed. "Split the floors between groups. If you find them empty, then head on down to the Atrium." She turned to face me and Taz, still standing slightly apart from the others. "You guys might want to stay here and keep safe."

My nervous anticipation had been rising, then Petra dismissed us so easily. Even Taz appeared to be having issues finding a suitable response, his mouth stuck on auto-gawp.

I might not have many skills, but if the others are fighting then I am too. Like Taz said, this is our home, and I belong with my friends.

"No," I said. "We're seeing this to the end if you don't mind, um, thank you."

A surging fire was starting in my toes and powering upward to tear at my inhibitions.

Petra eyed me for several excruciating seconds as the crowd outside disappeared in batches into the lift.

"I'm not responsible for the consequences," she warned.

Taz's hopeful expression, like Leo faced with a full cricket salad, was worth the imminent peril. *Almost.*

I nodded. "Understood."

Petra swept off into the empty corridor without another word. Taz shot me a grateful look and scampered after her. With no idea what to expect, I followed them into the lift.

I didn't dare ask what might be waiting for us, but noticed Petra had pressed the button for the Atrium.

Is she hoping to get us out somehow after all, or just guessing that's where the fight will be?

I tugged at the neck of my t-shirt in the absence of my satchel, which I still missed. No doubt Elvira had pulverised it out of pure spite, or stolen it.

"Ready?" Petra asked as the lift stopped.

"Abso-bloody-lutely." Taz at least sounded determined.

Elvira tried to get Leo taken away as well. I nodded, determined and petrified in one stomach-dropping swoop. *I'm as fired up and ready as someone with no gifts or abilities can be.*

I took a deep breath as Petra yanked the gate open and we emerged into absolute carnage.

Fairies stood in defensive stances around the reception desk in the centre, the clusters spanning out behind. All eyes were fixed on the crowd massing in front of the lift shaft as more and more bloodthirsty Fae spilled out of it.

A loud crack echoed through the Atrium seconds before a zig-zag of lightning blasted down and struck the reception desk. I gasped but already a multi-coloured glow was emanating between the smoking wood and the fairies still standing there, a force field to keep them safe.

Another crackle filled the air. I looked up to see a bright light growing brighter and pushed Taz to the floor.

"MOVE."

Petra's voice blasted in my ears as she shoved against me and sent me sprawling on top of Taz. I rolled off him and hit the unforgiving marble floor next, twisting onto my side to look up.

Instead of being hit by lightning, Petra had one arm raised as daisies and dandelions floated down around her. Her face was pinched with concentration and, in that moment, I realised just how much effort wielding a powerful gift must take.

With the sound of fighting around us, I scrambled to my feet and dragged Taz up as well.

"What do we do?" I asked as a shockwave shook the marble underneath our feet.

Taz looked around, his expression stricken. "I- I don't know."

Beryl, Meryl and Cheryl charged out of the lift with a feral battle cry, and I knew anything had to be better than nothing. A group of Fae rushed the reception desk, only for ivy to whip out from the arches nearby and send them flying like bowling pins.

Arcanium is fighting back on our side, that's got to stand for something.

"They're using the lift shaft as a skip-way somehow." Ace appeared beside us. "One of my friends has the ability to break stuff, so we were thinking we could take one of these pillars down and roll it at them."

"And half of Arcanium with it," I reminded him. "No, we can't just try to knock them down with a big battering ram. They'll just get up again, or be crushed."

Taz glared at me. "So?!"

I noticed a girl about our age on Ace's other side, watching everything going on around us with wide, dark eyes. Ace caught me looking and grimaced.

"Oh, this is my sister, Sarah. She insisted on coming with us even though she's only sixteen and far too young to be in the middle of a Fae battle."

I wanted to point out that Taz and I were only sixteen and in the middle of a Fae battle. I settled for an awkward smile instead.

"Sarah, this is Demi and Taz," Ace introduced us. "Now, for the sake of my sanity, stay right beside me, okay?"

Sarah nodded, but as Ace turned away, I noticed a belligerent gleam in her eyes.

Before I could address the issue of what we could actually do to help, I spied a bigger problem stepping out of the lift shaft.

Elvira emerged dressed in a white, wide-legged trouser-suit, with fluted lapels and flouncy sleeves. She had her dark hair pinned atop her head in an elegant creation, but her keen eyes swept the room and landed right on me. She strode forward with intent, Luchia and Draven scuttling at her heels to keep up.

"We've got trouble coming," I called out. *And I haven't the faintest idea what to do about it.*

Only having Taz on one side and Ace on the other stopped me from fleeing in the other direction as Elvira drew closer.

"Three little piglets, left all alone," she sang. "Nobody around, the future unknown."

Taz rolled his eyes, standing tense and ready.

"Very poetic but the rhyming is awful. We know you're

impervious to weather and that you can glamour at will. I'm sure you have other tricks, but we bested you last time."

"Your friends entertained me briefly." Elvira laughed. "But you three are no match."

Taz grabbed my hand seconds before the prickling of an attack needled over my skin.

"Still three against one," he taunted through clenched teeth. "We may not have gifts, but we have blood."

Elvira curled her lip as her gaze swept over me. "Barely."

I ignored the burn of shame in my cheeks, but knew Elvira could see it, like she'd happily stripped away the flimsy walls of self-esteem I had spent years building.

Without the oddity of being born with fairy blood somehow, I'm nothing. I'd have to go back home to be kicked around by my sisters forever.

Taz's fingers tightened around my hand, his nails pinching the skin.

"She's trying to play with your fears." He forced the words out with effort. "Don't listen to the voice in your head."

Cursing, Elvira lifted her attack and I sagged as though I'd just run fifty laps of a playing field with an Oricadae on my shoulders.

Speaking of beasts...

"Oh, enough of this," Elvira flicked her gaze down to her pets. "Get them!"

I snorted. "Oh, that's original."

Original or not, the Oricadae obeyed, stalking forward.

I veered back and swung around, aware that Taz was spinning with his hand still in mine. I tried to shake him off, but he clung on, his knuckle bones almost boring right through my fingers.

"Don't let them separate us," he shouted. "If they do, we'll have no hope of beating her."

"We have no hope of beating her now!" Ace pointed out. "Even if we do stay together, the giant mutant Leos will eat us."

"Don't call them that!" I objected, panting.

I stumbled then, literally and mentally as I had a brainwave. I almost pulled Taz down with me but focused forward and powered on toward a large wooden door.

"What's through there?" I pointed.

Taz shook his head. "It's just a staff room for the receptionists, I think. Pretty sure the cleaners keep their stuff in there. I'm *not* hiding, if that's what you're thinking."

"It's not."

I stumbled to a halt in front of the door and fumbled with the handle. I threw it wide open and turned to Ace.

"Any chance you could do your whole running and distracting thing again?" I asked. "If we can separate one of the Oricadae from the other somehow, that might give us a better shot. Lead it back to the crowd and hopefully someone will know what to do."

Ace's face twisted, his expression uncertain. He opened his mouth, no doubt to start debating, but an ear-piercing whistle tore through the air before he could.

CHAPTER TWENTY TWO
AN ILL-ADVISED PLAN

Sarah whistled through her fingers a second time, then took an apple out of her bag and threw it into the air. It sailed with deathly precision and hit Draven right between the eyes. The furious Oricadae opened his mouth and threw out a feral hiss like boiling acid.

Before Ace could react, he found himself being dragged along in the wake of a sprinting sixteen-year-old, followed by a very irate Oricadae.

"I like that girl already," I muttered. "What's the plan then?"

Luchia had been watching her companion, but now her attention was back on us.

"Incoming!" Taz shouted.

He pushed me sideways as something sailed between our heads, two seconds after mine had vacated that exact spot. A woman darted toward us, dressed all in black with every essence of her screaming 'trained for elite combat', from the red bandana tied around her fizzy blonde hair to her lithely muscled bare shoulders.

Taz darted in front of me, his hand out. The woman seemed to falter, her feet slowing as if they'd been embedded in treacle. She leaned forward, her face contorting. I couldn't work out what Taz was doing to hold her back, but I would do whatever I could to help him.

I found my connection and threw up a hand, the ribbons of rainbow light twirling themselves around him. Casting a warding is like one of those practical practice things; once you've done it

223

a couple of times, it's easy, and I'd been practicing over the past few days any chance I got. So easy I could revel in it. So easy, I focused on protecting Taz and nothing else.

Fingers landed on my shoulder, digging in with talon-like sharpness. I winced and turned my head to the side, convinced Luchia or Draven had me. The talons were human and red, attached to a pale, claw-like hand.

Elvira didn't even bother to taunt me as her free hand clamped on my arm, pinning it behind me. I struggled, trying to get my balance weighted so I could kick back, but she seemed to have super-Fae strength. It was all I could do to keep upright as she started pulling me backwards, fear digging its own talons around my throat.

I opened my mouth to call out, but Taz had his own warding up now to protect him from two attackers, a young man with a ruthless grin having joined the fray against him.

I can't help him like this.

I renewed my effort, twisting and dropping my weight to the floor in the hope of unbalancing Elvira.

"Stop struggling, brat." Her voice rang clear over the chaos of the fighting. "I have a strength gift, so you will only tire yourself out. Although, considering what I intend for you, tiredness might be a *kindness*."

She spoke the word like ash on her tongue, a disgusting taint she couldn't bear to say. I flung my free arm out to grab a doorframe as it loomed past me, but Elvira's strength pulling against me almost snapped my fingers off.

As Elvira spun us around, I recognised the angle of the atrium through the doorway. I had no idea why she'd brought me into the storeroom, but then a large chest came into view.

She can't be intending to lock me inside.

Elvira pushed me forward with vitriolic strength. I opened my lips to scream, but her fingers wrapped around my mouth, her nails digging grooves in my cheek.

"I know a young man who has a skill with mind-reading." Her breath tickled my ear and my skin crawled so much I almost wriggled free in anguish. "He was most delighted to tell me the horrors that lurk in your pretty little head."

The next push sent me sprawling forwards and her fingers disappeared. My shins hit the side of the chest. No amount of screaming was working as Elvira forced me into the sturdy wooden chest, like a coffin lined with thick, folded fabric.

My insides writhed in horror as she let go, hands grasping for the lid. I braced my arms against the sides and lurched up, my fingers clutching the lip of the box. Elvira stamped on them with a vengeful boot and I yelled out, but nobody was coming. I had to draw my fingers toward me, cradling them to my chest, the agony blistering through them as they started to throb.

"They'll assume you've deserted." Elvira shoved her hands on my shoulders and held me as I railed against her, legs flailing to stamp my way out. "They'll think you've hidden, or been dealt with already." She grinned as one final shove sent me onto my back. "Besides, who would bother looking for a *fairy* like you?"

I cried out as the lid slammed, the darkness weighting around me like a suffocating shroud. Sickening panic pounded around in my head, louder in the sudden darkness.

Something rattled near my arm. *The lock.*

Another slam echoed, extra loud as if Elvira wanted me to hear her closing the storeroom door.

Okay, okay, okay. Think. Breathe. Think. Breathe.

I forced every instinct back, the need to claw and bang and scream rising like acid in my throat.

They will search places but I don't have time for that. Taz will know you wouldn't just run off, he has to.

In the darkness with my eyes shut tight, the vision of Taz holding up against two grown Fae bloomed with unerring clarity. I couldn't leave him fighting on his own. I kept my eyes closed and my movements slow, knowing if I knocked the side of the box and it didn't move, my anxiety would spill over and I'd lose all sense. My feet kept up an agitated tapping, and I made that movement, the control of it, hold the panic in check.

Reaching into my pocket, I ran my fingertips over my orb. With my other hand, I found the penknife Xavio had gifted me. I could orb for help.

"Who would bother looking for a fairy like you?"

Harsh, but everyone else was busy fighting already so I couldn't ask them to come and get me. I couldn't risk Trevor landing the rickshaw on the box or inside it, squashing me to death.

I fumbled around until I found the little knife attachment and flicked it out, but it wouldn't even slide into the tiny gap between the lid and the box.

The one gift I get given and it can't even help me. Frustration boiled in my chest and I slammed my fist sideways against the wood. *All it's been good for is opening a stupid cabinet which almost lost me Leo.*

I dropped my hand. Lifted it again, feeling along the rear side of the box. I flinched as my fingertips slid over something cold. With some effort, I managed to find two rough circles. With feverish hope making my hands shake, it took me several moments to find the right attachment on the penknife.

I almost cried with relief when the first screw on the back hinge started to turn.

Thank Faerie for whoever made this box with the screws and hinges on the inside.

The first screw dropped. I renewed my enthusiasm, hands

beginning to smart as I gripped and fumbled, failed and started again.

The second screw dropped. My upper back muscles screamed with aching as I stayed twisted. I heaved against the lid and felt it begin to give, but there was still another hinge holding it shut at the other end. Grimacing into the darkness, I ran frantic fingertips along the side of the box.

If it's too far down, or I can't bend enough...

I grazed the hinge and almost dropped the pen knife in my desperation. The angle of my hand was all wrong, and the screwdriver slipped and slithered as the anxiety started clawing back in, like an Oricadae at my throat.

The third screw dropped. One more, and I would find out if there was any way of busting the box open. Right now, even a glimpse of light, of fresh air, would be-

The fourth screw dropped. I shoved my fingers into the gap and heaved, expecting resistance.

The lid swung up, but almost banged back down on my fingers as I fumbled to push it with shaking arms. I pushed again and finally the lid fell backwards.

Light streamed in to kiss my cheeks, air filling my grateful lungs. My arms were shaking, legs wobbling as I climbed like Bambi out of the box. The lid was still attached, but I could see that the lock was one of those flap hinge ones that needed to be padlocked shut. Again, I thanked whatever wonderful person had made the box so escape-friendly. Then I remembered Elvira.

I'm going to kill her. I'm going to force her to watch us beat the Forgotten, then I'll end her.

The knowledge that I had zero gifts to use against her didn't so much as pinch my fury as I stormed toward the door. I swung it open and saw a face hovering right in front of me.

I screamed.

The sound, pure belated anguish, peeled across the atrium and attracted attention, but I couldn't claw it back in.

Taz blinked back at me, his mouth open in horror.

"What the hell, are you okay? Took me a while to fend them off." As he caught sight of the wreckage behind me, his face darkened. "Did she lock you in that chest? Oh hell, sorry, I came to get you out but two of them tackled me."

"I know, but I got myself out."

I didn't have time to be touched by his concern. Over his shoulder, I could see Elvira striding toward us with a cruel smile. I grabbed Taz's hand. Ignoring his startled squawk, I dragged him into the storeroom and slammed the door shut behind us. Taz stared in horror as I grabbed a nearby armchair and hauled it with much grunting against the door.

"I told you, I'm not hiding-" Taz fell silent when I held up a hand, looking around at the room.

It had wooden bench table in the middle of the room, just behind the ruined chest, and a big cupboard on the far wall. Apart from a couple of sofas and chairs, the rest of the room was taken up with what looked like cleaning supplies, and a huge, dubious-looking plastic tub that had 'air freshener' scrawled on the side in black marker.

Perfect.

Something hit the door. Seconds later, the handle rattled.

I grabbed a broom, aware of Taz staring at me like I was demented.

"You can glamour, can't you?" I asked. "Could you glamour someone else, like you did with Leo and the spider legs?"

The door bounced twice against the back of the armchair with increasing force.

Taz frowned, confused. "Yes, if I'm touching them or if they're small animals like Leo, but-"

228

"When that door opens, you have to stop her looking like herself. I'm going to do the rest. If we can get rid of the Oricadae, then it's just her. She always has them nearby so she must have a weakness without them, somewhere."

A loud crash sent the armchair sprawling across the room. Taz bounded over and grabbed my hand as the door swung open.

Elvira stalked into the room with Luchia at her heels, the sound of shouting and banging from outside following them in.

"You really are entirely tiresome," Elvira grumbled. "Now there are only two of you, against a grown Fae with gifts and an Oricadae that could tear you apart. But there is little fun in that."

She reached into her white suit jacket and pulled out three small vials full of colourful liquid, one purple, one green and one blue.

Same colours as Beryl, Meryl and Cheryl's hair. I shook the thought away.

We just had to get close enough to her for Taz to change her appearance.

"What do they do then?" Taz asked.

He made a show of shuffling forward to peer closer, but Elvira held up a hand.

"That is quite close enough, children."

Taz shot me a weary look, every essence of his being saying 'knew it wouldn't work'. Elvira clinked the vials together to get our attention.

"These are just a few little potions I've been brewing. The only useful part of my position here has been the opportunity to realm-skip and gather various ingredients from different realms of Faerie."

I knew I had to keep her talking as Taz inched us closer, one shuffle at a time. I frowned and aimed for distracting Elvira with corrections.

"That can't be why your Forbidden people sent you here though? What about stealing the Book of Faerie?"

"You mean the Forgotten," Elvira sneered. "Really, this place doesn't teach anything useful at all anymore. I wouldn't expect much from your kind, but not even knowing the proper histories. The Forgotten aren't aware of my little side-project, but then it's none of their business what I do in my own time. And I told you before, I had nothing to do with that stupid book disappearing. I wish I had taken it, to burn on the altar of our triumph! Now, as much as I would like to let you trip around trying to distract me, let's see. Shall I go for memory loss?"

She held up the purple vial in one hand. "Or ever-lasting rage?"

Then the green. "Or maybe it will be Misery. Each of these potions should give you an effect, although I haven't had much time to test them."

I had been hanging valiantly onto the hope that we'd have the slim chance of pulling off my plan. Taz's hand started to shake around mine and my last strand of hope frayed as Elvira eyed us with a malicious smile.

"You can be the gentleman." She pointed a finger at Taz. "Manners are so important. You may decide which one your bloodless little friend gets."

"Well, no point giving her the rage one," Taz said. "I mean, you've met her."

His nails dug hard into my palm as he surged forward. His hand broke away from mine and he clamped his fingers around Elvira's wrists.

Luchia hissed as Elvira swung her arms up and round in a wide circle, disabling Taz's strength. Pain flashed on his face as Elvira turned him and slammed him into the wall, pinning his arms behind his back. I panicked and focused all my attention on the performance of a lifetime.

"GGGRRRRRRRAAAAAASSNNNNAAAARRRRGGH."

I put all my frustration and fear into the roar and threw it out of the door.

Luchia's gaze, fixed on her mistress, swivelled around to survey the Atrium. She stalked to the door and stared out, no doubt expecting to see some kind of feral beast come flying toward us.

The noise had even distracted Elvira, and Taz took full advantage. He jammed one of his heels into the toe of her shoe and balanced on it to swing his other foot back into her leg.

"Ouch, you brat!" Elvira recovered in time to tighten her grip on Taz's arms. "You're going to regret that."

I barrelled forward and went shoulder first into her back. She fell forward onto Taz, who managed an artful twist to the side just in time. Elvira crashed into the wall with a nasty thump to her head and stumbled straight past us in an attempt to regain balance. As she wheeled around and made another attempt to catch Taz, I grabbed the broom. Without thinking, I raised it and uttered a strangled war-cry that sounded somewhat similar to a constipated chicken.

The broom thudded down on the back of Elvira's head. I held my breath.

Elvira stopped grappling to hold Taz, and I waited for the inevitable sickening thud of her falling. Knowing my luck, she'd knock her head on the way down and tumble to her death. I'd be accused. There might not even be a trial. I'd never get to become an FDP now. Worst of all, I'd have to go back home.

Elvira turned, her face bright red. Her eyes rolled white and bulged. She raised her arms, hands outstretched toward my throat.

At least she let go of Taz, I panicked as I backed away. *He can flee and I'll just- oh, hell.* I raised my arms to protect myself.

"Oh no you don't!"

Something shoved into my arm, pushing me to the side. I braced myself against the wall and lifted my head in time to see Petra stride past.

Elvira readjusted the dark haystack that was her once-fancy hairdo and glowered as Taz slipped past her, fists clenched and teeth grinding.

"The Forgotten are fleeing," Petra announced. "Queenie has reversed your skip-way to a holding location in Faerie. It was a mistake to attack us when we're still strong, when we still remember what side we're on. Leave now and you might just hold onto some dignity."

Elvira stormed toward her, wagged a finger in Petra's unimpressed face with poisonous ire in her eyes.

"You are weak, all of you. Your sentimentality for the lesser folk will be your undoing."

A wave of power burned my skin as Elvira sent out another gift to attack us with, but Petra threw up an arm and the feeling dissipated.

"You're powerless here with your party tricks," Petra insisted. "And there aren't lesser folk, just different ones, that's *your* mistake, your arrogance."

In the upheaval, I had forgotten one very large, important thing. A wash of grey flickered in the corner of my eye. I turned to see Luchia charging toward Petra with her fangs bared.

"Grab her now!" I yelled.

It only took Taz a split second to understand. He clamped his hands onto Elvira's arm as I hared past them, hurdling over a sofa to grab a huge plastic tub. I prised open the lid on my way back, relieved but dizzy as an overwhelming scent of lavender and jasmine smothered me. It reminded me vaguely of the residents' hall after cleaning day, and I knew I'd never feel comfortable with the scent ever again.

"Demi, hurry!" Taz shouted.

He fought to hold onto a struggling Elvira, who now looked like Sandra once more thanks to his shared glamour, while Petra used the broom to fend off Luchia. The beast snapped her mouth at the bristles, but she seemed hesitant to attack now that her mistress looked different.

Sight fixed.

I said a silent apology in advance to Taz and threw the contents of the tub as hard as I could.

Scent fixed.

Taz and Elvira-Sandra disappeared under a tidal-wave of nauseating floral notes. I turned my back so Luchia couldn't see my mouth, pretending to put the tub away.

Sound fixed.

"Flee, precious," I shouted in a perfect imitation of Elvira. "Back home the way we came, Draven too. Go now!"

The shout sounded as though it came from the Atrium. Elvira opened her mouth, spluttering through the face-full of air-freshener, but Taz helpfully shoved a bundle of his sleeve in there to keep her quiet.

"Come on, darlings, home now!" I tried again, wondering if I was choosing the wrong words.

Luchia tilted her head to the side. A second of hesitation passed, then she scrambled out of the room and took flight toward the lift shaft like a squat, scaly arrow.

"Come back you stupid creature!" Elvira managed to spit out the sleeve, but Luchia was already disappearing out of sight.

"You're almost alone," Petra said. "Is this really the choice you want to make?"

I didn't expect Elvira to just give up. I guessed the awful

woman would likely have a back-up plan of some kind.

Unfortunately, Elvira shoving Taz to the floor, grabbing the broom from Petra and turning it into a shining sword wasn't the sort of plan I had envisioned.

CHAPTER TWENTY THREE
AN UNLIKELY RETURN

"OUT."

Petra darted forward to grab me and Taz and hustled us out to the Atrium. I gawped as she pulled a hair from her head and a second later, a thin, serrated blade formed in her hand.

"You think you can challenge me?" Elvira scorned. "You're little more than a child yourself."

Petra laughed. "I may be young, but I'm no child. I've probably seen realms you've not even had nightmares about, doing the job I do."

I wanted to applaud as they edged into the Atrium, face to face, blade to blade. Nearby, clusters of fairies stopped congratulating each other and turned their way. In moments, nobody else in the Atrium was moving a muscle, spellbound.

"We are given this power as a responsibility," Petra continued. "It isn't our prize, or birth right, it's our duty."

Elvira growled. With her dark hair unravelling and eyes aglow with hatred, she could have passed for a demented hag. She lunged forward, sword outstretched. Petra feinted back and the crowd gasped as one buzzing unit. I had a moment of admiring Petra's ornate silver hilt encrusted with blue gems. Then sword met blade with a loud clang.

Elvira moved with speed and precision, but Petra held her own. She blocked every strike Elvira made with a grim smile on her face. I watched with my mouth open, horrified and chilled right to the core. Beside me, Taz stood like a coiled spring, as if ready to jump in if needed. Elvira swung her sword back and aimed a punch instead.

Petra ducked to the side, but not quick enough. The blow caught her shoulder and she staggered, dropping her blade.

Elvira vanished her sword into thin air, her arms hanging at her sides as she advanced on Petra, a gleeful smile stretching her face.

Flashes filled my head of my sister Jenny holding me down. My other sister laughing, egging her on. Something in that smile, that grotesque mask of cruelty, made me snap.

I ran forward and grabbed Elvira's wrists, yanking them behind her back. She screamed as I hooked a foot around her ankle and sent her tumbling to her knees.

She twisted, her nails tearing my sleeve as she tried to get a hold on me, the smile now a vicious snarl. I yanked back, flinching as potion vials spilled out of her cloak. Her gaze moved as her hand reached out.

I lunged forward, legs gunning like pistons and kicked at the vials, desperate to move them away. My toe nudged a bulbous one full of yellow liquid. It rolled slowly, right into Elvira's waiting fingers.

She twisted out of reach and rose to her feet, her gaze fixed on me.

I searched my body for my connection.

Come on, please!

A spark at my elbow, the tingling swelling through my limbs.

Panting and red-faced, Elvira lifted the vial aloft.

As she dashed it down at my feet, I wove the strongest image of rainbow colours, my protection warding knitting together around me.

A noxious cloud of dark yellow smoke exploded up into the air, obscuring me from view. I could just see everyone else covering their faces nearby.

Even with my warding up, lingering hints of the awful smell crept around me. I gagged and recalled the smell of my sisters' room before cleaning day.

The moment the scent started to fade and the smoke began to thin, Elvira darted toward me.

As she reached into the smoke with eager hands, I whirled past and pinned her arms behind her back again. She opened her mouth to scream in anger and inhaled a savage waft of smoke for her trouble.

Petra appeared beside me, her blade ready in her hand.

"A dirty trick." She raised her voice for the crowd to hear.

I whipped my leg forward to pull Elvira back to her knees, wincing as my body shook and I almost fell over on top of her.

Elvira finished spluttering as the last of the smoke tendrils cleared, exhibiting us once again to the gawping crowd of onlookers. I eyed the faces but couldn't tell if they were mostly Arcanium people or if some of the Forgotten were still among us.

A couple of FDPs rushed across to help Petra escort Elvira toward the lift shaft, and I almost forgot to let go of her.

"This isn't the end," Elvira snarled. She lifted her head high and shouted into the crowd. "Remember your true allegiances, because the time *will* come to choose the right side, and we will not be forgiving to those who choose badly."

I pressed a shaking hand to my chest, my insides still pounding with leftover adrenalin.

At the lift entrance, Petra and her companions let Elvira go and stepped back. Queenie stood tall and blew a breath of air outward, the fabric of Arcanium responding to her will. The lift shaft seemed to gasp in one rushing breath, pulling Elvira toward it. The last I saw of her was a pair of flailing legs disappearing upwards like a rocket launching.

Silence reigned for several moments. Someone muttered something to the person next to them, setting of a chain reaction of buzzing conversations as the realisation that we'd won the battle dawned across the crowd.

"*SILENCE,*" Queenie bellowed. "No celebrations until we've had this place cleaned up and back to normal."

I looked around, glad to see Taz, Ace, Petra and the Eastwick sisters now clustered beside me. Amid the grumbling crowd, Queenie turned her stony expression on us.

"You lot, my office, now."

She pointed to the lift, the golden gate hanging off one hinge. Ace hurried forward to fix it back on as the rest of us trooped into the lift. As we shot upwards, I noticed that Queenie had already disappeared, no doubt having translocated up to her office to prepare some awful fate for us.

"Well, that was something," Meryl said.

Ace grinned. "*That* was fun."

I shared a dubious look with Taz as Petra shook her head.

"It's not over yet," she muttered.

We hurried out of the lift and along to Queenie's office in demure silence. I eyed the seven wooden chairs lined up against the wall, three on the left side of Queenie's doors and four on the right.

"Guessing those are for us," Beryl said.

Before I could sit down, Emil came stomping toward us. He pointed at Petra and she followed him straight into Queenie's office.

"So, what are the chances of us getting the boot, do you think?" Cheryl asked.

I cringed away and hunched my shoulders up to my ears.

All of this, and I'll probably get sent home now in disgrace. I tried so hard.

I sniffed and focused on keeping the tears from falling, my insides squishing tight at the mere thought.

Depressive silence descended. Not even Queenie's usual bellowing could be heard through the doors, which somehow seemed worse for being abnormal. After some minutes, a raised voice ricocheted out of the office, muffled beyond distinction by the door. It only issued what sounded like one long, emphatic statement, then fell silent again.

Moments later, the door opened. As I was sitting right beside it, I was the first to jump. I turned my head as Petra came out and closed it behind her.

"Good work, guys," she murmured. I froze as she looked directly down at me. "And Demi, that was really clever voice throwing, nicely done."

She strode off down the hall toward the lift, but I couldn't bring myself to be jubilant at the compliment. Taz prodded my elbow.

"You're so lucky," he whispered. "I still can't believe Petra even knows your name, she's only like The. Best. Mentor in the hub."

I blinked. "Well, that's a nice, bittersweet memory to take with me when they send me home."

Taz opened his mouth, most likely to call me an idiot or something, but the office door opened again and saved him the trouble.

Emil poked his head out. "All of you, come on."

I tried to think of stoic things as we lined up in front of Queenie's desk. The thought of going home for a holiday was all but unbearable. The idea that I might not get to come back at all was unthinkable. I couldn't stem the breathless panic fluttering in my chest, but I could still do my best not to burst into tears.

"It appears that Arcanium is in your debt." Queenie

announced.

I lifted my head and tried to keep my jaw from dropping. I failed, my mouth gaping open. Taz leaned over and nudged a knuckle under my chin as if to shut it for me, his lips already lifted in amusement. I batted him off.

"You mean you are." He turned his attention to Queenie.

She gave him a look but didn't disagree. "Now, I believe the best we can offer our second year students is the invitation to take the trial as FDP initiates when they finish next year?"

She looked to the Eastwick sisters and Ace, all of whom nodded frantically. I forgot my own troubles for a moment and found a small smile of relief for my friends.

"You will be on probation of course, but at least we know your loyalties are true. Now, what about you, Demi? I'm led to believe, mainly because Petra only seems to have one volume, that you in particular played a very big part in our success today."

I bit my lip. "Well, it was Taz's plan really. He was the one who suggested Beryl go and get the FDPs, and then Ace-"

Taz elbowed me hard in the ribs. "Just tell her what you want, idiot."

My mind funnelled through the possibilities. It wasn't done to ask for gifts, I knew that. I could ask to be made an FDP initiate like the others, but a small voice in the back of my mind said that was something I should earn the normal way, not be given.

"Um, to clarify, I'm still a student here, right?" I asked. "As in, if I wish for something else, I'm not going to be sent home or anything?"

I heard Taz muttering in anguish next to me about wishes being for genies, but focused on Queenie's fearsome gaze as best as I could without flinching. I couldn't be sure, but I thought I saw the slightest quiver of a smile dip the middle of Queenie's

240

top lip.

"It wouldn't look too clever on our part if we dismissed you after today," she said.

"Oh, thank you." I took that to mean yes. "There is one thing I'd ask, if it's possible. Can I have a pet? Can I keep my chameleon? Without him needing to go to quarantine or anything awful happening to him? If I can find him again, I mean."

Queenie pursed her lips, her fingers forming a steeple in front of her face.

"It's true there isn't actually any rule in place, however the customary practice in making or amending them is to put the matter to the council-"

"The elders are busy with many important Faerie matters," Emil cut in. "Would it be wise to disturb them on an internal matter? Perhaps we can take a short lesson from this lot, who seem to have mastered the art of 'assuming yes until told no'. The lizard did look harmless, and it was here a while apparently without causing any drama."

Queenie sighed.

"Fine," she said. "If the rules change though, or it starts terrorising anyone, or anything, it'll have to go."

"Thanks!" I squeaked.

I took several steadying breaths to try and calm the roiling leap of excitement in my chest and pressed my hands into my pockets to keep them from wringing out the excess energy in front of everyone. I tapped my toes inside my shoes instead, desperate to run up to Trevor and go find Leo. It only then occurred to me Queenie had probably expected me to ask for something much more difficult to agree to.

At least Leo can come home now. What if Alannah's already set him loose though? I might never find him. I can't exactly just go realm-skipping without a reason either, not now they've said

I can stay. I can't go back now, not when home is here. Maybe I can orb Alannah and ask first.

"Well, if that's all, get out." Queenie's pleasantries dried up like summer rain. "You've caused me a lot of very tedious paperwork, and the Atrium pongs like a month's supply of budget air-freshener."

Taz snorted. "That's because you probably only give them a month's supp-"

He squeaked as Emil clapped a hand on his shoulder, swivelled him around and marched him out of the office before he could do any serious damage.

I followed the others out with a final mumbled thank you over my shoulder to Queenie, overwhelmed at how things had suddenly gone my way. I half expected Queenie to come raging out and change her mind, or pop into existence in the hall and say 'only joking, you're all out of here'.

The Eastwick sisters hurried off toward the lift, but I dawdled at the back. I almost didn't notice Emil until I walked right into him.

"I'm sorry to do this." Emil grinned, not looking sorry at all. "I'm a bit worried that Alannah wasn't in the group of FDPs that returned in the end. Would you mind just popping over and seeing if she's alright?"

I knew full well that Emil could just orb Alannah and ask her to report in. He could probably also commandeer one of the trolls and go visit her himself.

He knows exactly where Leo's been all this time, I realised.

"Um, yes, sure, I can do that." I beamed. "I've figured out how to tell Trevor the right instructions now as well, so I can definitely do that!"

I straightened up and hurried toward the lift with Ace and Taz right behind me.

"Just try not to come back with anything you're not allowed to keep this time!" Emil called after me.

I shut the lift gate with a huge grin threatening to break my face, reassured to hear Emil's chortling rolling down the hall.

"That was a spot of luck," Ace said.

Taz wiped his face with his sleeve. "Luck? I almost thought you were going to ask for something really dim then, Sparky."

I caught his eye and, in the spirit of childish relief, stuck my tongue out at him.

"You know what, *Oakthorn*, I almost did," I retorted with a smile.

Taz grumbled at me using his official Fae name, but the smile lurking on his face suggested he didn't mind this once.

The moment we got out of the lift, Trevor came rushing up with his rickshaw.

"Thank you for the sweets," he said. "I have to hide them up here and take them down a few at a time. It's lovely to see her little face light up each evening."

Wow, Call Me Henry is efficient!

I guessed Trevor meant his daughter, and shrugged modestly. "That's okay."

"She's been asking to meet you as well, because she thinks you're the sweet fairy. I said you're very busy though and for once she believed me."

"I guess I am kind of the sweet fairy then, in a way, to her at least." I wasn't sure how I felt about that title. "It would be nice to meet your family though, especially after keeping you so busy this last month."

I hesitated then.

It's been almost a month already. I can't even think of anywhere else as home now, not even, well, home.

I looked back at Taz and Ace, my friends, standing by me like

243

they had done since the day I arrived.

"We'll wait here," Taz suggested. "Don't do anything dim."

Ace grumbled something under his breath, which sounded a bit like 'give the girl a break', but he threw me a grin and a thumbs up. I got into the rickshaw and focused forwards.

"Okay Trevor, could you please take me to Alannah like before, wherever she is, but drop me off somewhere discreet so nobody sees me? Within walking distance preferably, if right nearby isn't possible. Oh, and stop gradually please, like no sudden halts?"

Trevor nodded. "Absolutely can do."

I closed my eyes as the rickshaw jolted forward. It was only a few moments of rushing air, but those few moments were peaceful. When I opened my eyes again, I was in a grand stone hallway, the flagstone floor laid with a royal blue runner. I hopped out of the rickshaw.

"Thanks, Trevor. I won't be long, but I'll call when I'm ready."

Trevor nodded. "Okay, I'll be waiting."

The air shivered as he disappeared and I glanced up and down, just in time to see someone turn a corner and come toward me.

CHAPTER TWENTY FOUR
ALL'S WELL THAT ENDS-

Alannah did a double-take before speeding up to meet me.

"I did what you said." I forgot about greeting her in the face of my latest achievement. "I told Trevor exactly what to do and here I am, landing on my feet and not startling any of your royalty."

Alannah laughed. "Well, I'm impressed then. What brings you here though?"

"I'm allowed to take Leo back, if he's still here. Emil also asked me to come and check you're okay, as you weren't there today when the Forgotten invaded, but I think that's his way of being kind and giving me a reason to come here."

Alannah looked up and down, then beckoned me to follow her. She led the way down the hall to a wooden door, opened it and stood aside to let me pass. Before I could even assess the room, I saw the most beautiful sight in all of Faerie.

"Leo!"

I hurried around the piles of random fabric on the floor toward the lizard lounging on the dressing table. A chameleon could apparently make themselves look completely at home wherever they happened to be.

"Well, I'm glad Emil cares enough to send someone, apparently," Alannah said, amused. "So, the Forgotten plot has been foiled."

I gathered Leo against my chest and nodded.

"Yes, there were so many of them, but luckily we were prepared and kicked them back out. Hopefully they'll think twice before trying that again."

I turned to face Alannah with Leo making a lazy bid to climb up my arm to my shoulder. He curled his tail around the front of my neck, and I chose to see this as a joyful reunion hug rather than him trying to throttle me for leaving him behind.

"I wouldn't count on it." Alannah shook her head. "Remember what I told you before about trusting nobody? Well, there are always bigger fish out there, and the first stab is usually just a tester. But that won't be immediate, and you've all saved the day for Arcanium today at least."

She was smiling, but I could hear the undertone in her voice, the warning that said *but it's only one day*.

"Yeah, I guess." I tried to find my previous jubilant mood. "My old mentor at fairy lessons always says just one step at a time. So, if there is more to come, well, we've taken that next step at least."

"Well, there you are then." Alannah turned her head back to the doorway as if she'd heard a noise in the hall outside.

Light from the window caught the pendant at her throat. The crystal cast its prisms and threw rainbow colours onto the stone wall, but it was the setting around the stone that caught my attention, a diamond-shaped cloudy crystal split into eight sections.

"It was you!" I gawped at her. "You were the cloaked person that orbed realm-wide to warn us about the attack."

Alannah closed the door. "What makes you say that?"

I searched her face for signs of potential anger or threat of throttling, but her expression was decidedly neutral.

I pointed to her pendant.

"Your necklace. The crystal on a diamond split into eight sections. Whoever orbed in was wearing one just like it, and they had a female voice."

I knew that the necklace could be one of many, but I also knew that as a fairy, Alannah couldn't lie to me without consequence. We stared at each other for so long I started wondering if she was casting some really long gift effect on me.

"It was my mother's, a family heirloom," she said. "It's not exactly a symbol that would be popular nowadays, but it's the only keepsake I have of her. My position means I couldn't leave here when the summons came earlier, but I did do my best to sound the alarm before. Were many hurt?"

"Not that I saw. If I'm honest, it was over very quickly. My friend Taz and I were up against one, but most of them ended up back in the reversed skip-way going back the way they came. I think if it hadn't been for your warning, Queenie might not have believed us about everything else, so thank you."

Alannah smiled. "That message was the least I could do for my people, as I can't leave here for long at all. I'm already likely being missed even now."

I heard the veiled dismissal but couldn't help risking one final question, curious about potential other entrances to Arcanium.

"So, you were able to go back and forth by troll really quickly, like I can? I mean, you've been chosen for transport?"

Alannah folded her arms with a laugh, our brief uneasiness apparently at an end.

"Is there any other way to get back and forth? But look at you, using all the right terminology like a true FDP."

I thought about the broken skip-way beside Emil's office and the one between the classroom and the girls' floor, then blushed when I finally recognised the compliment.

"I'm just glad we were able to beat them," I diverted the conversation away from my mad blushing.

Alannah frowned then.

"Remember what I said about big fish? Groups like that won't just slink away, or take defeat well either. The Forgotten are remorseless, and even their minions aren't to be taken lightly."

"Yeah, I've run into real 'traditionals' at Arcanium." I pulled a face. "Diana thought me being called Demi was very appropriate, and she's awful."

Alannah eyed her for a moment. "Diana?"

I wondered then if I should mind my tongue. I had no idea who knew who in Faerie or Fae circles.

"Diana Hemlock." I bit my lip. "She doesn't like me much."

Alannah nodded. "Ah, yeah the Hemlocks are a very powerful family, old blood, old ways."

"I did wonder if they maybe had something to do with the Forgotten, she seemed really keen on defending the old ways against the Queen's in our first class." I left the suggestion hanging.

Alannah shrugged. "Nobody knows who to trust, so we trust nobody."

Not exactly an answer.

I clutched Leo tighter to me, well aware that I had what I'd come for but still wasn't making any attempt to leave.

"That's sad," I said instead. "They still haven't found the Book of Faerie either, which is weird, but the Forgotten were adamant they hadn't taken it."

"They wouldn't have much use for it. Their only motivation for taking it would be to cause public embarrassment over the loss, or to suggest incompetence."

"So, it's someone who wants to discredit Arcanium, not for what's in the book?"

Alannah chuckled at that. "We're Fae. Fae wouldn't bother to steal the book itself, we'd just take its information, or rather, get someone in the ranks to take its information and report back."

A loud crash outside made us both jump.

"I would offer to be hospitable, but you should probably go." She pulled a rueful face. "Your last visit was kind of a shock for the royals and, even though I tried to say you weren't an evil sorceress, Prince Lucastrian still has people keeping an eye out for you."

I dug in my pocket for my orb.

"I don't like the sound of that. Okay, Trevor, I'm ready to return to hub now."

I stepped back as the air shivered around us, even though I trusted that Trevor wouldn't ever land the rickshaw on top of my head or anything.

"That was quick." Trevor grinned. "In you hop. Hi, Alannah."

I made sure I had a firm hold on Leo and clambered into the rickshaw.

"Thanks, Alannah." I leaned out to wave. "Good luck with the royals."

She chuckled. "Good luck to you too Demi, remember what I said and be careful. I'm sure we'll be seeing each other again."

Trevor started running on the spot and I pulled myself back into the rickshaw.

Time to go home.

I closed my eyes to the rushing air and focused on keeping both hands around Leo's now rather much larger middle. I tapped my feet in a lively rhythm, giddy at knowing he could finally come home with me.

The moment the rickshaw glided to a stop, I opened my eyes to see the dazzling sparkle of the Quartz wall. Ace and Taz were still standing beside it, waiting for me. I clambered out of the rickshaw and grinned at Trevor.

"I think I'm getting used to that," I joked.

Trevor beamed. "I'm glad. If you wanted to lend my services by the way, if you're going to be focusing on your studies from now on, well it'd keep me busy."

"Can I do that?"

"Of course. Being idle is never good for a troll."

I considered this and inched closer, aware of Taz and Ace watching nearby.

"If Taz ever needs you, or Ace, that's fine," I murmured into Trevor's waiting ear. "But I reckon if anyone else asks, I should probably know why first." Then, remembering Beryl's part in commandeering Trevor's services, I added the necessary caveat. "From now on, of course. I'm sorry I couldn't bring the message for Beryl myself earlier, but I'm fine with that. Does she owe anything?"

Trevor stepped back and gave me a broad wink.

"No, not anymore. My deal to her was she owed me a *big* favour until you said otherwise. I think she was hoping your good nature would hold out for her. Still, you've got time until the next mentee break. Plenty of room for more adventures."

I groaned. "I don't know about that. I think a few quiet weeks will do for me."

Trevor chortled and set off with his rickshaw, but I stayed still for a moment, enjoying in the realisation that this was my life now. The house and my human family all seemed so far away, and so much had happened.

So much has changed.

I shook the thoughts to the back of my mind and took Leo over to Taz and Ace. One thing caught my attention though, an item hanging over Taz's shoulder. He noticed me staring and rolled his eyes.

"I thought you might want this." He pulled the satchel off and held it out. "Elvira took most of the stuff out and threw the bag in after us, so your sweets and whatever was in the first aid kit thing are long gone, but I asked Emil last night if someone could realm-skip quick and retrieve it for you. The strap's fixed as well."

"Wow, thank you."

Astonished, I took my satchel, featherlight without anything in it now. I hung the strap over my head so that it rested diagonal across my chest and sighed with relief. Leo uttered a strange yipping noise of delight and wriggled out of my hands to dive straight inside.

"I had it cleaned quick and everything," Taz said, his cheeks pink enough to sharpen his freckles. "You always seemed really attached to it, what with clutching at it all the time. Also, why exactly did you carry around a first aid kit?"

I shrugged, not wanting to tell him the real answer. Whenever I mentioned anything real or in-depth to do with my family, people tended to pity me, and I didn't want that from Taz or Ace.

"You never know when something like that might come in handy." I peeked into the bag to find Leo getting himself comfortable and gave the others a goofy grin. "At least he preferred getting fat in a castle to exploring the wilderness, or I'd never have found him again."

"I'm glad you got him back in the end," Ace said.

I lifted a tentative finger and stroked the top of Leo's head. His eyes half-closed in contentment and he made a quiet crooning noise.

"Alannah was really kind to keep him for me," I admitted. "I thought she'd just release him into the wild, but he seemed quite happy in her room. She did say something else though."

I looked up and down the platform to make sure we weren't being overheard. Taz and Ace huddled closer.

"She admitted she was the mysterious cloaked figure that orbed in when we were down in the Ogle. Also, she said that even though we'd saved the day, there are always bigger fish and that I should still not trust anyone. I didn't really get a chance to ask her what she meant, but she sounded really serious about it."

"I doubt the Forgotten will take their defeat as the end," Ace whispered.

Taz nodded. "They'll need to regroup if they're going to try again, but one thing's for sure, we need to keep an eye out just in case."

"And everyone else seems so certain the Forgotten wouldn't have taken the Book of Faerie," I added. "Alannah said they'd only have reason to take it to discredit Arcanium, that they wouldn't have need for anything inside it and wouldn't stoop to nicking a book, just the information inside it."

"So we're back to the speed-stealing thing, but no motive." Taz sighed.

"Um, yeah." Ace rubbed the back of his neck, looking sheepish. "I'm guessing there's nothing much we can do about that for now. Until then, I've got an appointment to keep."

He nodded to where Cheryl was waiting for him by the lift.

"Okay," I shrugged. "See you later."

Ace set off toward the lift, joining Cheryl as both of them got into it together. Taz started after them, but I reached out without thinking.

My hand landed on his shoulder, a fleeting moment of unbridled instinct.

Taz stared at my hand. I stared at my hand. Then I promptly removed it with my cheeks burning a sudden fever.

"I just, wanted to say thank you." I hurried on as Taz frowned back at me. "Seriously, thank you. I wouldn't have Leo if it weren't for all your help, and I wouldn't have had such an interesting first term here. Actually, I'd probably be vaporised or something by now."

Taz shrugged his shoulder as if he was trying to brush off the feel of my fingers. I pushed down my own awkwardness as he turned toward the lift, although I couldn't do anything about my burning cheeks.

"I know, Sparky," he said. "Don't get soft on me."

I thought I sensed a tiny dash of pride blended in the large portion of embarrassment soup that was his tone as he walked away.

I tailed after him and smiled to myself as we entered the lift.

"The one thing unsolved now is the missing book." I sighed. "The only person we know of with a speed gift is Avril, and everyone's adamant it can't be her. I don't think she would either."

Taz tapped the button for the canteen and folded his arms.

"Yeah, agreed. It can't be someone glamouring as her either, as you don't get their gifts or anything when you do. If I glamoured to look like you, I wouldn't get yours."

I snorted. "Probably just as well, I don't have any."

"Yeah, you do." Taz rolled his eyes. "You can do that voice throwing thing, you're loyal and a great friend, and you can imitate any sound. People like you are proof that it's not the blood or the heritage that matters."

I shrugged as if that could sweep away the deep blush creeping back across my face.

"Demi by name, Demi in blood," I joked. "I'm sure Diana would agree. I remember that first time I met her and she said my name was fitting, and that I should choose my contacts better because she and her brother had all these gifts-"

I stared at Taz in dawning horror. He eyed me for a moment, a frown descending as he took a step closer.

"You okay?" he asked.

"I know who stole the book."

CHAPTER TWENTY FIVE
A REVELATION OR FEW

I blinked at Taz, still floundering through my memories.

"At least, I think I know who stole it." I hesitated. "Diana said she had a speed skill, right? When we first met, it was one of the things she said she and her brother had between them. They're so traditional it pretty much drips off them. What if they stole the book?"

Taz's frown deepened as the lift came to a stop. I saw a couple of students I didn't recognise heading toward the lift and reached out for the gate. Taz batted my hand back down and pressed the button for the library floor instead. I shot an apologetic look at the indignant couple as the lift took off again without them.

"What makes you think that though? And why would they?"

I hesitated. *At least he's not shutting me down straight away.*

"Diana has a speed skill," I said, thinking fast. "She could have zipped in and stolen it when nobody was looking, possibly fast enough to get in and out without ever being seen."

"It disappeared right before class though. She would have had it on her."

I replayed that day in my head, my first ever class with Avril, and Diana stopping by our desk to torment us.

"She swapped bags with Kainen." I stared at Taz in horror. "Remember? He came into class and said they'd gotten their bags mixed up. I mean, how unlikely is that? Even though they looked similar, same colour and material and everything, I'd never make that mistake and I'm betting she wouldn't either."

Taz bit his lip. "You might have a point, but we can't prove anything. They'd never admit it unless we could."

"But maybe we can scare them into putting it back." My brain clonked onto auto-scheme. "The alarms would have gone off wouldn't they, if they tried to take it outside, so it must still be here, unless there's like a magic skip-way they know of which doesn't raise any alarms."

Taz started to smile. "What are you saying we do then?"

"Be where they are, say we overheard that someone saw who stole the Book of Faerie and that they'll probably go to Queenie."

He rubbed the back of his head. "Not if it's a lie we can't."

"Let me think for a while, and I'll come up with something." I sighed, my mood dipping instantly.

The lift stopped and Taz opened the gate, standing aside to let me out first. I walked around the library platform and into the usual nook we used, slowing only to dredge up a smile for Gnat. Remembering my previous paranoia that even he might somehow be one of the Forgotten, Alannah's foreboding warning echoed in my head.

"Nobody knows who to trust so we trust nobody," I quoted.

Taz sank into the nearest chair with an arched eyebrow. "Dark, I like it. Very Fae."

"It's what Alannah said to me. I was thinking how it was silly of me to suspect everyone of potentially being the enemy, but anyone *could* be anyone. That's even true of the human world, I think. How well do you really know a person?"

Taz spread his fingers wide on the tabletop.

"Actions. That's the only real currency in either world, actions and effort."

I put my satchel on the table, sparing a smile for it, folded my arms and settled my head on them. I would get up eventually and see if the Braunees could sneak me something to take to my room. Then I would get a shower and sleep for a week. But for now, the peaceful silence of the library with the odd sound of a page being turned somewhere nearby, the scribble of a pen on paper, and the quiet snoring of a chameleon at home, was the best environment my weary brain could imagine.

"I overheard someone say, 'someone saw who stole the Book of Faerie' and the best thing to do there would be to go straight to Queenie."

Taz's voice reached my ears and I lifted my head with a grunt. "Wha'?"

He smirked at me, and I realised I'd been all but asleep on the desk. I froze when he reached a hand toward my face, but he just swiped a warm thumb over my forehead and sat back again.

"Smudge," he said.

I took a sharp breath as the small flurry of anxiety in my chest at the action.

He's just being kind. I shook the unsettling feelings aside. *Like me putting my hand on his shoulder, it's just a friendly thing.*

Taz carried on, apparently not as affected by his actions as I was.

"If we happen to be where Diana and Kainen are, you can say you overheard that someone saw who stole the book. You literally just overheard me say it, so it's *technically* not a lie, you're just parroting what you overheard me say just now. If that doesn't rattle them into doing something rash, I don't think anything will."

I wiped my eyes with my forefinger and thumb and sat up straighter.

"You think that'll be enough?"

Taz nodded. "Imagine the shame a Fae family would face if two of their own were kicked out for theft. They wouldn't risk it."

"Worth a shot." I grinned and stood up. "Where do you think they'll be?"

Taz laughed. "Whoa, Sparky. We can't rush into this. Might be best to get some food, sleep on it, chat to Ace first-"

I shook my head, stepping away from the chair and making sure Leo was still slumbering in my bag.

"The Forgotten have had a blow, so the power has shifted our way. The gruesome twosome won't want to be seen as on the wrong side right now, so they might well try to get rid of it. Can't give them any more time to manage it, or we may never see the book again."

Taz got to his feet with a grumble.

"I hope for your sake they're in the canteen then, because I'm starving."

I led the way to the lift, but we couldn't find Diana or Kainen in the study rooms, the class rooms, the training hall or the canteen. Taz refused to leave without food, so we had to hang around while the Braunees whipped up sandwiches and what looked like the biggest cricket salad ever known to fairy, human or Fae. Admitting defeat for the moment, I plodded back into the lift and took the sandwich half Taz held out to me, a mess of more melted cheese than bread.

"It might be better to spread the word generally," Taz suggested, pressing the button for the residents' floor. "Then someone will eventually get it back to them."

I shook my head. "No, it needs to come from us. They need to know we know it's them, so they don't chance getting rid of the book to hide all proof."

Taz finished his sandwich half and gave me a look.

"I hate to say this, but I think we've been a really bad influence on you."

I stuck my tongue out. "No, just you."

He chuckled, his eyes fixed on the gate as the lift stopped and the residents' floor came into view. I stifled a yawn behind the back of my hand.

"Well I'm going to crash out in the common area for a bit, if you want to join me?" he asked. "I think we've more than earned a break. I bet you haven't seen *Demolition Ducks* yet, and that's so much fun. It's like a religion around here, nobody dares try to use the orb-box when someone's watching it."

I opened the gate and stepped out, still pulling errant strands of cheese off my fingers with my teeth.

"Orb-box?"

"Yeah, that flat black rectangle hanging on the wall in the common area."

I blinked at him. "You mean the television?"

"Eh?"

"You don't call it a television?" I hesitated then shook my head. "You're making fun of me, aren't you."

Taz grinned as we reached the next hall. "You make it too easy, Sparky."

"I'll get you back for that." I laughed and lifted my satchel. "I'll just drop stuff off in my room and meet you at the orb-box then."

I didn't need to keep Leo a secret anymore, but I didn't want everyone taking an interest in him, not until I'd sorted out some kind of lizard-proofing routine. Taz sauntered off down the corridor to the right and I hurried left to my room. I unlocked the door and closed it behind me.

"There you go, Leo," I murmured. "Back home and with permission this time. First chance I get, I'll go up to the human world and get you some proper food and stuff. The Braunees have given you a mega cricket salad for now though, and I'll leave your drawer open."

Leo crooned back at me and slid quite happily into his drawer. I lifted the satchel over my head, loathe to part with it even for a moment. But I'd been wearing the same clothing for what felt like ages, and I was sure I'd be smelling the awful floral air freshener on my skin forever more.

I found one of my neater woollen cardigans, jewel green to make my hair less dull-looking, and changed my jeans, then left my room with my door locked and only my key in my pocket.

It'll be nice just to have some time to chill for a bit after so much excitement. I bet Demolition Ducks is some kind of mad fairy reality show.

With everything that had happened in the past few weeks, I should have been way more alert as I wandered down the corridor.

"So Taz calls you Sparky. What an *adorable* little nickname."

I froze at the sound of Diana's voice. With my gut muscles clenched to hide my outward reaction, I faced the enemy.

I can't say I know it's her, but she already knows I don't like her. I started to smile. *No harm in telling her exactly what I think.*

"So, the Forgotten have been sent back to the gutter where they belong." I said the first thing that came into my head.

Diana curled her lip, taking a step closer. "For now, but not for long."

Alannah's almost identical warning echoed jangled in my ears, but I focused on Diana stalking toward me.

"The only thing that hasn't been solved is who took the Book of Faerie," I said. "But I'm sure people have theories. All it would take is a speed gift and a place to hide it so the Arcanium alarms aren't set off."

A puff of air brushed my face before I could say any more. A hand closed around my throat. I yelped as my back crashed against the wall.

I never even saw her move.

I gulped, the bob of my throat pressing against Diana's palm.

"Don't make the mistake of thinking you've had a victory today," she snarled. "The Forgotten may have had a setback, but *you* haven't won anything. I could kill you as easily as breathing right now. I should, I still owe you from object training. It's not like anyone would even miss you, right?"

Something glinted lower down and I looked to see a penknife with a short, thin blade in Diana's free hand. She lifted it level with our faces as her features sharpened, the hawk-like effect of Fae blood shining clear.

She's stronger and faster. I'm outclassed in every single way, and we both know it.

Fear grabbed the breath from my chest as I eyed the blade. The golden hilt was encrusted with diamonds and monogrammed with an ornate 'D'.

Think, idiot. You know about the book. But she's Fae. You can't possibly outdo her in trickery.

That only left one weapon, a tactic I hadn't used since I was about five and really didn't like the idea of using, even now.

I kept one part of my attention on the blade as I met Diana's gleeful green eyes. I pushed my chin forward as far as I could with the hand to my throat.

"Where's the fun in that?" I asked and spat in her face.

The hand disappeared from my throat as Diana wailed in disgust. I used my wrist to bat the hand holding the knife away as she wiped at her face with frantic fingers. The knife thudded to the carpet and I lunged to get it before Diana came to her senses. My fingers were inches away when the toe of a dirty pair of boots tapped on top of the blade.

Taz stooped to pick the penknife up just in time as Diana turned to face us, her face a feral picture of pink cheeks, flashing eyes and lips pressed so thin she looked monstrously mouthless.

"Here, Dem, I overheard 'someone saw who stole the Book of Faerie'." Taz grinned.

I froze as he wrapped an arm around my shoulders, but I guessed it was more for group protection against Diana's potential gift-use than anything emotionally meaningful.

Just him being protective of a friend.

I pushed the more flustered thoughts away and pulled myself together.

"Oh, that's great news," I said. "What would happen to whoever stole it? Have they gone to Queenie yet?"

Taz pretended to be thinking and I risked a grin at Diana, who stood with her fists clenched in a seething rage, her widened eyes the only sign our word-tangling had hit its mark.

"They'd be kicked out I reckon," he said. "Shame on the family, outcasts in respectable society, destined for *menial jobs.*"

He boomed the last part in the tone of a cheesy horror film narrator and I couldn't help snickering.

"It's a shame the idiot who stole it doesn't just put it back before they're caught," I suggested. "Do they do room searches here, if they haven't already? Check all the hidden skip-ways?"

A low growl rumbled in Diana's throat. She looked up and down the hall before taking a step closer.

"Don't think I'll forget you crossed me, *Sparky,*" she said, her attention for me alone. "I'll get you back for this, and it'll come sooner than you think."

She stalked off toward the lift but Taz called after her. "Catch!"

He threw her knife underarm with a swift aim. Diana didn't turn or slow down. She shot out a hand at the last minute and snagged the knife without so much as a look back for it.

"Okay, I want to know how to do that," Taz admitted once

Diana was in the lift and long gone.

I bit my lip.

"She only threatened me, I notice."

I tried not to sound bothered, but having a target on my back was a worry I didn't want to have to carry right now, or preferably ever. I'd completely forgotten Taz's arm still around my shoulders and flinched when he squeezed briefly before letting go.

"I could offer you my family's protection, if you wanted?" He sounded completely serious. "It would mean you're in debt to us though, and I get the feeling that isn't something you'd be up for."

I shrugged. "Not if I can avoid it. Being in debt to people is always trouble. I've not actually asked you anything about your home, or your family. Are they important then?"

Taz hesitated. I shoved my hands in my pockets, avoiding his eye.

"Don't tell me if you don't want to," I added.

"Some would say they're important." He dodged the question. "My family live in Faerie, but my real home is here, at Arcanium."

I nodded. "Same for me. Not the family in Faerie bit obviously, and I doubt anyone would class my lot as important, but Arcanium is home now."

His anxious expression cleared like a new dawn. His eyes sparkled bright and his freckles deepened as he smiled.

"I meant to find out why she took it in the first place as well, the book I mean." I sighed, almost distracted by his sudden change in mood. "But she had me pinned before I could think."

"I imagine it was just to create confusion," Taz said.

"There's nothing in it she might want? She could have been copying all sorts out of it."

Taz rubbed his chin and shrugged.

"I can't say I've ever actually read it, but it holds the histories of Faerie. No doubt today's battle will be scribing itself inside as we speak. You might even get a mention."

"Don't say that." I groaned with as much dramatic flair as I could muster to hide the fact that sounded pretty damn cool. "I'll never live it down."

Taz grinned and held out his elbow like a gentleman.

"I won't breathe a word. So, *Demolition Ducks*? It's not for everyone, but it's totally bonkers so I reckon you'll love it as much as I do."

I laughed. "Alright, you're on."

I didn't take his arm, but walked beside him with the odd brush of his elbow against mine. Perhaps he would tell me more about his family in time. We'd not actually known each other long after all.

We've shared an almighty adventure though together, along with Ace, and Meryl, Beryl and Cheryl.

"Ah, there you are!"

We stopped dead at the sound of Emil's voice.

"What chance is there he's not talking to us?" Taz muttered out of the corner of his mouth.

I shook my head. "Zero."

We rotated back and waited for Emil to reach us.

"Wonderful news," he said, a little out of breath. "The Book of Faerie has been mysteriously returned. It just appeared on the pedestal like magic, so the council are putting it down to a childish prank."

I kept my responding snort in with great restraint.

Idiots. Given the derisive look on Taz's face, he was thinking much the same. *Probably in way more offensive language.*

"You came all the way up here to tell us that?" Taz asked.

"No." Emil gave him a weary look. "There will be celebrations of course, both for the return of the book and the victory over the Forgotten. Tales will be told, blind eyes will be turned to the drinking of Beast in the canteen for tonight only."

I didn't ask what Beast was, guessing it was some kind of Faerie wine or similar.

"But after that, thoughts will turn to the break in mentee classes we have soon approaching." Emil's stern frown turned to amusement. "Look, things are only going to get rockier from here. There are power plays at work behind the scenes and we need to be very careful."

I folded my arms. "This isn't exactly a great celebration speech, no offense."

"It's not meant to be. Demi, you should go home for the mentee break. Most students do, and you should keep your connection to the human world as much as you can."

I shrugged and avoided agreeing to anything, aware of Taz grinning at me. The thought of having to go home, even for a short visit, made me feel queasy and irritable. Time seemed to pass quickly here, but I still had a few weeks until the break.

Plenty of time to find an excuse not to go back.

Emil raised a knowing eyebrow at us.

"Your mother has called you home as well," he told Taz.

I smirked as Taz descended to glowering.

"Oh, hell."

Emil started to laugh. "The lockdown has been lifted and for tonight only, no curfew. We're hoping to still have everyone accounted for in the morning, but who knows. If you feel like running away, now would be the time. I'll advise your mother to discuss a carpool for the return after break, Taz."

He turned on his heel and set off with a jaunty whistle. I scowled at his departing back until he turned into the hall toward the lift.

"No curfew," Taz said. "Want to go up to the human world instead? *Demolition Ducks* can wait."

"Okay. I've only been up there about three times since I got here to send a quick message to my mum, so I probably should get some actual fresh air."

He grinned. "I can do better than that. There's a fish and chip place that stays open late, and I figured out how to get one of those human money boxes to actually give me the big paper money. Before I had to ask in the arcade and they kept giving me loads of these copper coins."

I snorted. "You mean 2ps? You didn't know how an ATM works, so you just used to go out spending loads of 2ps?"

Taz's cheeks went pink, but he just pulled a face at me and set off after Emil. We got into the lift and I jabbed the button for the atrium.

"So, I know why I don't want to go home," I said. "Why is it such a bad thing for you? At least you don't have to spend the whole week being shoved in cupboards or chased with hockey sticks."

I thought Taz would avoid the question or give me some glib retort, but he looked too tired to argue.

"Remember how we're learning about the Queen?"

I nodded. "The one who wrote the Book of Faerie and changed all the old traditional ways that the Forgotten want to get back so much? Sure."

"Well, that's kind of my mother. She's the Queen of Faerie."

I let that sink in as we left the lift and crossed the deserted atrium. Call-Me-Henry gave us a wave with a bottle of something in hand, and I realised I still needed to sort out payment for Trevor's Jelly Babies yet.

I followed Taz into the metal lift that led to the arcade and pounced the moment the doors were shut.

"Right, so you're saying you're a Fae prince?"

Taz rolled his eyes.

"Sort of. My siblings are all sisters so I guess you could say I'm the only Fae prince. But while I'm a half-breed, my sisters are all pure Fae. I grew up being the outcast. The rest of them all played pranks on each other, but they liked to gang up on me, to 'toughen me up' they called it."

I bit my lip. "Sounds like my sisters. How many do you have?"

"Five, and they're all older than I am. That's how I can glamour when I choose to without being a second year yet. I learned young but decided long ago that I wouldn't do it unless I had to. I don't want to be like them, using gifts on a whim and manipulating people for fun or gain."

I knew I had to be very diplomatic with my answer, but I was too exhausted for common sense.

"Can you do anything other than glamour? Have you been gifted? What's your part of Faerie like? I imagine it must have been kind of cool to have grown up immersed in it all."

As we stepped out of the lift, Taz halted and held up a hand between us.

"Stop right there. It's not 'cool'. Fae are always tricksters, always dangerous. It's not like when you're a kid and you spin around really fast hoping the world will have changed when you stop. There is no cool about it, and gifts aren't like magic pills. If you think that then you read too much."

I held up both hands in alarm. "Okay, okay, sorry. But we're FDPs, Faerie tales and magic are in our make-up."

Taz snorted as he started walking again.

"I thought you looked a bit red-cheeked today," he quipped.

I rolled my eyes as we stepped into the dingy arcade with the machines flashing their gaudy lights all around us.

"You know what I mean," I insisted. "Stop deflecting. We have these abilities to help people, that's the whole point of being an FDP. It might not be all gingerbread houses and glass slippers for us, but that's just how it is."

I tried not to let Taz bait me, knowing he was picking a fight on purpose. He didn't reply, barrelling out into the hot summer night. I stopped on the pavement and closed my eyes, breathing in the sweet food smells and the salty scent from the sea. I lifted my face to the dark sky and opened my eyes. If I squinted, I could make out the stars, and focused on them as I considered my final retort with care.

"I can't actually imagine you as a little boy spinning round really fast to make the world change," I said. "Was it like an arms out 'wheeee' kind of spinning or-"

I shrieked and dodged as Taz lunged toward me, but I could see he was trying not to laugh.

"Okay, truce!" I held my hands up again between us. "I won't ask you any more about your family. I just find it interesting. I'm stuck with two psychopathic sisters who both do sports and delight in tormenting me, so forgive me for being a tiny bit interested in someone else's traumatic upbringing."

Taz shrugged and pointed toward the pier, lit up for people to stroll along.

"Hold that thought," he taunted as we started walking. "You'll find out for yourself soon enough."

"What do you mean?"

"Oh, nothing much." He grinned. "Emil said he'd tell my mother to sort a carpool, by which he means we'll likely come to pick you up on our way back here at the end of the mentee break. Not sure why."

I stumbled to a halt but Taz powered on without waiting for

me.

The Queen of Faerie is going to be at my house.

I stared at Taz's broad shoulders and the easy swing of his legs as he walked along, like he didn't have a care in the world.

Taz and the Queen of Faerie are going to end up meeting my sisters. They're going to judge the tiny house we live in compared to what is no doubt a huge Faerie castle.

I took a deep breath to calm the uneasiness sloshing inside my gut. The mentee break was still two weeks away. Anything could happen between now and then, including a way to avoid having to go back home at all.

I broke into a jog until as I drew level with Taz again, strolling alongside him onto the pier.

I had no idea what might happen in the coming days, or what future adventures awaited me in Faerie with the Forgotten still lurking in the shadows, but I could be sure of one thing. I intended to have a great time finding out.

ACKNOWLEDGEMENTS

Where to even begin? I'm so lucky to have my family to support me, with a special forever place in my heart for my emotional therapy dog who walks me three times a day to keep me grounded!

Huge accolades must go to my superstar editor and amazing friend Anna Britton, who not only helped the story flourish but also gave me a complex about how many times I use 'just' and 'very'... (And picked me up every time I fell over, over-Tiggered or just lost faith - thank you <3)

To my writing family as well, your support has kept me going through the dark times more than you know - Debbie Roxburgh, Samantha Williams, Sally Doherty, Marisa Noelle, Emma Finlayson-Palmer, Stuart White, Susan Mann, writing Twitter, everyone who joins #ukteenchat, the WriteMentor Hub crew, my great critique groups, and so many more (I wish I could name everyone!)

Finally, it wouldn't be my acknowledgements without the biggest shout-out to the incomparable crew at WriteMentor. I was down and doubting when I found them over three years ago, but since then I've learned so much and met the most amazing people. It truly is my writing forever home, and this book wouldn't be here without all of you.

So thank you all - now you've made me cry!

ABOUT THE AUTHOR

While always convinced that there has to be something out there beyond the everyday, Emma focuses on weaving magic realms with words (the real world can wait a while). The idea of other worlds fascinates her and she's determined to find her own entrance to an alternate realm one day.

Raised in London, she now lives on the UK south coast with her husband and a very lazy black Labrador who occasionally condescends to take her out for a walk.

Aside from creative writing studies, an addiction to cereal and spending far too much time procrastinating on social media, Emma is still waiting for the arrival of her unicorn. Or a tank, she's not fussy.

For the latest new and updates, check the website or come say hi on social media:

www.emmaebradley.com
@EmmaEBradley

Lightning Source UK Ltd.
Milton Keynes UK
UKHW011829291121
394785UK00001B/88